FOR THE LOVE

A PERFECT MATCH NOVEL

C.R. ELLIS

Editor: Jennifer Archer, Archer Editing & Writing Services

Cover designer: Hang Le, ByHangLe

HarLex Publishing, LLC

E-book ISBN: 978-1-7323131-8-7

Paperback ISBN: 978-1-7323131-9-4

PROLOGUE
TRISTAN

"*Tristan! Were you aware of your parents' crimes?*"

"*Ms. Fitzgerald! Why did they do it?*"

"*Can you confirm you're no longer employed at Happy Hearts?*"

"*What do you say to those who believe you could be as guilty as your parents?*"

"*Is it true you only avoided charges because you agreed to help the district attorney?*"

The car door closes, finally offering me solitude, and I let my head fall back against the headrest, swallowing down the hot tears threatening to break free. By now, I've trained myself to ignore even the most outrageous questions flung my way by vicious reporters, trying to bait me into a front-page-worthy reaction.

Or so I thought.

Seconds later, my temporary bodyguard-slash-driver, Carl, pulls into traffic, weaving through mid-day Manhattan traffic. My eyes fall to a newspaper sitting on the front passenger seat, and as soon as Carl realizes what I'm looking at, he quickly swipes it off the seat and flips it over. "Apologies, Ms. Fitzgerald."

"It's fine," I tell him, waving off his concern.

He was fast, but not fast enough.

FROM GUCCI TO GUILTY—FITZGERALDS FALL FROM GRACE!

As headlines go, this one shouldn't stand out among the dozens I've seen lately. But the word *guilty* sears into my head like I've been branded with it. And in a way, I have been. By association, at the very least. A week ago, my parents were each sentenced to nine years in prison. And as of yesterday, I became the legal guardian of my three siblings. I'm a reasonably intelligent college graduate, but what that fancy degree didn't prepare me for? How to be both parents and sister to my siblings after the most traumatic experience of our lives. Or how to handle the valid-yet-impossible-to-answer questions they had about the situation. Or how to protect them from relentless reporters outside our building or from seeing the libelous headlines about me on gossip sites and trashy magazines.

And it definitely didn't prepare me for how to deal with the fallout they'd face at school, which is where I'm going now. Their head master called an hour ago and said it was imperative I get there as soon as possible, something about an issue with Liam and Genevieve. Last week, Maggie, my seventeen-year-old sister, had expletives spray-painted on her locker. I'd like to believe eight-year-olds wouldn't be that vicious, but my faith in people is pretty low lately.

"We're here," Carl announces, shaking me out of my thoughts. He scans the area, and my gaze instinctively follows, checking for reporters, before stepping into the chilly air.

By the time Head Master Johnston ushers me into his office, countless scenarios have run through my head, each one worse than the last. I'm on the verge of telling him to spit it out already when he thankfully closes the door and cuts to the chase without wasting time.

"I'll spare you the small talk and get right to the point," he begins, taking a seat behind his desk. Towering somewhere around six-foot-six, bald, with dark beady eyes and lips pressed into a thin line, it's easy to see why kids are intimidated by him. "This morning, a group of parents showed up, demanding to know why their children came home yesterday asking what the term "human traffickers" meant. Apparently, a few students in Genevieve's class started a rumor that her parents were sent to prison for human trafficking."

"What?" I cry in disbelief. "That's insane! I doubt they even know what it means; one kid probably found it online and ran with it. What did you tell them? Is Gen okay? I want to see her right now. And Liam."

My heart is simultaneously pounding away furiously and breaking for them. I've always been the protective big sister, but now that I'm essentially all they have, my instincts to shield them from all the negativity and hate are working overtime.

"We pulled them from class as soon as the situation came to light. It, unfortunately, is not the only reason you're here," he continues with a nod, keeping an annoyingly even tone. "Liam got into a physical altercation at recess minutes before my assistant went to get them both. It seems some students were giving Genevieve some issues at recess, and he took it upon himself to defend her. He suffered a black eye, but the other student is being evaluated for a possible concussion."

I flinch, knowing where this is going. Even so, my mouth opens to defend my brother, to justify his actions somehow even though he knows better, but Head Master Johnston holds a hand up and cuts me off. "Now, I am aware this is a rather…difficult time for your family. However, as you know, Eastwood Academy has a zero-tolerance policy regarding violence."

A nod is all I manage because whatever comes out of my mouth would likely be loaded with expletives, and that wouldn't do anything to mitigate the damage. *Expulsion.* Six months ago, the prospect of my sweet, goofball little brother being kicked out of school would have been laughable. Preposterous.

But that was before life as we knew it came to a screeching halt.

"…I'm sure you can appreciate the delicate situation this puts the academy in," he goes on, and the implication is clear. Keeping parents happy, especially ones with pockets deeper than the

Atlantic, is priority number one—always. "Unfortunately, my hands really are tied here…" He drones on, trying to remain PC in what ultimately boils down to expelling my brother and suggesting Genevieve might also benefit from a transfer as well.

Anger washes over me like a tidal wave. Only I can't tell which direction it's aimed—at the academy, the situation, or my parents, for being the whole reason behind the complete shitshow the last few months of our lives have been. But letting my mind drift down that road is a slippery slope, and I can't afford to let that energy out of its box right now.

"Don't worry," I snap, pushing up from my chair and cutting him off. "As of today, I'm withdrawing them from Eastwood. Now, I'd like to go see them, and then I'll sign whatever papers you need me to, and we'll be on our way."

He stutters through an agreement before showing me to a room down the hall from his office, where my siblings are seated on a couch. Genevieve jumps up and runs to me, throwing herself around my waist in a hug while Liam hangs back, a mixture of fear and frustration in his expression. But I shut that down and wave him over to join the hug. Later, we'll have words about the violence, but right now, he needs my support, not a lecture. The question of how my parents would handle the situation flits through my head, but I don't let it stick around because it's irrelevant now.

"I'm sorry," he mumbles into my shoulder. "I know I shouldn't have punched him."

"No, you shouldn't have, but we'll talk about it later," I reply, pulling back to get a look at his face. The left side around his eye is swollen and pink, definitely on its way to turning into a bruise. "How's your eye? Does it hurt?"

He grazes his fingertips over it and shrugs. "A little. I'll be okay, though."

"Good." I bend to kiss the tops of their heads and rustle their matching dirty blonde hair before releasing them from my grip. "Come on. We're leaving."

"We are?" Gen asks. "Where are we going?"

"How does ice cream sound?"

"Before lunch?" she asks, brows raised as her gap-toothed smile grows.

"Yep, before lunch."

Just a few days in, and I'm already almost certainly screwing this whole guardian thing up by pulling them out of school without a plan, but something snapped inside me while Head Master Johnston was talking. I wanted to keep things normal for my siblings, thinking that it would offer them stability by keeping up the routine of their daily lives. But this was a wakeup call; "normal" doesn't exist for us anymore, at least not here.

Guess that means we'll have to create our own normal.

1

TRISTAN

Three Months Later

*T*hree days after I pulled Liam and Genevieve out of school, we put Manhattan in our rearview mirror and set off for Arbor Cove, the small beach town in Connecticut, where my mom's stepsister Lorraine lives. She and my mom have never been close, but she's the only relative we have, and she offered me a job as her assistant, so it wasn't a tough decision. It's not like I was going to be overwhelmed with job offers in New York.

Life in Arbor Cove has been…different. Trading the concrete jungle and skyscrapers for a town where salt permeates the air, and most views feature the ocean wasn't all that difficult, but it wasn't an easy, overnight transition either. It took a while to get used to the silence of small-town life. Walking along the beach is soothing, but I still miss being able to wander down the streets and using the noise to drown out my own thoughts. But locals offer smiles and waves instead of suspicious glares, and I don't flinch when I hear my name called from across the street anymore, so that alone is a win for this place.

In the grand scheme of things, there's actually not much else I miss about New York. Except for my friends—Josie, in particular, who's been my ride-or-die since we were potluck roommates our freshman year at Columbia.

Between her hectic grad school and work schedule and my crazy life juggling work and taking care of my siblings, we've only had a handful of chances to talk over the last couple of months. So even though I'm technically running late in finishing some errands for Lorraine, seeing her name and face flash on my phone screen makes me stop and smile.

Hauling my purse over my shoulder, I swipe a finger across the screen and greet my best friend. "What are the odds this phone call is to tell me you're leaving NYC for the weekend to come kick it with us in Small Town, USA? After the week I've had, I could use a night out and about four margaritas."

"I wish. I'm scheduled to work every night this week. But that's not why I'm calling. Why do I never listen to you? I swear it's like I have a neon sign saying, 'GOOD GUYS NOT WELCOME!' plastered on my forehead."

I grimace, though I'm not at all surprised she and her boyfriend Jordan are apparently having issues with the long-distance thing, even if it's only been a couple of weeks since he traded the east coast for the west. "Back up. What happened?"

"It was originally what *didn't* happen that was the problem. We were supposed to FaceTime last week, but he was supposedly working late every night, and then he had the audacity to post a video to his Instagram story of him out drinking with the other interns on Friday."

If I liked Jordan, I'd consider defending his actions with a *maybe he forgot,* or *I'm sure it was a work-related thing,* but I haven't been a huge fan of his since I caught him blatantly staring at another girl's ass a month after they started dating. But Josie's loyal and loves hard, and that hasn't exactly worked in her favor in the romance department.

"So...did you eventually talk to him?"

"Sure did. This morning. He prefaced the conversation by saying he couldn't talk long because of some *work project* he had to get back to, and then launched right into the, 'So, I've been thinking...' routine and asks what my thoughts are on being non-exclusive for the summer, and then, and I quote, *seeing where things are for us in August.* WHO DOES THAT?! It totally means he's cheating on me. Or thought about cheating on me. I guess it's irrelevant because I told him to go enjoy sticking his dick in whatever LA bimbo he clearly wanted to hook up with because I'm done. For good this time."

"Ah, shit. I'm sorry, Jo. Maybe..." I stop myself from finishing that thought because she knows how I feel about him, and anything I said would be hollow.

"It's fine, really. I should've seen—" A loud crash interrupts Josie's response, eliciting some colorful curses instead. "Tina just knocked over like 400 plates. Guess my break is over. I'll call you later, 'kay?"

"FaceTime me after work, and we'll do a virtual happy hour or something. Good luck with the dish disaster."

"Sounds good. Thanks."

An hour later, I've picked up Lorraine's dry cleaning, her cat's medicine, and am about to take her car to get washed when my phone lights up with an incoming call from the last person I would've expected. I should probably send it to voicemail, but it's actually past time I give Jordan a piece of my mind.

"I'm sorry, you must have dialed the wrong number," I offer as a greeting. "I believe the one you're looking for is 1-800-IMA-DICK."

"Just hear me out. Please. Josie won't answer my calls; you're the only way I can think of to get through to her. Please, Tristan. You have to believe me. I messed up," he says.

He sounds genuinely distressed, but he's come to the wrong person if it's sympathy or help he's looking for.

"Gee, you think? Glad that fancy Cornell degree is paying off," I snap, hopping into Lorraine's Mercedes and slamming the door shut.

"I'm sorry, okay? I wasn't thinking. But she won't even let me apologize. I love her, and I don't want to lose her. Please," he tacks on, like saying the word one more time might have the power to convince me.

"Love? *Right.* See, now I must be the one who's confused because, silly me, I can't seem to find the connection between loving someone yet casually breaking up with them as if what you had was nothing more than a meaningless fling. Let me guess, you went and hooked up with whatever girl you've spent the last two weeks flirting with and realized the grass isn't always greener on the other side of the country?"

He's silent for long enough to make my blood simmer and my knuckles go white from gripping the steering wheel so hard. Finally, he sighs and mutters, "That's not...I know I fucked up with the non-exclusive bullshit, but it was a mistake. Josie means *everything* to me. You have to believe me. How do I make this right if she won't even hear me out?"

"You go back in time and un-bang someone who's not your freaking girlfriend," I practically yell. "And the fact that you called *me* to plead your case is laughable to the point of stupidity, Jordan. Why would I believe a word you're saying right now? You know, I've always thought Josie deserved better than a mediocre boyfriend with a wandering eye, but I tried to give you the benefit of the doubt. I won't repeat that mistake. If you call me again, I'll brush up on my Photoshop skills and take some creative liberties with those pictures from Halloween. I'm thinking a micropenis is in order, to go with your micro brain. I doubt you'd want those getting out and into the wrong hands, so do yourself a favor and lose my number."

Without waiting for a response, I hit the red button and drop my head back against the seat as the tension slowly uncoils from my shoulders. Between dealing with Liam and Maggie's shouting match this morning, a call from my parents' attorney, and my never-ending to-do list, Jordan's pathetic attempt to gain my sympathy was the perfect catalyst for a mini freak out tirade. And, actually, it didn't even scratch the surface of what I wanted to and could've said. But, God, it felt good. Really good. The last part was an empty threat considering I've never used Photoshop, but I could always learn. And he deserves to sweat.

I'm lost in my own thoughts when a sharp rap on the passenger window makes me jump halfway to the roof of the car. When I look over, I'm greeted by the scowl of a guy wearing a baseball cap pulled low and dark sunglasses that hide his eyes. He's on crutches, but I can't tell what his injury is beyond being of the lower body variety. Quickly surveying his features, I realize he's ridiculously, unequivocally attractive. Dark strands with a few dirty blond highlights spilling out from under the cap. A layer of scruff on his jawline, like he hasn't shaved in a couple of days. Plush lips I'd bet money weren't real if they belonged to a female. Wide shoulders and a broad chest that tapers down into a narrow waist. Golden biceps approximately half the width of a tree trunk. Under different circumstances, I'd admire his strong jaw and the muscular build his cut-off t-shirt puts on display. Maybe I'd also acknowledge the fact he's *exactly* the type of guy that attracts me. But, while I can't see his eyes, my gut tells me he's staring daggers at me.

Daggers I stare right back.

"Can I help you?" I ask, hitting the automatic lock button. Arbor Cove doesn't have much crime, but the summer season brings an influx of visitors. For all I know, the crutches are a rouse, and he's either the first reporter to dig deep enough to find us all the way out here, or he's here to rob me. I'm not sure which one would be worse.

"Okay, look, I can appreciate dedication, but you've taken it too far. Is there no line some of you people won't cross?" he snaps, arms folding over his chest as he mutters something else under his breath. It's irrational considering his less-than-pleasant tone, but I can't stop myself from swallowing at the sight of him. He's either a total lunatic or a total stoner, but there's no denying the man's allure between his looks and the faint accent I can't place.

Regardless, I'm pretty sure whatever he's insinuating wasn't a compliment, and any peace I had found by unleashing my wrath on Jordan is long gone.

"*You people?* What does that even mean? And, I'm sorry, are you seriously going to stand there and judge me for a *private* conversation you apparently eavesdropped on?"

He frowns and rolls his eyes like I'm testing his patience by asking a perfectly valid question. "I don't give a damn about your conversation, as disturbing as it was. I'm talking about the trespassing. Are you so bad at your job that you couldn't get decent shots from a distance and thought it would be a good idea to camp out *inside* my car? I've had stalkers with more stealth than that."

"*Your* car?! Stalkers?!" My voice is shrill, but I can't rein it in. This guy is clearly insane. "Listen, I don't know who you are, or if you're high or crazy or what, but this is my aunt's car. And I have Mace, so don't even think about trying anything."

I fish it out of my purse and shake it a little for good measure.

He tilts his head down to gaze at me over the top of his sunglasses, and for some reason, his stare makes my pulse spike. And, annoyingly, not in a *WARNING: STRANGER DANGER!* kind of way. I shouldn't even be thinking about how hot he is, and yet it's all my body seems to register. Thankfully, my brain is able to hold it together enough to put an end to my wayward thoughts.

"You really don't know who I am?" he asks, tone a little less gruff, like he's only just now considered that possibility.

The question is on the tip of my tongue to volley back, but I hold it in. If he's not here as a reporter, that would only serve to pique his interest and make it harder to fly under the radar.

"Nope, sorry to disappoint."

"So, you're not...paparazzi?" he probes, the wrinkle of annoyance between his brows softening marginally.

That elicits a genuine laugh from me, the kind I haven't experienced in months. It also means he really must not know who I am, either. "Me? Paparazzi? No. Hell no. Trust me, that is literally the last profession I would ever consider."

Something that wants to be a smile tries to break through, but he swallows it instead and nods at the camera dangling around my neck, semi-scowl back in place. "Then what's with the camera?"

So grumpy.

"Not that it's any of your business, but my aunt is Lorraine McDaniels," I explain, gesturing toward the billboard advertising her gallery behind him. "And I was taking photos of that for the website. Look, whoever-you-are, I realize you must be someone who's used to dealing with varying degrees of the stalker-azzi, but just so you know, minding my own business in the privacy of my car means I'm *not* trying to get pictures of you. Shocking, I know. But it's true."

He scoffs, and I somehow find his continued annoyance kind of…sexy? *That can't be right.*

And yet, the longer my eyes linger on the tanned column of his throat or his broad chest, the dryer my own throat goes.

Until he speaks, his tone dripping in enough disdain to smack those errant thoughts right out of my head. "Maybe another day I'd find it amusing that you keep calling this *your* car, but I'm waiting for someone, so I'm afraid I don't have the patience to keep this going right now."

My jaw drops. "Fine with me; you're not the only one running out of patience. I'm calling it *my* car because it is the car I am currently driving. But if you want to argue semantics, it's my aunt's car."

"No…I'm betting *that* is your aunt's car," he says, pointing two spots to my left. To an identical, *dirtier* black Mercedes SUV.

Oh.

My.

God.

I'm in the wrong car.

2

DOMINIC

*H*olding my right crutch against my body with my elbow, I lift my hand to unlock the doors with my key fob and watch my would-be stalker girl's face morph into fifty shades of mortified. Something between a groan and a laugh bubbles out of her, and I almost feel bad for rubbing salt in her wounded pride. I was already in a bad mood, and spotting her in my car while sporting a camera around her neck, only made things worse.

But now the whole situation is kind of...funny.

Too bad her face tells me she doesn't agree. Flustered and blushing furiously, I can't take my eyes off her. She's young, possibly even a decade my junior. But that doesn't stop me from taking her in. She's got dark, wavy hair, electric blue eyes a shade brighter than mine, and full lips stained hot pink. She's used to garnering stares, that's for sure, but my curiosity stems from more than that. Well, more than *just* that.

In the span of a few awkwardly silent seconds, I've racked my brain unsuccessfully for a way to fix this situation.

She breaks the silence before I can, locking eyes with me, a renewed sense of determination painted on her face. "Is it irony or just poetic justice that five minutes ago, I was convinced *you* were the lunatic?"

A laugh sputters out of me, rusty and gruff, like it's a foreign practice for my throat. Probably because it has been as of late. "If it makes you feel better, this was definitely the highlight of my day."

She gives me a look of disbelief and rolls her eyes. "So glad my humiliation could provide entertainment for you. *Not*," she says, jumping out of my car like it's on fire and jogging toward hers.

Somehow, this brief exchange has pulled me out of the fog of absolute misery I've been wallowing in for the past two weeks. I'm not sure why or how I feel about that, but before I can give it much thought, I'm hobbling after her. "Wait! What's your name?"

"Name? Never got one of those!"

She rips the door open and launches herself into the driver's seat without sparing me a glance.

"I'm Dominic," I offer, watching her closely for any kind of reaction. But she's still so flustered, nothing registers. It's not often I can get by without being recognized, so this is uncharted territory. Normally I'd relish the privacy, but something about this girl makes me wish she *did* know who I am. Maybe then she wouldn't be running away from me.

"Good for you!" she tosses back.

"You're really not going to give me a name?"

"Guess you'll just have to make one up for telling your friends about your encounter with the crazy, non-stalker girl. Victoria. Melanie. Emma. Geri. There, now I've given you four to work with."

"Pretty sure what you've given me is a preview of the Spice Girls' Wikipedia page."

A smile pulls at one corner of her mouth, but she quickly dismisses it. "Okay, driving away now. Good luck with all the other nonexistent paparazzi stalkers in Arbor Cove!"

And just like that, she's gone before I can get another word in. I watch the SUV until it's out of my line of sight, telling myself what I feel is a relief to have the misunderstanding sorted out. A relief that she wasn't some obsessed stalker or reporter. Not a disappointment at her departure.

That would be ridiculous.

Hobbling back over to my rental, I have to actively force myself to shove any lingering questions about her out of mind and focus on why I'm in this place to begin with—rehabbing my stupid leg. It's weird. I chose Arbor Cove for my recovery because my mom pointed out I'd be able to recuperate in peace here. I wanted to believe her, but we haven't vacationed here since my brother and I were kids, so there was no way to know if it would still be the same small town from back then. I got a little stir crazy while waiting in the car for Ellen to fill my prescription, so I figured a short trip down the block wouldn't hurt, considering the street was mostly deserted. After being in the spotlight for fifteen years, I'm usually not surprised when a reporter finds me or a fan seeks me out. And usually, I don't even mind. But my patience has run thin lately, so naturally, I jumped to conclusions after seeing a stranger getting into my car. *I blame the pain meds.*

I've never had an issue with the media before—they love me, in fact—but I'm not ready for the extent of my injury to become public knowledge unless it's on my own terms. Not when I know it'll bring up questions I've spent the last few years trying to outrun.

"Dominic? Are you even listening?" Gage's voice calls through the car speakers.

I'm not; I've been staring out my windshield at the billboard for Gallery 84—the same one pointed out to me four days ago. The memory of that exchange brings a half-smile to my face, the first one since that conversation, in fact. And before that, I hadn't smiled in…days? Weeks? Longer?

"Do I have your go-ahead with releasing the statement about the surgery?" he repeats, shattering my good mood with a reminder of my new reality.

Other than a heavy sigh on my end, I meet his question with

more silence. It's not the surgery I'm reluctant to disclose to the public anymore; it's telling the world I won't be back on a tennis court any time soon that I'd rather hold off on. It's a fate I'm not ready to face, even if the boot encasing my left foot is a constant reminder I won't be setting foot on a tennis court for months.

"We can wait," he relents, "but the longer we do, the more the rumors will fly."

I give him another sigh. *As if I don't already know that.* "I need a few days."

"Look, man, I know this is difficult for you," he says, switching from press communications chief mode to friend mode. "I know there's a part of you that thinks you can prove Dr. Shaw and Pierre wrong on your recovery window. And maybe you will. But I know you're also smart enough to consider the long run. You *just* started rehab. Taking some time off is not the end of the world. Pushing yourself to return before you're ready could be."

…*the end of your career.* He doesn't have to speak the words out loud for me to acknowledge their validity.

"Which one of my parents told you to slip that little tidbit into the conversation?"

"It was a joint effort. They're impossible to say no to."

I'm not surprised; Gabriel and Cordelia Moreau are the sport's golden couple and universally loved and respected. Back in their day, they were both tennis superstars in their own rights. Getting together and eventually married made the tennis world love them even more. I used to get annoyed by the constant questions from sports analysts and reporters about their relationship while recycling answers about how much I appreciate and value everything they've taught me. Still, the truth is, I really do love my parents. Even if living in their shadow, on and off the court, can be a bit much at times.

"Figures," I say with a sigh. "About the statement, though, just…hold off until Monday, if possible."

"Monday it is." The typing at his keyboard in the background comes to a halt, and he heaves a sigh after a second. "For fuck's sake, tell me that car alarm is on the TV you're supposed to be sitting in front of, not some public place."

"What are you, my babysitter? I'm injured, not under house arrest. Fresh air does a body good."

"Jesus, Dominic. Maybe you do need an actual babysitter," he mutters. "Being out and about is not the way to speed up recovery *or* stay off the press's radar. All it would take is one tweet, and that peace you were so insistent on finding in Nowhere, Connecticut would be gone."

He's right, but after a week of barely moving from the couch, I needed to do something—anything—outside the walls of my rented beach house. Most days having a spectacular view of the ocean only irritates me. The ocean's beauty means nothing when I can't even fucking walk without crutches.

"I'm sitting in my car by an empty basketball court. Not exactly the epicenter of trouble. Also, I'm happy to report there are definitely not any reporters camped out in Arbor Cove."

"You're a Moreau; trouble comes to you, regardless of geography."

"Think you've got me confused with my brother. Or Carter. Unlike them, I can handle myself when it comes to the media."

"I know you're capable of charming fans and reporters, Dominic, but you're forgetting that the press loved Carter once upon a time too."

"Good point. Guess I should cancel the massive party I'm throwing tonight."

He doesn't bother calling my bluff. "Just...try not to do anything that will make my job harder."

"No promises," I tell him, even though I have no intention of finding trouble or letting it find me. For what I pay Gage, he deserves to be kept on his toes.

He hangs up, muttering something about idiots like me being the source of his high blood pressure.

A few weeks ago, when the draw for the French Open came out, the stage was set for me to face off with my brother Max in the finals, provided we both made it that far. We've played against each other in semifinals or finals of every other grand slam tournament—Wimbledon, the U.S. Open, and the Australian Open—but somehow, never the French Open. Naturally, the tennis world exploded with excitement and anticipation.

But then, in the third game of my first-round match, one wrong move snapped my Achilles tendon. As a veteran professional tennis player with more than a couple of surgeries under my belt, I'm no stranger to ailments and injuries that come with my sport's territory, but this was another level of pain. I knew I was out for longer than just the tournament. Sure enough, the next day, my doctor said the MRI confirmed surgery would give me the best chance at preventing future injuries. It wasn't a tough decision to make; the conversation with my team mostly consisted of my physical therapist and trainer discussing recovery time and its impact on my schedule for the rest of the year while I sat there lost in my own thoughts, only halfway listening.

Now, instead of facing off with Max in the final, I'm thousands of miles away, almost wishing I didn't have to watch the match at all. But I could never actually let myself not watch Max play in the finals of a grand slam. From a young age, our parents always made sure Max and I understood that family comes before everything else, even in tennis. We're ruthlessly competitive on a tennis court, even—and maybe especially—against one another, but we're the other's biggest supporter when we're not across the net from each other. And after those matches, we switch from competitors to brothers in an instant. It wasn't always that way. As kids, we would pout and hold grudges and give dirty looks after playing each other, but we've come a long way since those days.

In fact, I should probably call him. We always talk before big matches, even if it's just a quick "good luck" kind of conversation. But this time…it's different. I've avoided his calls since my surgery. His name taunts me from my phone's screen, but before I can tap it, a sudden, rhythmic bouncing draws my attention to the basketball court's far side. It's a kid, and he looks young enough that I'm a little surprised to see he's alone. The last thing I need is for this kid to scream, "STRANGER DANGER!" at the top of his lungs, but the idea of leaving him here without an adult doesn't sit well with me.

Grabbing my crutches, I climb out of the car and slowly make my way over to the court. He sinks a few shots, dribbling around for different angles before one hits the rim, and the ball bounces toward me.

"You're pretty good," I tell him, using a crutch to roll the ball back to him.

He grabs the ball and slowly looks up at me, suspicion furrowing his brow. His mouth opens to reply, but before any words come out, his eyes go wide, and his jaw slackens as recognition dawns. "Whoa! You're Dominic Moreau," he exclaims, shock replacing the wariness from ten seconds ago.

"I am."

"This is so cool. I've seen you play before. I'm Liam," he says, coming over to offer me his hand.

"Nice to meet you, Liam. I take it you're a tennis fan?"

He hesitates for a second before nodding slowly. "Yep. Well...I do like tennis a lot, I guess, but not as much as basketball. Sorry."

His honest response draws another smile from me. "That's okay. I like basketball too." I scan the area again, searching for signs of an adult or someone else with him, but there are only a couple of teenagers on the far side of the park, sitting on top of a pair of monkey bars. "So, I gotta ask, do your parents know you're here?"

His face falls, and I immediately get the feeling that's a sore spot for him. "My sister's coming to get me. She'll be here soon."

"Oh. Well, how about I hang out with you until she gets here?"

He cocks an eyebrow and shrugs. "I don't need a babysitter, just so you know. But we could shoot hoops...if you wanna lose to a nine-year-old."

"Hoops, huh? Not sure how fair that would be. I'm clearly at a disadvantage."

"Excuses, excuses," he offers, taking off on a dribble. After easily making a lay-up, he turns to me with a brow arched in skepticism. "Can you play horse with one good leg? How about I play with one foot too? Then you can't use that as an excuse for losing."

This kid. I laugh and shake my head, hobbling behind him toward the hoop. He gives me a few much needed warm-up shots, firing off questions along the way. It's refreshing, though, because while his questions are ones I've been asked countless times in interviews, he soaks up my answers like a sponge, and I can tell they all come from innocent curiosity. I didn't even hesitate to tell him about my surgery when he asked about my foot.

"Does it still hurt?"

"Did you always want to go pro in tennis?"

"What would you do if you didn't play tennis?"

"Do you like being famous?"

"Have you ever met Steph Curry or Kevin Durant?"

Liam actually follows through with playing on one leg (so I "can't accuse him of cheating"), and after both getting "H" and "O," we find a groove for shooting on one foot and make our next few shots. He doesn't volunteer much information about himself, so I let him continue firing questions my way instead of prying into his life. At first, I found it amusing that he was willing to play one-footed, but when we're tied with only an "E" left, I realize his skills actually back up his trash talking. My one-handed shot from the baseline sails in, and I'm genuinely relieved.

"Damn it," he groans as the ball bounces off the rim. "I mean, *darn it.*"

I stifle a laugh at his correction. We just met half an hour ago, but I can tell he's a lot like I was at his age—*highly* competitive.

I take another look around the park on our walk to a table in the shade, but there's still no sign of an adult. Liam just shrugs and says, "You don't have to wait with me. My sister says I'm the most responsible nine-year-old she knows."

"That's a high compliment. Unless you're the *only* nine-year-old she knows."

"I'm not. I have a twin sister. But she always forgets her homework and loses her glasses. So she's *way* less responsible than me."

"My brother always lost stuff when we were kids too. Sometimes he'd even forget his racket when we'd go to practice," I say, smiling at the flash of memories from our childhood of all the times I'd have to bail him out by loaning him my spare racket.

Liam snickers and shakes his head. "Let's hope he doesn't do that on Sunday." He turns and looks up at me, tossing the ball between his hands. "It sucks he's in the finals, and you're not. I bet you would've made it if you hadn't gotten hurt."

"You're right. It does suck. But I'm also happy for him. He's played well and deserves to be in the finals."

"Yeah, he's pretty good. How come you're not going to be there to watch him in person?" he asks, before his eyes fall to my booted foot. "Oh, 'cause you can't travel after having surgery?"

I spend a second considering the question. A yes would be the easier answer. But it wouldn't be a completely honest one, and after spending the last two weeks drowning in half-truths, honesty has its appeal. Plus, it's not likely this kid is going to run off and sell my secrets to the highest bidder. "Truthfully," I finally manage, "right after I got injured, I wasn't sure I'd want to watch the finals at all. I knew he was playing really well and would probably make it. Knowing I missed out on not only the whole tournament but also potentially playing him in the finals was... tough to accept. But, at the end of the day, I'll always support my brother. Plus, I've never missed the finals of a major, whether I'm in it or just watching from afar."

"Never?" he asks, reeling back with his mouth hanging open in shock.

"Not for as long as I can remember. I'm a player, but also a fan of the sport in general."

His eyes fall to the ground. "My dad played tennis in college, so he still plays and watches all the time. I don't watch every tournament, but I like watching majors with him sometimes. Well, I used to like watching them with him. But he doesn't live with us anymore." He looks up and gives me a heartbreaking half-smile. "We actually went to the finals when you won in New York last year. It made me like tennis more—not more than basketball," he quickly clarifies, "but it was awesome. My dad said it was the best he'd ever seen you play."

Usually, a compliment like that would make my chest swell with pride. But his use of the past tense is unmistakable, and it cracks my heart for him instead. "Sounds like a great dad."

"Yeah," he replies, his voice thick with emotion as he tries to subtly swipe away a lone tear.

Shit. Bringing him to tears was not my intention, and now I feel terrible.

"Liam!" a voice calls from across the court before I can come up with a response.

We both look over and see who I assume is Liam's sister walking toward us. Her eyes widen when they land on me, and she quickly pulls her phone away from her ear and hangs up. It only takes another second for me to make the same realization she just did. Her hair is straight today, but it's the same bright blue eyes that meet mine.

And that same rosy blush is creeping over her cheeks.

Something twists in my gut—the same feeling from the other day, but I refuse to analyze it.

"Hey," Liam says, oblivious to the recognition between us. He turns back to me. "That's my sister Tristan. Tris, this is—"

"Dominic Moreau. I see that," she finishes, plastering a neutral expression on her face. *So she knows who I am, after all.* It makes me wonder if she looked me up or already knew before we crossed paths. I've gotta hand it to her; she's a great actress. If not for the faint blush and brief, unfiltered reaction to seeing me, I'd think she didn't even remember our run-in. "But you were supposed to meet me at the center. Where there are adults around—ones that *aren't* total strangers."

The look she gives him is a cross between concern and frustration, and I get the distinct feeling this isn't the first time he's been on the receiving end of such a look.

But it only affects him for a second before he scoffs. "Puh-lease. He's on crutches. It's not like he's in any condition to kidnap me. All I'd have to do is take a crutch and run if he tried."

I fake cough to cover up my laugh because the kid's got a point, but I'm smart enough not to voice that opinion.

"That's not the point. It could've been anyone in the park. Next time, ask *before* you leave the center without permission."

"I thought Maggie was picking me up, not you. I texted her I was coming here."

She frowns apologetically and glances down at her phone. "Sorry, bud, she had to stay at work, and I guess she just forgot to pass along the message."

"That's okay," he offers, picking up his ball and pushing off the bench. "If it makes you feel better, I was only here by myself for a little while before Dominic said he'd keep me company while I waited for you. We played horse." He turns to me with narrowed eyes and a determined grin. "I still want a rematch."

"You got it," I agree with a grin to match his.

Tristan's eyes finally meet mine for a beat before going back to her brother. "That was…kind of him. Did you thank him for hanging out with you?"

He looks over and mimics her tone when he says, "Thank you for hanging out with me. I had fun."

"Me too," I reply, holding my fist out for him to bump. And I mean it. I'd say I've been cooped up for long enough to enjoy anyone's company, but I genuinely like the kid, which is more than I can say for a lot of people these days.

"Seriously, thank you," Tristan says, meeting my eyes. "I'm sure meeting you will be the highlight of his summer."

"Don't mention it, happy to help. Even here in Arbor Cove, you never know what kind of *high* or *crazy* people might be lurking around. No telling what someone like that might be capable of."

"T-true," she says, fighting a losing battle against a smile that breaks through before she bites her lip to contain it. It's the kind that simultaneously pulls you in and punches you in the gut, and I can't help but smile back. "Well, thanks again, Dominic, for keeping my brother company. I'm sure you're busy, so we won't monopolize any more of your time. C'mon, Liam, grab your bag so we can go."

"Aw," Liam whines, though complies with her request. "Do we have to? Dominic owes me a horse rematch."

"Yes, I'm sorry, we do need to go. But guess what?"

"What?" he asks with minimal enthusiasm.

"Jo's almost here! For two sleepovers!"

The news makes his face light up. "Really? Okay, we can go!"

"Thought so," she says, wrapping her arm around his shoulders.

Liam looks back at me. "Maybe I'll see you around another time for that rematch? I know for a fact you're not busy practicing."

I nod through a laugh and hold out my hand to shake on it. "You're right; my schedule is pretty open."

"Cool. See ya later, then. And tell your brother I said good luck."

"Thanks, I will. And nice meeting you...*Tristan*? Or was it Victoria?" She might not want to acknowledge the other day, but that doesn't mean I won't.

Tristan studies me for half a second before rolling her eyes and biting back what can only be described as a half-smile-half-grimace.

"It's Tristan," Liam clarifies for her, one brow raised in confusion. "Victoria isn't even close, dude."

"Yeah, I thought that sounded wrong. Tristan definitely suits you better."

"Uh huh, okay, yeah, good talk," she rattles off, flustered and unwilling to indulge this conversation any longer. Her arm around Liam urges him to pick up the pace. She clicks the locks on her car before glancing back for one last look. "See you around...apparently," she adds under her breath.

Once again, she drives off, leaving me with a smile and even more questions than the first time.

At least this time, I know there will be a next time.

And I'm pretty sure we'd both be lying if we said Liam was the only one looking forward to it.

3

TRISTAN

*C*lick. *Clack. Click.*

My head whips up at the distinct sound of crutches moving against the restaurant's tile. "You've got to be *freaking* kidding me," I groan the second my suspicion is confirmed. *Three times in one week? Seriously?* In a town this small, I shouldn't be surprised, but it's going to be difficult to forget the most mortifying incident of my life if I keep seeing his face around every corner. It doesn't help that Josie and I came to the most popular restaurant in town for dinner. He stops at the to-go counter, and I can't help feeling relieved he's not dining in.

"What?" Josie asks as she swivels around to see what I'm seeing. *Great.* After dumping Jordan, she went full speed ahead with her traditional post-breakup makeover. Now sporting lilac-colored hair, she's pretty hard to miss. The mixture of a sigh and moan that escapes her throat tells me exactly where her eyes landed. "My god, he looks even bigger and hotter in person. Pixels on a screen really don't do that man justice. And that accent..." she says, shaking her head as she fans herself off dramatically.

Last night, meeting Dominic was all Liam could talk about. Then, after the twins went to bed, I told Josie about *the incident,* and she spent the next hour doing the kind of online stalking that should qualify her for a restraining order. She's not wrong though —the slight twinge of a French accent, thanks to his dual citizenship between the U.S. and France (one of the countless "fun facts" Josie dug up last night), is what tips the sexiness scale into the *how-is-he-real* category.

"Jo, you've seen plenty of famous, hot athletes in person," I counter with an eye-roll. Sure, Dominic is too hot for words, but her parents own a sports management firm in the city, so she practically grew up around all kinds of athletes. "Stop looking, or he's going to notice. And I'd rather dive under this table than awkwardly wave hello and hope he doesn't think I'm actually a crazy stalker."

She laughs at my attempt to sink into the booth and hide behind a drink menu.

"You're one to talk. So what if his first impression of you was overhearing you yell the word micropenis? I'm sure he thought it was funny. And if he knew the whole story, he'd probably agree Jordan deserved a swift kick to the ego."

I lean around the side of the menu to give her a glare. "Except it wasn't just the micropenis comment. I basically called a global superstar a stoner or a crazy person *while sitting inside his freaking car!* Not to mention, I didn't even realize it was him! I seriously don't think I could have embarrassed myself more. And that's exactly my point—I'm not someone who gets star struck; I should be able to shake it off, be more composed. But if yesterday was any indication, he's not about to let me keep any of my dignity. Plus, can we please remember he was kind of a dick when he thought I was a freaking paparazzo?"

"Oh, come on, don't you think you're being a little unfair? He can't be that bad if he spent what, an hour with Liam?"

"Fine, that was really nice. I'll give him that."

"And he didn't recognize you," she says softly, making me drop the menu to meet her hazel eyes. "That's a check in the pros list these days. But really, though, I still can't get over the fact that *you* didn't recognize *him.* I'm pretty sure he's been on half the billboards of New York at one point or another."

"Well, excuse me for being flustered! He was wearing sunglasses and a cap. Plus, it's not like I walk around Arbor Cove expecting to run into a celebrity."

"Fair enough," she concedes. "But he *is* here, and you've now run into him multiple times. I'd say that's a sign…"

When she doesn't elaborate, I look up and catch her brows waggling in dramatic fashion.

I roll my eyes at her implication. "Really, Jo? A sign I should hook up with a celebrity? First of all, you're insane for even going there. He's literally one of the world's most famous athletes who probably only dates supermodels and actresses, not daughters of disgraced felons. And, secondly, that's actually another reason *not* to interact with him. You spent how long Googling him? The last time he was seen in public was, like, two weeks ago in Paris, when he got injured. Pretty sure it's only a matter of time before him being here attracts at least a few reporters. Things are finally going well for Maggie and the twins. I won't risk messing things up for us here. Fame factor aside, a hookup is the last thing on my list of priorities right now."

I expect Josie to argue or disagree, but she just gives me a sympathetic smile and reaches across the table to squeeze my hand. "I know. I'm sorry. You're right, and I know you've got a lot on your plate right now."

"Good. Now can we drop it and move on?"

"Fine. If that's what you really want," she agrees with a shrug that tells me she still disagrees but won't fight me on it anymore.

"It is. Is he still standing at the counter?" I ask, still halfway hiding behind a drink menu.

She fake stretches in a poor attempt at subtlety to glance back. "No, he's definitely not at the counter."

"Really?" I ask, sitting back up. At the same time, I hear the *click-clack-click* of his crutches right before my eyes find his. *As he walks our way.* "You are a dirty liar, Josephine Holt!" I hiss, darting my attention to her for only a second before lifting my gaze back to him.

Heads turn, and it's not just women looking. If he notices the stares, he doesn't show it. Doesn't even break stride on his way over. His attention never wavers from our table, and I have to force myself not to blatantly stare like everyone else, even though that's all I want to do. Messy hair spilling out of his backward cap, a perfect layer of scruff lining his jaw, a particular air of self-assurance that only comes from being one of the world's sexiest humans. On most, that distinction would feed into arrogance, but with Dominic, it's confidence, and it's part of his appeal.

"Hope I'm not interrupting," he greets, flashing Josie a smile. "Hi, I'm Dominic."

"Josie," she replies, returning his smile and reaching her hand out. "And you're not interrupting. I've actually heard a lot about you."

"From Liam," I clarify quickly. "He told Jo all about meeting you when she got into town last night," I explain, praying my cheeks aren't betraying my mortification. His lips pull into a smirk that tells me they are, so I rush to continue the conversation before he can. "Just so you know, he will hold you to the rematch. He's already been practicing. And he's not the most gracious loser, in case you couldn't tell."

"Yeah, I sorta got that impression. But he really is good. Had me worried I was going to have to use my injury as an excuse for losing. Speaking of Liam, though, I actually came over here to see…" He shifts on his crutches, a flash of uncertainty crossing his features. "He mentioned something about how he used to watch tennis with your dad, and seemed to be having a tough time, so I just thought I'd offer for him to watch the finals tomorrow with me. But only if that's something you're comfortable with. I don't want to overstep."

His unexpected invitation catches me off guard, but it's the part about our dad that shocks me most. "He talked about him? About our dad?"

"Yeah. It was right before you showed up, though, so he didn't say much."

I nod, weighing it all out in my head. I've spent months trying to get Liam to open up about how he's handling everything, but so far, all he does is shut down when I bring up our parents. And if meeting Dominic was enough for Liam to spend the last twenty-four hours walking on cloud 9, I can't imagine how happy watching tennis together would make him. I'd never deny him that chance, especially not when he's gone through so much the last six months.

"Are you sure? That's an incredibly generous offer, and I'm sure Liam would love it, but it's totally unnecessary. I'm sure you've already got plans…"

He shakes his head. "Positive. No other plans."

"I, uh…would it be all right if I come too? It's just…" *super awkward to leave him alone with a grown adult who's basically a stranger.*

His lips twitch. "What, you're not comfortable leaving him with some possible stoner crazy person?"

My mouth falls open, but I refuse to let the reference fluster me, yet again. "Yeah, actually, something like that."

That gets a full smile out of him, and I swear it's a sight I could see a million times and still want more of. "Anyone ever tell you you're full of surprises?"

"Maybe once or twice," I answer with a casual shrug.

"I don't doubt it. Of course, by the way. And your sister is welcome as well."

"My sister?"

"Liam mentioned he has a twin sister. I just assume you wouldn't want to leave her home alone? You're both welcome as well."

"Oh, right," I reply, nodding. "Yeah, that would be great. What time?"

"It starts at nine our time. Here," he says, picking up one of the napkins on the table. "Got a pen? I'll give you the address and gate code for where I'm staying."

"Here you go," Josie offers, pulling a pen out of her purse when I'm slow to react.

She flashes me a quick look that says *hello? Earth to Tristan*, but I'm too busy thinking about the last time I can remember seeing

Liam and our dad watch tennis together. Because I'm suddenly flooded with guilt. Not just about forgetting their finals tradition, but for neglecting all the other things we used to do as a family, like weekly pizza competitions or movie and game nights. I've spent the last few months focused on leaving all traces of our old life in New York that I didn't even consider incorporating pieces of it into our new life. But just as swiftly as the guilt came, a tiny seed of hope blooms in my chest. A hope that maybe tomorrow can be a step in the right direction to remedy that.

Dominic props a crutch against the table, balances himself on the other, and scribbles an address before picking it up and holding it out for me.

"Thanks," I tell him with a smile, forcing my thoughts back to the present. When I take the napkin, our fingers brush, sending a little zing through me. I suck a sharp breath and try to shake off the heat, now flooding my neck and cheeks and summon a look of indifference before meeting his gaze. I'm halfway expecting him to subtly acknowledge my reaction, but he's just studying me with his brows drawn and blue eyes narrowed ever so slightly. It's an unreadable look, reminiscent of the way he looked at me when we first met.

And I have no clue what to make of it because before I can fully register the accompanying frown, it fades, and he pushes off the table to pick up his other crutch, inadvertently drawing my eyes to his broad chest. It's outlined perfectly by his t-shirt in a way that makes my hands itch to explore that plane of solid muscle.

Jesus, Tristan. Get a grip.

I quickly pick up my margarita glass and take a healthy gulp, just to have something to do that doesn't involve staring at him.

"So...I'll see you three tomorrow?" he asks after a few awkwardly silent seconds.

"Yep, we'll be there."

He nods and turns to Jo. "Josie, it was a pleasure meeting you. Enjoy your dinner, ladies."

He walks back to pick up his order and stops along the way for a couple of selfies with a group of high school kids.

"See? He indulges his fans even when he's injured and hungry. Marry him," Josie insists the second he's out of earshot. "If you won't, I certainly will."

"Let me know where you're registered, so I can send a gift," I tell her with an eye roll.

"Fine, marriage can be put on the back burner. But seriously, Tris, he's not your average mega-famous, the-world-revolves-around-me athlete. Trust me. I've met enough of them to know. Plus, I was thinking about it while watching you two just now," she says, pausing until I look up at her. "He told Liam he'll be in Arbor Cove for a while, right? I'm assuming however long it takes to recover from the leg injury?"

"Sure, let's say that's the case. What's your point?"

"My point is, my beautiful-but-blind best friend, he might be here for *months*. I think a summer fling with possibly the hottest human being either of us will ever lay eyes on is *exactly* what you need."

She's wrong; a fling is the last thing I need right now, regardless of how hot he is.

"You're either delusional or a little too tipsy," I counter, reaching across to pull her half-empty margarita glass away from her. "Either way, not going to happen. For the same reasons I listed five minutes ago. And it's worth repeating that it doesn't even matter because he's so far out of my league, it's laughable."

"Uh, I'm sorry, did you or did you not date an Olympic gold medalist who shall remain nameless for an entire summer? And a current NBA player before that?"

So, maybe I have a type. Sue me.

"Not the same. They're nobodies compared to him, and you know it."

"I'm just saying...world-famous athlete or not, he wouldn't have hobbled all the way over here on a bum leg to invite you over if he wasn't at least a little interested in seeing you naked."

"You did hear the part where he invited *Liam* over, and I basically invited myself, right?"

"You're crazy if you actually believe inviting Liam over wasn't at least partially motivated by his desire to see you again. A monkey could've seen the sparks between you two."

"I think you're confusing sparks with lingering weirdness from when we first met."

"Uh-huh. So, that banter and joking back and forth was 'weirdness'? And you say *I'm* the delusional one."

I sigh and take a drink from my margarita glass. "You should've gone to law school; you could probably argue whatever point you want until the other person dies from exhaustion."

"Probably," she agrees before leaning in and grabbing her glass back. "So, what are you going to wear tomorrow?"

"I don't know, Jo, probably a muumuu. Or a turtleneck. Or a chastity belt. Just for you, so you'll know there's zero chance of a hookup or a fling or anything remotely romantic happening."

She frowns. "You're a real buzzkill; you know that? The Tristan from last year would've been all over this golden opportunity. Hell, forget the Dominic opportunity, she would've been all over *any* opportunity for a little fun in the romance department."

"Yeah, well, the Tristan from last year had to grow up fast and accept some responsibility. That means thinking about more than just herself," I fire back, a little harsher than I meant.

"God, you're right. I'm the worst. I promise I'll stop, okay? No more talk about Dominic or guys or romance."

I wave a hand to dismiss her apology and pick up the menu again. "It's fine, really. Let's just order food, and you can help me figure out how to decipher the teenage brain. I really thought it wouldn't be that hard, considering I was one not that long ago, but I can't seem to get more than ten words at a time out of Maggie."

She nods and picks up her menu. "Okay, but if we're delving into the world of teen drama, I'm going to need another drink."

Agreed.

4

TRISTAN

I should never have let Josie talk me into having a third margarita last night.

That becomes glaringly obvious when Dominic shows Liam and Genevieve the theater room in his house. Inside, a giant screen is currently showing announcers talking about the match and various breakfast foods cover the coffee table. The twins both jump up and down like little gremlins, going on and on about how awesome his house is. *Loudly.*

I hold back a grimace and excuse myself to the bathroom down the hall.

Waterfront, with a beautiful backyard pool area overlooking the beach, a massive porch in the front, an open kitchen full of high-end appliances, a bright, inviting living room, and a freaking home theater — the house looks like a home featured in a magazine spread. It's a little sparse on the decor and lacks personal touches, but that's not surprising, considering it's a rental. Once upon a time, my parents might've rented a place like this for a family getaway weekend. Now, I was damn lucky to find a decent four-bedroom house to rent without completely draining my savings account.

By the time I trudge back into the kitchen, Dominic is perched on a stool at the oversized island, sipping from a coffee cup and scrolling on his phone. He's wearing a black t-shirt with its sleeves cut off, athletic shorts, and a backward baseball cap with what I now recognize as his logo on it. I want to pull the hat off to see what he looks like without it for once, but I know from Josie's internet stalking session that he looks just as good with messy hat hair.

Before it becomes awkward because he doesn't realize I'm here, I clear my throat and nod toward the theater room. "You really didn't have to go through the trouble of getting breakfast set up," I tell him, though the lingering aroma of fresh baked goods makes my stomach rumble in disagreement. Especially since between getting Josie to the train station and wrangling the twins, I barely remembered to grab Pop-Tarts for everyone on our way out the door.

"What kind of animal invites people over at 8 a.m. and doesn't at least offer to feed them? I can't take the credit, though, it all came from that bakery over on Tulip Street, and they delivered."

"Ah, you mean Molly's. Those must be blueberry scones I smell. Good choice," I say, doing my best not to let any drool escape my mouth.

He nods before gesturing toward a coffee maker. "Feel free to grab some if you'd like. Cups are in the cabinet above it. Sugar's to the left, and there's milk in the fridge."

I'm already halfway there by the time he finishes the offer. "If I ever turn down coffee, something is seriously wrong."

"Noted," he says with a laugh.

I quickly pour my cup and add a splash of milk, and Dominic and I fall into a silence that's not exactly awkward, but it isn't comfortable either. He's alternating between texting and sipping his coffee. It suddenly occurs to me; this has to be weird for him—watching his brother compete in one of the biggest stages of their sport, from another country, with virtual strangers. When I think about it like that, it's hard not to wonder what's going through his head. Liam told me Dominic said he watches every finals match of the majors, but I assume he usually watches with his family or someone from his team. Plus, I looked it up; he's been in the semis or finals of almost every major for the last eight years, so it's not like he even has much experience watching them as a spectator.

"Are you nervous?" I blurt out, causing him to look up. "For your brother, for the match?"

"A little," he replies, shrugging. "I think we both get nervous for each other, though, whether it's a first-round match or the finals. He's been playing well all tournament, so I know he's ready. But it's just...I don't know, hard to watch, I guess."

He doesn't elaborate, so I can't tell if he means hard to watch his brother from here or hard to watch because he was expected to be in this match and is laid up with an injury, instead. Either way, it would explain why he was willing to invite us over. Maybe Liam's not the only one who needs a tennis watching companion today.

"I bet. I can't imagine being in your shoes."

My eyes fall to his left leg, and he answers my question before I can even ask it. "Torn Achilles. One second, I was chasing the ball down, and the next, my left leg was on fire. Had surgery three days later."

"Wait, you just had surgery, and you're here by yourself? Shouldn't you have, I don't know, at least a few people around helping?"

He shrugs and waves off my questions. "My mom was with me for the surgery and helped right after, but I told her she should go back to Paris after Max won his quarterfinal match. I came here, to Arbor Cove, specifically to avoid being around people. Gave my team some time off; it's not like I can train anyway. And I'm not completely alone. We have a family friend who lives a few minutes away. She's been looking after me."

Oh, I'm sure she has. The thought comes out of nowhere, accompanied by a completely irrational and unwelcome bolt of something that feels acutely like jealousy, and I immediately shut it down.

"I get that. The wanting to get away thing." Our situations are vastly different, but it's kind of comforting, in a way, that we both know what it's like to need a change of scenery. "Why'd you choose Arbor Cove?"

"My mom grew up in Bridgeport, and when Max and I were kids, we spent our summers here. Once our training schedules picked up, we weren't able to travel for much other than tournaments. So, when I wanted peace and quiet for my recovery, this was the first place that came to mind."

"Ah yes, peace and quiet…let me guess, a basketball hustling nine-year-old and a crazy wannabe carjacker-slash non-stalker were exactly what you had in mind?"

Our eyes catch, and we both realize I've just opened the door for him to steer the conversation to the one topic I've been trying *not* to acknowledge in his presence.

A corner of his mouth pulls up as he slowly shakes his head. "Not exactly. Although, I meant what I said, walking up to find a woman in my car, shouting something about a microp—"

"Oh god, please don't remind me!" I groan, pulling a hand up to cover my face.

"Remind you of what? Oh, you mean that time you were threatening to give some poor man a micropenis using Photoshop and send it into the world? Don't remind you of that?"

Inhaling a breath, I drop my hand and force myself to meet his gaze. He's biting back a smile, and the sight of a teasing, playful Dominic is enough to bring long-dormant butterflies to life in my stomach. But I only let them flutter for a second before reality swats them down. *Liam—I'm here to make Liam happy, not get caught up in Dominic's charms.*

"Listen, in my defense, that was Josie's ex on the other side of the conversation, and he probably deserves a lot more than a lame empty threat. In a nutshell, he's an asshole, and that was my first opportunity to give him an honest piece of my mind. Definitely not my finest moment, but I also don't regret it. Just the part where, you know, I was in a stranger's car then yelled at him for being the crazy one. That part was definitely regrettable."

"I don't know," he says with a slow shake of his head. "I'm not so sure regrettable is the right word."

The smirk he's wearing, accompanied by the way he said that, sounds...*flirty?* I try to convince myself otherwise, but my skin is already tingling.

He's about to elaborate when Liam's voice carries into the kitchen, cutting our conversation short. "Dominic! Tristan! They're warming up, hurry!"

"Guess that's our cue," he says, pushing up to collect his crutches.

I nod and turn to top off my coffee before grabbing his as well and following behind him. Probably best we don't venture down whatever road that was about to turn into.

When we get to the theater room, Liam pats the spot on the couch next to him, waving Dominic over like he's saved him the last empty seat. It's actually adorable, seeing him this excited. Genevieve sprawls out on the couch on the raised platform behind them, so I plop down next to her. Totally coincidental that this vantage point gives me a view of the screen *and* Dominic.

By the time the match starts, I've filled a plate up with scones and fresh fruit to share with Gen, ignored Josie's text of a GIF with cartoon characters kissing, and managed to only glance at Dominic a handful of times. But really, though, does it even count if I'm mostly watching because it's ridiculously adorable to see Liam so giddy and excited about both the match *and* being around Dominic? He played it cool the day they met, but this—being in Dominic's house and watching the finals of a major he has actually played in and won—is entirely different. He mimics Dominic's fist pumps when Max hits a good shot or wins a point and occasionally asks a question about Max or Matteo Amaro, his opponent. I don't think I've seen Liam smile this much over the last three months combined.

Eventually, Gen ditches me to join Liam and Dominic, her excitement and enthusiasm matching Liam's. I can't even be mad; it's making my heart swell to see them this happy. It doesn't hurt that Dominic is a really good sport about it, even though I'm sure they're making it harder for him to pay attention as closely as he'd like.

I'm so distracted by their interactions that I don't even notice what's going on in the match until both Liam and Genevieve jump up, whooping and cheering like lunatics. Somehow Max has already won the first set, and I've only paid attention to a handful of points. Dominic gives high fives and fist bumps but quickly refocuses on the match when the second set gets underway.

I've seen pictures of Dominic and Max together, so I knew they shared physical characteristics, but when the camera zooms in on Max, I realize I hadn't actually paid that much attention to the younger Moreau in those photos. His hair is a bit lighter, but his eyes are as striking and blue as Dominic's. The Moreau gene pool must run deep because there's no mistaking their resemblance. Or the fact a key component of their genes is apparently hotness. Good lord. Those two in one room together would be enough to make any woman forget her own name.

For the next hour, I'm consumed by the second set. Max's level of play remains, but Matteo's rises to make the match more competitive, and it's riveting. They glide across the court and make shots that should be impossible look effortless. Watching this makes me wish I hadn't been so quick to dismiss my dad when he tried to get me interested in tennis as a kid.

Just as Max is set to serve for the second set, the front door opens, and a female voice calls out, "We're here! Sorry we're late!"

Moments later, she appears in the doorway, along with a kid who looks to be around Liam and Gen's age. His eyes bounce from me to Liam to Gen to Dominic and back, before looking back up at the woman. She's pretty, with light green eyes and a short blonde bob. In contrast, the kid has dark green eyes, and his jet black hair styled into a faux-hawk. They share a certain resemblance, but also look completely different.

"Go ahead, honey," she says, nudging him forward.

"What's up, my man?" Dominic says, peeling his attention from the screen and offering him a fist bump. "This is Liam, that's Genevieve, and she's Tristan. Guys, this is Kai."

He gives us each a nod and shy smile before hesitantly joining

Gen and Liam on the couch. And just like that, all four of them are laser-focused on the match again.

"Hi, I'm Ellen," the woman tells me, smiling sweetly as she comes into the room. She's close enough now for me to realize that she's older than I initially thought—there are faint lines at the corner of her eyes and some rogue gray hairs, putting her somewhere around sixty.

"Tristan," I reply, shaking her hand.

I'm curious about Ellen and Kai, but decide to hold off on questions. The kids erupt into cheers as Max wins the set, and Dominic indulges their high five requests before pulling out his phone to fire off a text.

"So, Tristan, you're Lorraine McDaniels' niece, right? And you're working at the gallery?" Ellen asks over the surrounding chaos.

I nod, praying she doesn't ask more questions about our family. When we first arrived in Arbor Cove, I wondered if we'd have to deal with small-town gossip or any kind of adversity after word got out about who we are. So far, though, all we've gotten is the occasional eyebrow raise at the grocery store or a lingering stare at the coffee shop. For the most part, the people of Arbor Cove have been nothing but welcoming.

Thankfully, Ellen doesn't even hesitate or give me a curious look.

"I just love her work. In fact," she says, looking around, "I've been wanting to redecorate. I'd love to have a consultation and maybe brainstorm some ideas sometime this week, if possible."

"Sure, I'd be happy to check Lorraine's schedule and get back to you…" I trail off, trying to put the pieces together.

She must read the confusion on my face because she quickly explains, "I own this house and a few others in the area as rental properties. I've known Cordelia since childhood, and when Dominic and Max were kids, we'd all spend summers together out here. So when Dominic needed a place, they knew who to call."

So, Ellen is the "family friend" who's been helping Dominic since the surgery. *Good to know.*

With the third set underway, I redirect my attention to the screen, watching Max and Matteo as they continue to throw everything they've got at each other. It's astounding, really, how effortless they make it look to hit shots no normal person could ever hope to return.

My ringtone tears my attention away, and when I click to silence it, the name on the screen makes my stomach sink.

Frank Belford.

I should answer, but all I manage to do is stare at the device until the letters blur together. Thankfully, everyone else's attention is on the match, so I quietly excuse myself from the room. I pace in front of the floor-to-ceiling glass windows in the living room after letting it go to voicemail when my screen lights up with his name again. The thought of speaking with my parents' attorney shouldn't fill me with this much dread. After a deep breath, I connect with his call and resume pacing. "Hi, Mr. Belford. Is something wrong? Now's not really a good time for me to talk."

"Well then," he says with a scoff. "In that case, I guess I should be grateful you managed to answer my call at all, Ms. Fitzgerald. Especially considering you haven't answered the last three."

I try to focus on the crashing waves in the distance to keep my frustration at bay, but it's not working. Unclenching my jaw, I manage to channel the same fake sweetness I'd give my father's former bitchy assistants and say, "I'm so sorry; working full time and taking care of my siblings leaves me with little free time. You understand."

"Of course. Of course, you're absolutely right," he backtracks. "Speaking of, how is everyone? No more violent incidents with Liam, I take it? And the other one, Gwen? How's she doing? And your job at the art store?"

For the thousandth time, I regret telling him about Liam's altercation at school. He was skeptical about my abilities to care for my siblings before that, and telling him only fueled his doubt.

"*Gen* is fine. Liam is doing well. As is Maggie. She got a job at a dance studio for the summer, and the twins are enrolled in a summer program at the community center," I tell him proudly. The smile tugging my lips up isn't faked, not when I genuinely am proud of how far the four of us have come. "And my job at the *gallery* is great. So, we're all good here."

"Wonderful. It certainly seems as though things are on the right track for you kids," he comments, sounding surprised.

I'm tempted to call him out on it, but it's not like that would accomplish anything, and the cheers ringing out in the other room remind me what I'm missing. "Uh-huh, sure. Like I said, Mr. Belford, I'm actually in the middle of something, so is there something specific you needed to discuss?"

"Ah, yes, we'll get right to business then. Your father tells me you're not taking his calls. And your mother said you've yet to go visit."

And there are no fewer than a dozen reasons for that.

"I have nothing to say to them. And frankly, I don't really see how that's any of your business."

He sighs like I'm being dramatic, but I stand by that statement. My parents lost the right to summon me at their leisure when they became felons. "They're still your *parents*, young lady, and you left them no choice but to involve me to relay their message."

Now I'm the one releasing a heavy sigh. "And what exactly is it they need you to relay?"

"It's about your family's finances. Specifically, an account they opened in your name…"

What feels like an eternity later, I'm still going back and forth with Mr. Belford when deafening cheers erupt from the theater room. My stomach sinks when I realize I've probably missed the end of Max's match.

"Mr. Belford, I'm going to have to call you back," I tell him, not even remotely apologetic about interrupting. "But I can tell you now; I won't change my mind."

He huffs in indignation. "Ms. Fitzgerald, I must insist you

reconsider. At the very least, you shouldn't be rushing to a decision. Take some time to think things over."

"I appreciate where you're coming from, but more time won't change my mind."

"Very well, then. You'll still have to come back to the city to sign some paperwork. I'd be remiss if I didn't urge you, once again, to speak with your parents before making a final decision. You could even see your mother on the way here."

The thought of going back to New York—of seeing my parents, of going to Mr. Belford's office, of reopening the door to what feels like a different life entirely—paralyzes me, momentarily suspending my urgency to hang up.

But then Dominic storms out of the room, moving entirely too quickly for someone on crutches with a look of pure anger on his face. I rush to hang up, but he brushes past me without slowing down, only stopping long enough to throw open the sliding door to the back yard.

After watching him for a second, I scramble to the theater room in time to catch Ellen directing the kids to play foosball in the room across the hall. Whatever happened, it doesn't seem like they were affected.

"What in the world happened?" I ask, flicking my attention between Ellen and the TV, where the trophy presentation is currently taking place. The screen splits between Max's smiling face and his parents and team in the stands, all smiling and snapping picture after picture—a scene I can't imagine Dominic would want to miss.

"The commentators were talking about Max, going on about how well he's been playing lately, and it was all fine and dandy until the conversation temporarily shifted to Dominic. At first, it was just speculation about his injury and wishing him a smooth recovery. But then they mentioned Dominic's recent struggles on the court, and one of them made some idiotic, dubious remarks about a successful comeback at his age if the reports of surgery are true."

"His age?" My brows knit together in confusion. "Isn't he, like, thirty-three? Why does that matter? That's hardly old, even for a professional athlete."

"You're right, but age is a little bit different as a tennis player. The sport is grueling and incredibly demanding on a player's body regardless of age or how fit they may be, and unlike other sports, players must constantly adapt to the different court surfaces and the challenges each presents. Some believe age is also relative to how long a player has been part of the professional tour. In Dominic's case, that would be seventeen years."

My eyebrows skyrocket up. "I had no idea he's been playing that long."

She nods. "And then, of course, injuries also play a big part in a player's longevity, especially if they require surgery."

Suddenly, I wish I had let Josie do more online snooping. I thought the best way to squash my curiosity about Dominic was to shut it down completely. But now I feel like he's one giant puzzle with a bunch of missing pieces.

Maybe I should just step away from the puzzle box altogether.

"Come on," she says, pulling me out of my thoughts. "I'll see what he's got that I can use to throw together for lunch."

"I don't know; maybe it would be best if we just go..."

"Nonsense," she dismisses, continuing into the kitchen. "The kids can play for a while, and you can indulge an old lady in some grown-up conversation. Don't get me wrong, I love my grandson, but there's only so much Minecraft or video game talk I can take."

Her comment makes me smile. "I know exactly what you mean."

Ellen rummages around for a few minutes until she has the ingredients for chicken salad, and we quickly fall into conversation about the trials and difficulties of parenting young kids these days. Without going into detail, she divulges that she recently became Kai's sole guardian, and it's been a somewhat rough transition for them. I'm tempted to ask about it, but she was kind enough to not press for details about my family dynamics, so I respect hers too. Eventually, our conversation shifts to her history with the Moreau family, and I learn she and Cordelia were neighbors as kids, but lost touch once Cordelia's tennis career took off, and she moved away. They reconnected when the Moreaus came to Arbor Cove for vacation, and they discovered their sons were the same age.

By the time she finishes telling me stories of their shared summers here, I have a pretty distinct picture of a miniature version of Dominic running around the beach, all lanky limbs, with an infectious smile and a shaggy mop of maple syrup colored hair flying in every direction.

I don't even realize I'm scanning the back yard, subconsciously seeking out Dominic's all-grown-up frame until Ellen follows my gaze and hums when he's nowhere to be seen. "He probably went around to the garage. Would you mind going to let him know lunch is ready, and I'll get the kids?"

"Sure." It's on the tip of my tongue to question if she should go instead, but my own curiosity wins out, propelling me out the same door he stormed through earlier. When I round the corner from the back yard, the sight in front of me stops me cold. He's turned part of the three-car garage into a makeshift gym with every type of workout equipment imaginable, and he's currently putting the pull-up bar to good use. I'm not sure what I expected to find, but a sweaty, shirtless Dominic working out was definitely not it.

Holy hell.

He's facing away from me, providing the perfect view of his back and shoulders, glistening with sweat as he pulls himself up time after time. The carefully controlled way his body moves makes it seem effortless, like it's not a big deal he's lifting his bodyweight so many times I've lost track now. Too many seconds tick by before I realize my staring is venturing dangerously close to creepy, and yet I can't seem to stop myself. The man is an Adonis, and there's no harm in looking, right?

I finally get myself together enough to clear my throat, but he doesn't slow down or even seem to register my presence. Taking a couple of steps deeper into the garage, I spy two white buds in his ears. For a second, I'm tempted to continue my little spy session. But then he lowers himself completely and drops gently onto his feet, keeping his weight only on his right leg. He bends over and grabs a towel, running it over his face before hanging it around his shoulders. I swallow at the sight, willing my tongue not to fall out of my mouth.

When he turns around, there's so much tension and frustration etched into his features that it's heart-wrenching. And a little scary. He looks up and sees me, and his expression softens just enough so that he isn't glowering at me, before pulling an earbud out.

"S-sorry," I sputter, swallowing thickly because if I thought the unobstructed view of his back was drool-worthy, boy was I mistaken. The sight of his broad chest and carved abs—slick with sweat and tanned to golden perfection—is enough to make me temporarily forget how words work. "I, uh…Ellen made lunch, so I just wanted to let you know."

"Thanks." He nods, but shuffles over to another piece of equipment and hoists himself up, resting his weight on his fore-arms and gripping a bar before lifting his legs up to create a ninety-degree angle.

It's a glaring dismissal, so I take the hint and turn to go back inside without another word. It's hard to reconcile this version of Dominic with the laughing, playful one from just this morning. Part of me considers trying to find the right words to offer, to see if he wants to talk, but he's so locked inside his own head I'm not sure anyone could break through right now, much less someone he barely knows.

"Don't take it personally," Ellen says after the door to the garage slams behind Dominic. "He's still the same giant grump he turned into on Sunday. I've known him nearly all his life, and he's barely offered more than a grunt or the occasional two-word response for three days now."

I didn't think my raised-eyebrow reaction to his lack of enthusiasm for finding me at his kitchen table was noticeable, but apparently, she caught it.

After his cold demeanor lingered on Sunday, even when the kids begged him to play foosball with them, I was prepared to bury every question and ounce of curiosity I had about Dominic Moreau. But then Lorraine delegated the task of coming to Ellen's rental properties to do walkthroughs and take photos of her current decor collections to me. Yesterday wasn't an issue; we were at a house between renters for the day. Today, I spent half the morning walking through and photographing Dominic's living space. I know it's not *his*, technically, but it still felt like an invasion of privacy on some level. Ellen brushed off my concern when I implied as much, saying she'd promised Cordelia she would drop in on Dominic anyway.

I manage to redirect the conversation back to the task at hand, and, thankfully, the rest of our meeting goes smoothly, without another mention or sighting of Dominic.

"So, I'm thinking we start with this property because it's the most accessible currently and has the same layout as the one on Beagle Street. I spoke with Lorraine, and she said it would be no problem for you to come out and get started right away. I was hoping we could have everything ready to go into Beagle Street by the end of next week. That weekend is the only time it's vacant for back to back days through August."

"I'm sure we can make that happen," I assure her with a smile. For the hundredth time, I remind myself that it doesn't matter how Dominic acts, anyway. Ellen's right; I really shouldn't take it personally if he's in a perpetually shitty mood.

And yet, the next day when I arrive to meet Ellen and he's working out in the garage *again*, the way his eyes bore into me upon my arrival—brows pulled together, jaw tight—sure *feels* personal.

Or maybe I'm just imagining things.

Either way, I think that tiny little seed of curiosity I'd tried to kill off by not feeding it just grew roots.

For the next week, this becomes my routine. I arrive a few minutes early and linger in my car while sneaking glances at Dominic from afar as he works out in his makeshift garage gym. Is it borderline inappropriate? Maybe. But I justify my newfound creeper status by convincing myself I'm mostly watching to make sure he's not overdoing his workouts. Really, I'm just looking out for the millions of fans who would be devastated if his recovery was even more delayed because he refuses to accept his body's limits. The fact he's sometimes shirtless and always sweaty is merely a happy coincidence.

Every day, I expect him to eventually come inside at some point while I'm there, but he never does. And every day, my curiosity about how he spends that time grows. It's not like he's doing full-body workouts; I doubt he's even supposed to be doing much of any type of training, yet.

Not surprisingly, today's meeting with Ellen comes and goes without an appearance from Dominic. But when I get back to my car, there's a note tucked under the windshield wiper.

You'll have a better view if you park in the driveway tomorrow.

So much for thinking I wasn't obvious. In true Dominic fashion, I can't tell if he's being flirty or if there's an underlying tone of annoyance in his words. *Guess I'll find out tomorrow.*

5

DOMINIC

"*W*hy are you in such a shitty mood?" Max asks. I should've known better than to accept a FaceTime call from my brother. He's too perceptive, even sixty seconds into a conversation. He's lounging in his oversized hot tub, his preferred way to unwind after a grueling day of practice. I, on the other hand, am wound up and contemplating another workout.

"Not sure if you heard, but I had surgery last month that derailed the hell out of my career," I snap.

"Nah, that's not it. Mom just told me your rehab is going well. This is...different from your 'woe is me' mood. And don't tell me it's those bullshit comments about your age. John's always been a dick who shit talks any player better than he was, and they've never bothered you before. You're pissed about something else."

He's right, but I'm not about to tell him my annoyance stems from the absence of a bombshell brunette I have zero business even thinking about. Over the last week, I saw her stealing glances of me on her way into the house, and each day I've been torn between wanting her to stop or linger on her way out and being relieved when she doesn't. But today, she just didn't show at all, and it's been bothering me all afternoon.

"Yeah, well, I wasn't staring down the barrel of my mid-thirties before." Not a lie—comments and speculation about how long

I'll remain at the top of my game have rolled off my back in the past, motivated me even. But with my thirty-fourth birthday a couple of months away, combined with the fact I'm going to miss the rest of this year, the comments hit a little harder.

Which is why I can't afford a distraction, and that's exactly what Tristan is. A ridiculously hot, intriguing, and possibly too-young-for-me-anyway distraction. I've stuck to short-lived relationships and casual dating for the last decade for a reason—tennis is the love of my life, and I've never been tempted to let a woman come between us. I barely know Tristan, but that hasn't stopped my mind from wandering into completely uncharted territory. So keeping my distance from her is the best and only option.

"You say 'mid-thirties' like it's a death sentence," Max admonishes. When I don't say anything, he sits up, an uncharacteristically serious look coming over his face. "Dom. You're called the iron man of tennis for a reason. You'll probably still be married to tennis long after I hang my racket up."

"Speaking of marriage…you getting nervous? Big day's almost here." Changing the subject to his love life is one way to ensure he forgets whatever he was previously talking about. I love to give Max a hard time about how domesticated he's become, but the truth is I'm beyond happy for him. I can't imagine a better match for him than Chloe.

He shakes his head as an obnoxious grin spreads wide. "Nerves are for matches, big bro. Not for marrying your soulmate. I can't wait."

I make a whip cracking sound effect at the same time I catch Chloe's head pop out of the water next to him before she wraps herself around Max, wasting no time before leaning in to nip his earlobe. Within seconds, the scene turns into a make-out session that's veering into R-rated territory.

"All right, save something for the honeymoon. Jesus," I mutter, though I'm not surprised at the turn things took. "You two clearly have other things going on, so I'm going to let you go. Talk soon."

An hour later, I'm slowly making my way—crutch free—around the Arbor Cove Rec Center's walking trail when a familiar face catches my eye from a bench outside the center. He's looking down at the ground and swinging his legs.

"Hey," I say before dropping onto the bench next to the one Liam's on.

A smile flashes as he looks up and sees me, but it's nothing like the ones that lit up his face last Sunday. "Hey, Dominic. You don't need crutches anymore?"

"Not full-time. Just got permission this morning to start walking without them a little at a time. Which means we can shoot hoops using both legs before too long," I tell him, trying to infuse as much positivity in my voice as possible.

"Cool," he replies without an ounce of enthusiasm.

His somber tone makes me frown. Something must be off if he isn't even remotely excited about his shot at revenge. "You okay?"

He shrugs and keeps his gaze on the ground.

I don't have a lot of experience with nine-year-olds, but it doesn't take an expert to tell he's not okay. Then I look up and see a group of kids playing basketball on a court outside the rec center and realize they look about his age, and they're playing with seven players. "Those guys your friends? Looks like they could use another player."

He swivels around to look but quickly shakes his head, his brows pulling down. "They're *not* my friends."

The way he emphasized *not* gives me the distinct impression there's more to the story. But before I can find a way to ask about it, he looks around and pulls out his phone.

"Your sister on her way?" I ask, trying to temper my excitement about the idea of seeing Tristan.

He nods. "Yeah. But she has to pick Gen up from her art class and drop her off with Tristan first."

My brows shoot up. "You have another sister?"

"Uh-huh. *Three* sisters. And none of them will ever let me forget I'm the youngest."

"This might not make sense yet, but one day you'll appreciate growing up surrounded by so many ladies. It'll give you some unique insight when you're having girl troubles."

"Yeah, Tristan told me that too. She said having them around means they'll be able to make sure I'm 'one of the good guys,' whatever that means. I say having them around gives me a headache."

I shake my head with a laugh. Never know what's going to come out of this kid's mouth. "Well, I don't know about the headaches, but she's right. So, uh, how is she?"

He eyes me with a brow raised as if he's trying to figure out my intentions, before lowering it and shrugging. For a nine-year-old, Liam has the suspicious brother look down well. "Good, I guess. She works a lot." He pauses for a second, a flash of something crossing his features. "Sometimes I think she likes it that way. But mostly, I think she misses her old job in New York and her old friends, and she works a lot so that she doesn't have the time to be sad. She doesn't want us to know she's sad, though, but I can just tell."

My brain soaks in this information like a sponge, but all it does is leave me with more questions. "She lived in New York?"

"Yep. We all moved here a few months ago. After," he pauses, his brows knitting, "after my parents did something bad and had to go away for a long time."

Whoa. Was not expecting that.

"I see," I say slowly, waiting to see if he wants to elaborate.

"Do you think..." After a second, he looks up and meets my eyes with his. "Is it bad that I don't miss them? Sometimes I do, but I'm mostly just mad at them. They ruined *everything*."

"Well, I think there's not always a 'good' or a 'bad' way to feel about certain situations. Your feelings are valid, no matter what they are. You know, your sister seems like a pretty good listener. Do you talk to her about how you're feeling? I bet she could help."

"Nah. She's always worried and stressed, and I don't want her to worry more."

"I'm sure—"

Loud laughter draws Liam's attention back to the group of kids on the court behind us, and I follow his gaze to see several of the kids laughing and joking around while they're getting water. He lets out a sigh and clenches his jaw, clearly bothered by something he saw.

"Did those kids do something to upset you?" I probe, already feeling the urge to go over there and set them straight if my hunch is correct.

He nods.

"Wanna talk about it?"

"Dominic! I know you're here!" a loud voice calls from the porch between heavy bangs on the front door.

Using the crutch-free skip slash hobble I've perfected in the last few days, I get to the door as quickly as I can manage and throw it open. "Tristan? Hey, how's it —"

I don't even have time to finish my sentence or fully appreciate seeing her before she brushes past me into the house. I can practically feel daggers in my chest from the glare she's giving me. "Look, I know you were probably trying to help, but," she says, interrupting herself by whirling toward me to keep us face-to-face. Her chest is heaving, and there's a fire in her eyes. "What did you do? What the hell did you tell him?"

I wonder if she knows how hot she is when she's angry.

I quickly shove that inappropriate thought down deep and bury it. "What did I tell who? What are you talking about?"

"Liam!" she wails, her arms cutting through the air in frustration. "He said *you* were the one who told him how to deal with the kids who were apparently bullying him at camp?"

"Oh. That." I grimace, scratching my jaw and thinking back to our conversation. "I should explain—"

"Yes, please explain," she interjects, hands flying to her hips now. "Explain what exactly you were thinking when you told a nine-year-old the best way to deescalate the situation was to defend himself *with his fists!*"

"Whoa, no, that's not what I said. I told him bullies feed off of fear, so he shouldn't be afraid to stand up for himself, and that in doing so, the kids would probably back off."

She starts pacing up and down the hallway, the clicking of her heels against the wood the only sound between us for several seconds. There's a strong possibility her silence right now means she's either trying to rein in her anger or plotting my demise. Either way, I'd be lying if I said the sight of her like this didn't stir something in my blood.

"Did you even think to clarify what you meant by 'stand up for himself'?" she demands, using air quotes for emphasis. "You can't just leave things open to interpretation for kids! That's not how it works, especially when it comes to Liam. You had no right to tell him *anything!*"

My hands go up in surrender. "Hey, look, I'm sorry. I was just trying to help."

She spins around, her braid cutting through the air in a chestnut wave. "Yeah? Well, your *help* led to him sucker-punching the kid. Which then led to Liam getting kicked out of the entire fucking program, Dominic! So thank you *so much* for your 'help'!"

"Oh shit. Fuck. I really am sorry. I'll make this right. What can I do?" The need to fix this burns through me, driving me to step in front of her to cut off her pacing, so she'll read my sincerity.

"Oh, I think you've done more than enough, don't you?"

"I'm serious. I want to make this right. Is there another summer program he can join? Or I can talk to the director of this program. Maybe if I just explain—"

"No," she says, her jaw tense and eyes still burning holes into me. "Arbor Cove is small. There's only one full-time summer program. And there's no way they'd consider giving him another chance. Not now, at least. You don't understand. We moved here a few months ago, and part of that move was prompted by Liam getting expelled from his school—*for violence*. He had been dealing with a lot at the time, and I knew he was having difficulty adjusting to some, uh…changes at home." She pauses, darting her eyes away from me. Her shoulders deflate on a sigh, and it makes me feel a thousand times worse. "He was doing so well here, I thought. I had no idea he was even being bullied," she admits, keeping her attention on the crashing waves beyond the window. "Why wouldn't he tell me? I would've done something."

I'm pretty sure her question is rhetorical, but I answer anyway. "I suggested that. He said you already have enough to worry about, and that he didn't want to cause you any more stress."

"He told you that?" She turns to look at me, her expression softened but tinged with surprise.

I nod. "He did. I get the impression he's a pretty observant kid. But he's been through a lot of changes; he needs an outlet to work through them in a constructive way. I really am sorry, Tristan. I didn't mean to overstep. I know that doesn't fix the situation, but I truly was just trying to help."

"I believe you." She folds her arms across her body and sighs. "I guess this was a reminder that, for all his wisecracks and jokes and smiles, he's still a little kid who's dealt with more adversity than any nine-year-old should ever know about. Did he tell you anything about why we moved here?"

"A little. He just mentioned that your parents had to go away because they did something bad."

"Something bad," she repeats, a sarcastic laugh spilling from her lips. "That's one way to describe getting convicted of multiple felonies. Robbing people of their retirement money. Defrauding *charities*. Being selfish enough to destroy your family without considering the consequences."

She studies my face, searching for a reaction to her disclosure, I assume, and shakes her head when I don't have one. "You really haven't Googled my family, have you? Why?"

"Probably for the same reason you haven't Googled me. The internet is a wasteland of libel and misinformation. Trying to sort fact from fiction is a fool's errand." I glance down at her, meeting her eyes. There's strength and compassion in them, and I know in an instant she's nothing like her parents. "I'd rather hear the truth from you."

One side of her mouth turns up in a distractingly sexy smirk. "How do you know I haven't Googled you?"

I walk over to the couch, and she follows, taking a seat on the adjacent couch. "Have you?"

"No, but full disclosure, technically Josie did. And either she left out all the scandalous parts, or there really isn't any dirt to be dug up on you. Not even a messy break-up story or a dramatic showdown with reporters. I can't decide if it's refreshing or disturbing."

"So you're saying Liam wasn't the *only* one talking about me after we met?" I ask, raising a brow playfully.

"I might've mentioned the car mix-up debacle. Casually. It's not like I went all fangirl, don't get too excited."

The thought makes me want to laugh. If there's one thing I could tell after our first meeting, it's that Tristan wasn't some deranged fan or paparazzi, despite my initial accusation. In fact, I knew then she wasn't like any of the women I'm used to meeting.

And it seems every interaction since then has only served to reiterate that truth.

"Uh-huh. *Casually.* Kind of like you've been *casually* watching me work out from your car when you come to meet Ellen?"

Her mouth gapes for a second before pulling into a smile. "You make it sound so creepy! I was just making sure you weren't, you know, overexerting yourself. I doubt your trainer or coach or whatever would be happy with you if you re-injured yourself before you've even made it back to one hundred percent. And your actual fangirls *definitely* wouldn't be happy. So, really, I was just looking out for you *and* them. You're welcome."

"How thoughtful of you. I'd say I hope it wasn't too much of a chore for you, but I noticed a little bit of drool fall from the corner of your mouth on Tuesday."

"And I'd say you're kind of an arrogant egomaniac for making comments like that, but you know what? I'm woman enough to admit I did enjoy the show. You're a professional athlete with a body that puts the Magic Mike cast to shame. A body, I might add, you were not shy about putting on display even knowing I was coming. So, fine, I'll admit to a little ogling. It's not exactly a secret you're ridiculously easy to look at, Dominic."

Does acknowledging that women generally find me attractive make me arrogant? Maybe. I'm used to getting compliments about my looks, but there's something about Tristan's admission that just feels...different. Gratifying in a whole new way. She gives meaning and weight to words that I usually find empty.

"The same could be said about you," I tell her in French.

She shakes her head and shifts back on the couch, trying to reel in her smile. "And charming, too, apparently. The plain ol' sexy accent wasn't enough; you just *had* to pull out the French, huh? I don't even need to know what you said to know it was smooth." She gives me an eye roll when I raise a brow in question. "Please. You know exactly how women feel about accents."

"It's not like I can take credit for being raised bilingual; blame my parents," I reply.

"Fair enough. How's the rehab going, by the way? I see you're off the crutches."

"It's...okay, I guess. More painful some days than others, but nothing I can't handle. A little slower than I'd like, but I've experienced enough injuries to know that's usually how it goes after surgery. I've got a long way to go, but I'm hopeful things will pick up once the boot comes off next month. And I'm not quite done with the crutches entirely, just a little at a time."

"I don't know that I'd call it slow if you're already weaning off the crutches. Then again, you don't exactly strike me as a patient guy."

I take a second to consider the right response because she's right; I'm usually not patient. But... "I can be. When I know it'll pay off in certain situations."

"Do you think you'll stay here for the duration of your recovery? Or will you jet off back to France at the end of the summer?"

"I haven't decided. I have to be in France for my brother's wedding, but other than that, I have no idea. I won't play any more matches this year, so there's no rush to get back. Think you could handle seeing me around for a while?"

"Eh," she replies, shrugging. "I could probably manage that. I'm sure Liam would be thrilled to keep bugging you for a rematch every chance he got."

Bringing her brother up turns the mood somber in an instant. Just like that, we're back on the subject that brought her storming into my house to begin with.

"I was thinking," I start after a few seconds of silence hangs between us. "About Liam...what if he hangs out here, with me, during the day while you work? My physical therapist comes to the house, and rehab is all done from here, and other than errands here and there, I don't really have anything else going on."

"Dominic, no, that's way too generous," she insists, immediately shaking her head. "Maggie and I can work something out."

"It's not. If I hadn't told him to stick up for himself, he'd probably still be in the program. Please, Tristan, let me do this. Let me help you. It can be temporary, until or if you find somewhere else for him to go. Don't say no."

"I don't know. Do you even have experience around kids? What if you find out after a day you can't handle having him around all day, asking a million questions?"

"Honestly, no, I don't have a ton of experience with kids. But from the time I have spent around him, I can tell he's a good kid. Ellen even lives nearby, and Liam and Kai seemed to hit it off the other day. They could play together."

"You said it yourself; he's dealt with so much change. Plus, getting kicked out of his program shouldn't lead to being rewarded by spending time with his newest idol. I'm new to parenting, but even I know that much."

"So, I'll give him a mile-long list of chores the first day or week or whatever. You can set any parameters you want. I'll follow your lead." The more the wheels turn and click into place in my head, the more convinced I am that this could work. I *want* this to work, and not just because it would give me a reason to see Tristan every day. "Stay for dinner, or a drink, if you're not convinced, and we can talk it out. If nothing else, I owe you dinner for my role in his actions."

She scoots forward on the couch, bringing us close enough that our knees almost touch. "You're serious, aren't you?"

"I am. I wouldn't have made the offer otherwise."

"Why? Why would you volunteer to let a nine-year-old you barely know hang around all summer? I thought you came here to recover in peace."

I run a hand over my jaw, scratching the stubble there while considering her question. *Because it means I'd have a reason to see you every day.* It's the truth, but not the one she needs to hear right now. "Because I think it could be really good for him. And peace is overrated. You're right. I don't know him that well. But for whatever reason, he trusts me enough to open up about your parents. It's a start, at least."

She thinks about my points for a minute, worrying her lip between her teeth. "If we did this, it couldn't be every day; Maggie can change her work schedule, and he can come with me to the gallery sometimes. And it would only be temporary until I find something more permanent for him."

"That's fine. Like I said, you set the parameters. So is that an actual yes?"

"I don't know," she says. "I was kind of looking forward to making you work for it over dinner."

"Yeah? That can be arranged," I say, pushing up from the couch to stand.

"Wait, you just meant a casual dinner here, right?"

"Is the thought of sharing a meal with me in public terrible?"

"*So* terrible," she says, though her lips pull up into a smile that makes my own smile appear. But just as soon as it came, her smile falls. "I just mean...Arbor Cove is a small town. And I can tell you right now, not everyone adopted your philosophy of not Googling the Fitzgerald family. They've respected our privacy, and nobody's come out and said anything to us, but still, gossip is the favorite pastime of a small town. Combine that with the fact you're...*you*, and there's no way people wouldn't talk."

"Dinner on the back patio it is, then. But just so you know, I don't need to know the details about your family's ordeal to know I don't have any reservations about being seen in public with you. You're not your parents, Tristan."

"Speaking of the 'ordeal'," she says, glancing up to meet my eyes. "I owe you the full explanation. And it's definitely going to require some wine."

"Red or white? I'll throw dinner in the oven and meet you on the patio with the wine in a few."

She hums and taps a finger against her lips in thought, and it's sexy enough to make me wish I hadn't asked. "Surprise me."

"I can do that."

6

TRISTAN

"That's my ride. I'm leaving!" Maggie shouts over her shoulder.

"Wait! You never answered my question—whose house are you going to, and who's going to be there?" I ask, catching up to her at the front door before she can make her escape. Since the start of summer, she's been increasingly tight-lipped about where she is after work and who she's with. I remember being seventeen, and I've tried to give her freedom, but I have my limits.

"What does it matter? You don't know them," she fires back, narrowing her green eyes in true dramatic teenage fashion and folding her arms over her chest. It draws my attention to the fact she's wearing a fringed crop top with holes that show off her neon pink bra underneath. Her blonde hair features green streaks, and while I don't *hate* how it looks on her, it was the source of our last argument.

Sometimes I fucking hate that I can't just be the cool big sister anymore.

"It matters because it's a house party thrown by teenagers; I don't need to know them to know it's a recipe for trouble. I was seventeen once too, you know."

That gets an exaggerated eye-roll. "Shane Moss—that's whose

party it is, and I'll be with Shelby, Meredith, Tanner, and Andre. Happy now?"

I've heard some of those names on the rare occasion she actually told me about how things were going at school, but that's all I have to go off. But it's better than nothing, and this is one of those times when I have to pick my battles with her. "Was it so hard to tell me basic information?" I sigh, the will to go another round with her leaving my body. "Look, Mags, I'm not delusional; I know what goes on at these parties. I just want to know you're being safe, that's all. I'm not stopping you from being a normal teenager. But that only works if I can trust you and get information from you. You get that, right?"

She drops her arms, not making eye contact. "Yeah. I know. I promise to call you if I need a ride or if things get too crazy. I'll text you the address of the house when I find out from Shelby, okay?"

"Okay. Thank you. Have fun," I tell her, stepping into her for a quick hug.

Before our lives imploded, Maggie and I had a normal sisterly relationship. We'd go shopping and watch scary movies together and spend hours talking about everything from fashion to boys to plans for both of our futures. I was the first person she told about her dream to go to Juilliard for dance. She was the first person I called after I got my dream job at The Happy Hearts Foundation. Our age gap used to mean she was my annoying little sister who spied on my friends and me during sleepovers, but we were finally in a good place, and we even had plans for her to live with me while she was at Juilliard.

Now, I'm lucky if she'll even look up from her phone long enough to give input on what we should do for dinner.

Shrugging off the lingering uncertainty and apprehension I feel about Maggie's party, I go in search of Liam and Gen. *Thank God I have a while before they're teenagers.*

The best bonus feature of this house was the small treehouse in the backyard. If I'm ever in doubt about where they are, this is my first stop. I quickly climb the ladder attached to the back yard's giant oak tree and poke my head into the treehouse's window. "Boo! What are you two whispering about?"

"Uh, nothing!" Genevieve insists, grinning in a way that tells me it definitely *wasn't* nothing.

"We just thought, maybe, since you've had a long week, that we could be the ones to cook you dinner tomorrow, instead of you doing it. We already have a menu and a grocery list ready, so all you'll have to do is take us to the grocery store, and we'll do the rest."

"And maybe give us some money," Gen adds, punctuating by batting her long lashes and tacking on a huge fake grin.

They both clasp their hands together to plead, sticking their bottom lips out and flashing me their best puppy dog eyes. There's a reason these two have had my heart for the last nine years. I wish I could keep them little forever.

"Well, then how could I possibly say no?"

"*Yes!*" They cheer, giving each other high fives like I've just given them permission to eat chocolate cake for dinner, not prepare an actual dinner.

"Wait a minute. Is this dinner going to consist of more than a box of Kraft mac & cheese?"

"It is! We're going to do—"

"No!" Liam wails, interrupting Gen before she can give more information. "It's a surprise. You'll see tomorrow. But I know you'll like it. Chef Liam will not disappoint!"

"Is that so?" I ask with a laugh. For the past couple of years, Liam has sworn he's going to be a chef when he grows up. And to his credit, he's actually not bad at cooking. It's just been a while since I've seen him this excited about it.

He nods and picks up a notebook and pencil from the floor of the treehouse. "Now, we just need to finalize the dessert, so if you'll excuse us," he says, shooing me out of their sacred space.

I hold up my hands and nod. "Okay, okay. But I need my little chefs to come inside in ten minutes for dinner. I was also thinking we should build a fort to eat in, and maybe watch a movie after dinner. Good idea?"

"Yes, yes!" they chant, gap-toothed smiles lighting up their faces.

After a long day at the gallery, greeting guests and customers on my own while Lorraine was gone, entertaining and feeding two hooligans isn't exactly my preferred way to unwind. But when I think about them eventually becoming teenagers who are too cool for movie nights with their "old" sister, there's nothing else I want to do.

"What do you mean, 'it's not like that'? It can't *not* be like that with a man like him," Josie says from my phone's screen.

I'm sitting in the hammock of our back yard, with a glass of pinot grigio, giving the twins privacy to work their "chef magic," as Liam calls it. They really went all out and cleaned the kitchen and living room, and have kept their plans for the meal completely under wraps.

"I mean, I've barely seen him since the dinner at his house last week. We text, occasionally, mostly about Liam, but other than that I've been busy, and it sounds like he has too. Liam says he has FaceTime meetings with a bunch of his team back in France and the people who run his family's foundation. Plus, his rehab schedule and whatever training he's doing on top of it. Told you, Jo, I'm not doing the fling or hookup thing."

I'm beginning to feel like a broken record when it comes to this conversation with Josie. She understood me wanting to keep my distance at first, but since she found out about him having Liam over, she's convinced it means us hooking up is inevitable. Because it's clearly *impossible* for a guy to have pure intentions, if you ask her.

Her breakup might still be clouding her judgment.

"You should see what he's doing for the Fourth of July. My guess would be nothing because he's not used to being in America this time of year. It's casual, but a perfect excuse to see him. And if you happen to be at the beach in swimsuits, even better. Bikinis and booze will bust you right out of this friend-zone nonsense you're trying to cling to."

"Sometimes, I swear, it's like I'm talking to myself with you. You did hear the part about not looking for a fling, right?" I mean what I said, but the prospect of spending more time with Dominic makes me happy in a way I haven't allowed myself to feel lately.

"Sure, whatever," she says, waving a hand like she doesn't actually believe me. "You say that now, but talk to me in a month, when you're in the midst of a hot love affair with France's sexiest bachelor."

Josie's phone pings with a notification, and her eyes roll with annoyance.

"Jordan, again?" I ask.

"Yep. He's nothing if not persistent. He wants to buy me a plane ticket to LA, so we can, quote, work things out. Like I'm not just as busy as he is."

"Is there a chance…" I trail off, not sure if I can actually finish the thought.

"That he didn't actually sleep with Tits McBooberson? I don't know. But really, it doesn't matter. I know I say it every time, but this time we're really done. For good. I'm getting off the Jordan and Josie merry-go-round once and for all."

"You know I love you no matter what, but let me just say, *hallelujah*! I know you like the suit-and-tie, pretty boy type, but I'm pretty sure Jordan is going to be one of those guys who clings to the frat boy mentality until he's forty."

"I'm swearing off the pretty, preppy boy type. Maybe I should break my own rule and date someone in the sports world. Let's see, who's the hottest athlete I can think of that just so happens to be a mere train ride away?" she muses.

"Oh my god," I exclaim, jolting out of the hammock with my eyes glued to the scene unfolding in the living room. "He's here. In my living room. I have to go."

"What? Dominic? Damn, guess I'm too late," she says with a laugh. "If this is a setup by Liam and Gen, tell them I'm taking them out for ice cream next time I visit!"

"Yeah, right. They're going to be grounded for the next, I don't know, decade. I'll call you tomorrow."

By the time I get to the door, my heart is thumping a thousand miles an hour, though I don't really know why. For all I know, Liam left something at his house yesterday, and he's just dropping it by. There's no reason to jump to conclusions. Except he looks ridiculously handsome and uncharacteristically dressed up in a blue linen button-down shirt with the sleeves rolled up and white pants. His usual multi-day scruff is gone, and he's tamed his unruly locks down.

"What, uh, what's this?" I ask, looking between Genevieve and Liam before allowing myself to meet Dominic's sky blue gaze.

In addition to matching white shirts and black pants, the twins are both sporting dish towels thrown over their shoulders, and they move in sync to the dining room table that now features a candle, a single rose in a glass-turned-vase, two wine glasses, and a bottle of the cheap wine I keep stashed on the pantry's top-shelf.

"Allow us to seat you before dinner is served," Liam says, pulling out my chair. Gen does the same for the chair opposite my spot.

Dominic goes with it, smiling and thanking Gen.

They both turn toward the kitchen, but I'm not letting them off the hook that easy. "Stop. Come back. Explain."

Liam slowly turns back, wearing the most adorably mischievous grin. "Um, well, I just thought you both deserved a nice meal for helping me, and I knew neither one of you had plans tonight. Did I do something wrong?"

Releasing a sigh, I shake my head. "No, bud, you didn't do anything wrong. That was very thoughtful of you. But next time, you need to ask first."

He nods before they both make a hasty exit through the swinging door to the kitchen.

I turn to Dominic, heaving another sigh and tucking my hair behind my ear. "How exactly did he get you over here? Did you know about this devious little plan of theirs?"

He laughs, shaking his head. "No, not exactly. He called me earlier, saying you had given him and Genevieve permission to make a nice dinner tonight, and he wanted to cook for me too, as a thank you for helping him out. He didn't mention the part where he was kind of parent-trapping us into a date."

I laugh at his phrasing, though it's accurate. "Those two...I'm in trouble when they're teenagers. I'm having enough difficulty with the actual teenager in the family; I don't think I'm ready for them to start causing me stress."

"They meant well, at least. They're sweet kids."

"You're right. And at least I've hopefully got a couple of more years before that changes." Picking up the wine bottle, my hand freezes halfway to his glass. "Hey, listen, I'm sorry they sort of sprang this on you. They told me it was going to be the three of us; I had no idea he invited you over."

"Why are you sorry? Don't be. I'm not."

"You're not?" He shakes his head. "I guess I just didn't want you to get the wrong idea, and think I have some kind of expectation or something."

"Expectation about what?" he asks, taking a sip of the wine. I can't help but laugh at his failed attempt to hide his grimace. He grabs the bottle and studies the label.

"It's my 'in case of emergency' wine that's about $4 a bottle. It must be the only one we had. I mean about us, this, tonight. Like I might have the lines blurred and be confused about where you and I stand. I just—"

"Tristan, relax," he interrupts, an easy smile pulling at his lips. "I knew as soon as I saw your shocked face what the situation was. And as far as where you and I stand? We're good. This is just two people enjoying each other's company with hopefully an edible meal, okay? That's how I see it, and I'm guessing you feel the same."

"Okay, perfect," I reply, already feeling more at ease with the situation.

Just two people enjoying each other's company. It's exactly what this situation is and should be. And it *definitely* is how I feel.

For an entire laundry list of reasons. But a part of my mind refuses to accept that, and instead, I'm flooded with flashes of the way he looked at me by the end of our last dinner together, of the sexy smile I caught when he found me watching him work out one day, of the way my whole body lit up from a simple text from him yesterday. Of the way he listened intently when I told him about my parents' crimes and the horrible aftermath of their arrest and trial, and then gently squeezed my hand and reiterated that I'm not them and told me what I'm doing for my siblings is admirable, and I'm doing a great job.

A cheesy aroma floats through the room seconds before Liam and Gen appear, each carrying large serving bowls. Liam sets down chicken fettuccine alfredo and salad, and Gen places bowls of bread and some kind of vegetable medley on the other side of the table from Liam's. They look at each other for a beat before saying in unison, "bon Appétit!" with mini-bows and excuse themselves to the living room. Their dedication to remaining formal is adorable, and it makes us both smile.

We eat in comfortable silence for a few minutes before Dominic refills his plate. I'm not far behind in wanting seconds; Liam's fettuccine tastes like heaven in a bowl.

"This is really good," Dominic comments. "Liam told me last week he likes to cook, but I had no idea he's some kind of child culinary genius."

"So, I'm not just the biased big sister for thinking the kid's got serious skills in the kitchen, right? I used to be skeptical and watch over him like a hawk when he wanted to try new recipes, but he's earned my go-ahead for pretty much whatever he wants to try now."

"Definitely not biased; I'm going to need him to teach me some of his favorite recipes. I'm used to eating whatever meal plan my trainer comes up with while I'm in the middle of a tournament, but I give myself a little leeway during the off-season."

"You know," I say, tearing apart a piece of garlic bread. "Other than knowing the basics, I feel like I know nothing about your career and life as one of the world's most elite athletes. The other night, I went on and on about my family life and my background in school, when really, *you* are the interesting one with probably a million great stories. I feel like a jerk for not even asking before now."

"Don't; you have no idea how refreshing it is to not field those kinds of questions and inquiries all the time. You make me feel... normal. In the best way," he adds when I make a face at the word normal. "And that's not something I have the luxury of experiencing all the time. So, thank you."

"Not something I've ever been thanked for before, but...you're welcome."

We spend the rest of dinner talking about him and what it was like growing up with tennis legend parents, following in their footsteps, and even surpassing the number of titles both his parents won. He tells me stories about how he used to be a huge hothead and struggled with his temper on the court as a young teenager, and about his difficulty accepting how much the media loved him once he learned to control his temper and started rising in the rankings.

The media comment draws a sarcastic snort from me. "Must be nice to have the media's unwavering love."

He shrugs, and I get the impression he's genuinely humble about the attention he receives and the fact he has such a shining reputation. From what I've seen, it's completely deserved.

I didn't tell him the extent my name, specifically, got dragged through the mud, but the picture I painted told him enough to know it wasn't pretty. But apparently, Dominic is universally loved, and by more than just sports media and journalists. Because of his work with his family's foundation, he's been interviewed and written about in various business publications. If Gabriel and Cordelia Moreau were the tennis world's golden couple, Dominic certainly fits the bill as the tennis world's golden boy.

"And what about Max?" I ask.

"Max is...not necessarily a black sheep of our family, but he hasn't exactly garnered the same warmth and love of the journalists. He's come a long way, but also kind of prefers to fly under the radar these days."

"I can understand that. I probably would too, if I was in the shadow of you and your parents."

"Some of it is his own doing, like being known for partying and saying stupid things when he was younger. But I do think he's turned his image around over the years. Especially since he's been with Chloe. She's been really good for him. How they make it work is a mystery sometimes, but they do."

"You said they're getting married, right? This fall?"

"Uh-huh. September. Right after the U.S. Open," he says, putting his napkin on his plate and moving it out of the way.

"Oh, wow. I bet France is beautiful that time of year."

"It is. Though in the region where the wedding will be, most people prefer the summer months because that's when the lavender fields are in bloom. *That* is a truly beautiful time to visit."

"Good to know. For the next time I can take a vacation, oh, I don't know, after the twins graduate high school?" I muse with a half-sad-half-real laugh.

As if they knew I was talking about them, Liam and Genevieve slip into the dining room, towels over their shoulders, and still in their black and white waiter ensembles.

"May we clear your plates?" Gen asks, picking up the empty serving bowls.

"Sure. Thank you." Turning to Dominic, I ask, "Do you have anything else going on tonight, or can you hang out and watch a movie with us? I introduced them to the Teenage Mutant Ninja Turtles—the 90s movies, not new ones—and now they're obsessed. I was thinking we'd watch the second one."

"Well, how could I turn that offer down? I'm in," he replies, helping Liam pick up the rest of the dishes.

I tell the kids to leave the dishes. I'll get to them later, and we all get comfortable in the living room: Liam on a beanbag and Dominic, Gen, and I share the couch. It's a tight fit, but telling my sister to move would mean I have no excuse to sit close enough to get whiffs of Dominic's musky aftershave. *Fat chance.*

For half the movie, my attention is split between enjoying the twins' reactions and trying *not* to focus on the fact Dominic's arm is slung casually over the back of the couch, close enough that a minor adjustment in my position would put his hand in direct contact with my shoulder. Then Gen grabs a pillow, maneuvering herself until she's horizontal on the couch with her pillow on my lap, telling me to scoot down.

I do, eliminating the inches that separated me from Dominic.

And then, so softly I'm not even positive it's happening, his fingertips start to lightly trace from my neck, over my collar bone, and down my shoulder. It's a gentle, unhurried touch, and yet all it does is set off fireworks under my skin, making me crave a different kind of touch. I'm holding my breath, too afraid to move or even breathe and ruin the moment when his adept fingers start to press a little harder, applying just enough pressure to draw a slight moan of contentment from my lips.

Without a second thought, I adjust myself enough to grant him better access. Without exchanging a single word, the line we both agreed upon earlier gets thinner and thinner the longer his fingers work their magic on my body.

But for now, *for once*, I don't let logic catch up to me.

Until the harsh ring of my phone jolts me awake, and I realize, in a fog, I fell asleep at some point. And apparently helped myself to snuggle right into him. He stirs underneath me, and I quickly push up and dig around the couch for my phone, thankful to also realize Gen moved to a bean bag at some point and is completely oblivious to the sound of my ringtone.

"Maggie? Are you okay?" I ask after fishing it out from between couch cushions. It's late, and between dinner with Dominic and falling asleep, I forgot all about Maggie's curfew.

"Tristan, I...I did something stupid. I need you to come get me," she says, her words slurred and desperate. The background is full of loud music and shouts of teenagers jumping into a pool.

Those two sentences are all it takes to wake me right up and pop off the couch. "Where are you? I'm grabbing my keys now."

"Shane's. The one I told you about yesterday."

"Okay. I'll be there as soon as I can. Just stay where you are," I say, hanging up and slipping on shoes.

"Maggie's in trouble," I tell Dominic in a rush. I glance back at Gen and Liam, both fast asleep on their bean bags. "I really hate to ask, but would you mind—"

He shakes his head and gestures to the door. "Not at all. Go; I'll stay with them until you get back. It's not a problem."

"Thanks," I offer with a quick smile, even though the magnitude of the relief I feel makes me want to leap into his arms and kiss him.

I pull up Maggie's text from last night with this Shane kid's address and realize it's not exactly in the best part of town. After seeing our family's wealth vanish practically overnight, I'm not one to judge. But it still raises my hackles that Maggie has been spending so much time with a kid I barely know, in an area I've only heard described as "the part of town you stay away from," by Lorraine.

By the time I put the car in park and call Maggie, it's been over twenty minutes since we spoke, and I'm sitting in the parking lot of an apartment complex with at least seven buildings. I have no idea how to find her. When she doesn't answer, I follow the sounds of a party until it leads me to the pool, where I spot her sitting in a lounge chair, looking miserable and half asleep.

"Maggie, wake up," I say, gently shaking her shoulders to get her attention. "Time to go."

"I'm so sorry," she mutters, tears filling her eyes as she grips my arms and tries to focus her bleary green eyes on me.

"Mags, you can apologize later. Right now, we're just going to get you home, okay?"

She nods and stands up, leaning into me for support on our way back to the car. The whole time she mutters apologies, but it's not until I get her settled into the car that she clarifies why she's apologizing.

"I didn't know. I swear. I didn't know," she says, grimacing as I pull onto the road.

"Didn't know what?"

"That he was…recording us. I don't know how I could be so stupid."

My jaw clenches, and I pray to any higher power that she doesn't mean what I think she does. As much as I don't want the answer, I have to know. "Who? Who was recording you doing what?"

With every ounce of strength she has, she turns her head to me and peels her drunken eyes open. "Shane. He recorded us having sex and said he had big plans for the video."

Fuck.

A sinking feeling fills my stomach. "Maggie, did you tell him about our family? Does he know about Mom and Dad?"

"I'm so sorry," she sputters, nodding as tears fall from her eyes.

I grip the steering wheel with enough force to rival how tightly my jaw is clenched, fighting the urge to scream as a cocktail of panic and anger runs through my veins. But taking it out on Maggie right now won't help.

"Close your eyes," I tell her. There's no kindness in my voice, but it isn't as harsh as she deserves either. "I'll wake you up when we get home."

And wring your neck in the morning.

7

TRISTAN

$\mathcal{A}$fter spending hours tossing and turning, playing out a thousand scenarios for what's to come, wondering if I've given Maggie too much freedom, and thinking about the way it felt to have Dominic's hands on me, I finally gave up the idea of sleeping before the sun even came up.

Walking past Maggie's door, guilt overtakes me. As a teenager, our parents weren't overly strict with me—I never had a curfew; they took my word at face value when I told them with whom I'd be hanging out. I'd always been told they'd never get mad at me for calling if I felt unsafe, even if I'd been drinking. In the past six months, I've given Maggie many of the same ground rules. The realization of how incredibly wrong that was smacked me in the face on the ride home last night. I stupidly believed trading New York for a place like Arbor Cove meant Maggie wouldn't need strict rules. But I underestimated how easy it is for a teenager to find trouble, even in a small town, especially when said teenager is going through so much.

Coffee in hand, I settle onto the couch and pull out my phone. To do what, exactly, I'm not sure. Look up Shane Moss? Maggie told me the basics—he's 19, graduated last year, and works in a garage one town over. Do a Google search for 'Maggie Fitzgerald sex tape'? I'd rather crawl over hot coals. Reread the last few text exchanges with Dominic? Been there, done that. *And definitely shouldn't let it develop into a habit.* Dominic's name lights up my screen with a text in the midst of my internal debate, and I'm already smiling like a lovesick teenager before I even read it.

DOMINIC: I know you said you've got everything under control, but I'm here if you need anything, even if just to talk things out. Hope everything gets worked out today.

I'd be surprised he's even awake, but over the few short weeks I've known him, I've come to expect the unexpected when it comes to Dominic. Not only did he stay with Liam and Gen last night when I left, but they were both tucked into bed, and the kitchen was cleaned and the dishwasher running by the time I got back. It's not that I thought he'd be incapable of cleaning because he's a famous athlete who could afford to never touch a dirty dish in his life, but the gesture was wholly unexpected. And I can't even pretend that there's not something incredibly sexy about a man who cleans.

I left out the details of the situation with Maggie last night, but the need to get advice is gnawing at me. He already did so much more than I could have asked for last night, though; I can't drag him into this mess even more.

TRISTAN: I'm not sure if 'worked out' is the right term, but there's a strong chance I deck a teenage boy today. Okay, maybe not deck. But definitely confront with some choice words. We'll see.

DOMINIC: What happened?

TRISTAN: Oh, not much. Just realized what a shitty guardian I've been for Maggie. She might've made a reckless and stupid decision, but I'm the one who should've never let her get into that situation in the first place. Clearly I don't know much about parenting a teenager, but I do know this Shane kid is about to get a very rude wake-up call because unfortunately for him, I know exactly where he lives.

DOMINIC: Are you sure it's a good idea to go over there? Now?

TRISTAN: It's a time-sensitive issue, so yes.

DOMINIC: I'm coming with you. Wait for me.

TRISTAN: What?! No, you really don't need to do that. I'll be fine, Dominic.

When he doesn't respond, I panic that he's actually serious, so I run back to my bedroom and throw some leggings and a tank top on, use some dry shampoo to revive my unwashed hair, and brush my teeth. I meant it when I said I'm going over to confront Shane; it's the only way to know if he's bluffing or if he really does have "plans" for the sex tape. A rational, calm person might start off by pointing out Maggie is seventeen, and he's nineteen—not illegal in Connecticut, but also not a good look—but the longer I have to replay my conversation with Maggie from last night, the less rational I feel myself become.

Ten minutes later, there's a soft knock at the door, and I bite my lip, bracing myself for Dominic to try and talk me out of going over there. But when I open the door, it's not just Dominic on my porch.

"Hope you don't mind us tagging along," Ellen says with the same warm smile she always seems to wear. Kai waves and smiles briefly before going back to his Minecraft book. He's wearing a neon yellow shirt with a 'DM' logo and a bright orange cap on backward, mimicking Dominic's look. "Kai and I were going to grab some breakfast at Bernie's Diner, and I figured we'd see if Liam and Genevieve could come with us."

I'm not sure if the timing of Ellen's offer is actually coinciden- tal, or if Dominic realized I'd probably be having a conversation with Maggie that little ears shouldn't hear. Either way, the offer is sweet and kind of perfect for this morning.

"Oh, I'm sure they'd love that. Kai, I think I heard them turn on the TV a minute ago. You can go find them in the living room and let them know about breakfast."

He gives me a wordless nod and takes off for the living room in a neon blur.

When he's out of earshot, Ellen looks from Dominic to me and says, "Dominic didn't give me much information, but honey, Shane Moss is bad news. I know you haven't been in town long, but he's got a reputation around here—and has for years—and let's just say if your sister really is involved with him, it's best to get her *un*involved now."

My stomach knots with more guilt and unease, and for the thousandth time, I wish I'd kept a closer eye on her over the last few months. I thank Ellen for the insight, and she assures me she'll get the kids fed and keep them occupied while I'm gone.

Dominic and I sit in my car for a few seconds before his hand grips mine over the gearshift, and I realize I've just been staring out the windshield. "Hey," he says, drawing my attention. "It's going to be okay."

"He made a sex tape of them," I blurt out, only realizing a second too late that's Maggie's highly personal information and probably not something I should be telling Dominic. But he's coming with me to confront this kid, so he'd hear it there anyway. "And he basically implied that he's going to sell it or put it on the internet himself."

"That's not going to happen." His voice carries an undercurrent of finality, leaving no room for doubt. He pulls out his phone and spends the next minute furiously typing. I sneak a quick glance at his profile and find his brow furrowed and jaw set in a hard line. Despite the circumstances, the look combined with his signature backward cap and t-shirt with its sleeves cut off is enough to make my mouth go dry.

"Do you have any plans for the Fourth of July?" I ask. "There's a bonfire and barbecue on Brighton Beach with fireworks that Gen and Liam have been begging me to take them to. You should meet us there if you're free," I say without giving myself a chance to change my mind. A week ago, I practically balked at the idea of dinner together in public, but now, I'm asking him to meet us at an event most of the town probably attend.

"July fourth? Seems random. What's the occasion?" he asks, looking perfectly confused with a brow arched.

My mouth gapes on a gasp. "Um, Independence Day for the U.S.? And you say you have dual citizenship!"

A slow smile spreads from one corner of his mouth to the other before he breaks into full-on laughter.

"You jerk!" I groan and roll my eyes before reaching over and punching him in the bicep. "I can't believe I fell for that."

He rubs his arm, feigning actual injury, but it's only a second before we're both smiling, and I realize the mood has dramatically lightened. But then, I'm starting to feel that way *every* time I'm around him. Whether it's been a stressful day at the gallery or I'm ready to tear my hair out because of one of my siblings, five minutes around Dominic seems to melt away the day's stress. And I'm not sure that's a good thing considering he's only here temporarily, and once he's gone, our lives will certainly never have a reason to overlap.

"I don't have plans, and I'm probably overdue for a proper American celebration."

"Well, then, let's hope Ellen and Kai invite you to celebrate because my invitation just got revoked," I counter, proud of myself for keeping a straight face.

"That so? What if I just so happen to show up at the same time and continuously bump into you guys?"

"I'd say you might be turning into a little bit of a stalker, so I'm gonna have to cut you loose."

"Just like that, huh? Ouch."

I shrug casually. "Somebody's gotta keep France's most eligible athlete humble."

He just shakes his head and groans, and I swear I catch a faint blush creep into his cheeks.

It only adds more dimension to his appeal.

"Speaking of France," I say, darting my eyes over to him for a second. "How is it that you grew up there, but your accent is so...faint?"

"I grew up speaking both languages equally thanks to my mom. She insisted Max and I become just as confident in our English as our French, and she was our main source of learning. Plus, she knew we'd probably learn English eventually, anyway, so she just started us out earlier than usual."

I nod. "Smart lady."

"She is."

I pull into the same apartment complex from last night and quickly check for confirmation on his apartment number before following the signs to building four. "Maybe you should stay in the car," I tell Dominic, once the car is in park. "You're not exactly unrecognizable, and I'm not going to drag you into a mess of my sister's creation. Not when this dickbag is already threatening to use what slight recognition Maggie's name will even have across the internet."

He's already shaking his head before I even finish, and unbuckles his seatbelt. "I don't care. You're not going up there alone. That's not happening."

I turn toward him with arched brows and arms folded across my chest. "And what if he recognizes you? Decides you're a better target than Maggie?"

"I could be Scarlett Johansson, and he wouldn't recognize me right now. The kid is a stoner who was partying last night. There's no way he's firing on all cylinders this early. Assuming he even opens the door. Either way, I'm coming with you."

He's up and out of the car before I can formulate a response. For a guy whose foot is still in a boot, he practically bounds up the stairs to Shane's apartment just a half-step behind me. At the last step, I turn to him, almost making us collide before his hands grip my biceps to keep us from doing just that.

"What's wrong?"

"Here," I tell him, plucking his cap off and turning it to face forward, then taking the sunglasses from his hand and putting them back on his face. The way they frame his face and highlight his carved jawline isn't even fair.

"Better?"

Ha. Not even remotely. I swallow down my *how-are-you-this-hot* reaction and nod. "It'll do. At least hang back a little—to the side or something—and I'll let you know if I need you." His broad chest heaves, like he's not a fan of this plan. I lift a hand to his shoulder. The stairs separating us negate our height difference, making it easy to meet his bright blue eyes with mine. "Promise."

He gives me a single nod and squeezes my waist in as much of an agreement as I'm going to get.

After a minute of knocking on apartment 412's door, I finally hear sounds of life behind it. "What the fuck? I'm fuckin' coming," a haggard, deep voice shouts. The door slowly opens until I'm face to face with a guy who looks almost exactly like I imagined he would: tall, slender build, overgrown straw-colored hair down to his shoulders, heavily-lidded eyes, and a plethora of tattoos splayed across his bare chest.

"Yeah? Do I know you?" His eyes narrow on me as they sweep up and down my body, slowly coming into focus as his lips curl into an unappreciated smile. "'Cuz if I don't, I feel like I should. Biblically."

"Not even in your wildest fucking dream, asshole," I reply, pulling my tank top down to cover the sliver of stomach that was showing. "But I'm told you do know my sister. Maggie."

There isn't even a flash of hesitation before her name makes his expression twist into a smirk I'm painfully tempted to slap straight off his face. "Ohhh, *Maggie*. You know," he says, leisurely leaning against the door frame and licking his lips. "Based on the pics I saw of you online, I have to say, I wasn't sure which one of you would be more bangable, but now...fuck if that's not an impossible decision."

"You're disgusting," I hiss, wondering what the hell Maggie was thinking to ever even hang out with him. "And it's irrelevant because you're done having any contact with my sister."

"Oh yeah? Doesn't matter. I already got everything I wanted from her, anyway. And then some, if you know what I mean."

Instantly, I can feel Dominic step up behind me, and I know he's done waiting in the wings. But it doesn't matter because I'm too enraged to think straight. I step into him and lift a knee, swiftly making contact with his family jewels. His eyes were on Dominic, so he's caught off guard and falls to his knees, whimpering on the way down.

"You crazy bitch," he groans, hands flying to his crotch. "I should have you arrested!"

"Yeah? And explain to them *why* I'm here? I'm sure they'd be glad to know."

He rolls over, his glare going even sharper before he grips the door frame to pull himself up. "Sex tapes aren't illegal, you know. And that one is the crown jewel of my collection. I'm thinking it'll fetch a pretty penny from a few sites. Unless there's something you're willing to give me instead."

My eyebrows fly halfway up my forehead. "You're actually going to try and blackmail me? Seriously? You're a bigger idiot than I thought. She's seventeen. You'll get arrested. Just delete it—now—and we can all go on our merry way, pretending this never happened. Or I can get the cops involved myself."

Calling attention to the situation, making a spectacle of this whole ordeal, and shining a light on my family is the absolute *last* thing I want to do, but he doesn't have to know that.

"You sure that's a good idea, given your family's history of trouble with the law?" he sneers. I'm a second away from kneeing him again when Dominic pulls me back, drawing Shane's attention. I guess amidst the pain emanating from his favorite appendage, he'd forgotten Dominic was here. "Oh, look, you brought a steroid-infused bodyguard; I'm *so* scared," he says, waving his hands around mockingly.

I'm not sure if Shane is still high or just incredibly stupid, but pissing Dominic off right now was a big mistake. He's tall, but Dominic's taller and has a build every average-sized man would be intimidated by, walking boot and all.

"You *should* be scared, asshole," Dominic says, taking a purposeful step forward. It's clear Shane isn't immune to Dominic's intimidation factor. Dominic flickers his gaze over to me. "Tristan, I need a minute with Shane."

I want to say *no fucking way* for multiple reasons, but the fire in his eyes leaves no room for discussion. "I don't think that's a good idea," I tell him, instead. He can't just go around threatening nineteen-year-old kids, not when he has even more to lose than I do.

"This won't take long. It'll be fine. Isn't that right, Shane?" he asks, practically daring him to say no and openly admit to being scared shitless of Dominic.

"Three minutes, and not a second more," I tell him, slowly backing away but fully intending to haul ass like it's on fire back up here if he doesn't come down within those three minutes.

I watch the seconds tick down for two minutes and fifty-eight seconds before Dominic rounds the corner and calmly comes to a stop in front of me. "It's done. He won't be bothering Maggie again, and the video might as well have never happened."

My mouth falls open.

What the hell did he just do in under three minutes?

8

DOMINIC

*O*n a list of all the regrettable things I've done over the course of my life, this ranks pretty fucking high.

Not going with Tristan to the idiot stoner's apartment. Not even the part where I led him to believe I have connections with law enforcement and wouldn't hesitate to call in a favor if he didn't delete the video and leave Maggie alone. That, I don't regret for a second. What I do regret is telling Gage about Tristan and her siblings, thinking he'd listen as a friend instead of my chief of press communications. Without going into much detail, I mentioned that I took care of the Shane situation, and he damn near lost his mind, chastising me for getting involved in something that could lead to any kind of scandal. *Good thing I didn't give him Tristan's full name—he'd probably have a coronary.*

Over the years, Gage and my agent, Nash, have become not only integral parts of my team but also some of my closest friends.

But right now, I'm tempted to fire his ass.

"With whom I spend my time is none of your concern, Gage. I mean it. You're being ridiculous."

"Oh, *I'm* being ridiculous? Do you hear yourself? You're supposed to be recovering from what could've been a career-ending injury, but instead, you're playing babysitter for a kid just to get into his sister's pants *and* putting yourself in a position to potentially damage your image. In all the years I've known you, I've never known you to let your dick do the decision making. At least not this irresponsibly. Call Svetlana or Margot or Chastity; they're all in New York, aren't they? And I'm sure more than willing to be a temporary bedmate."

They're models from a magazine shoot I did a few months back, and at the time, he made a joke about how I should hook up with all three of them. I didn't—but I did take Svetlana out on a date before realizing I was just...over it. I spent my twenties and the first part of my thirties thinking there couldn't possibly be anything better than short-lived flings with women who were also just interested in a good time, nothing more. It was perfect. But that night, fielding the same questions and hearing the same stories from Svetlana that I'd answered and heard countless times before, I realized I wasn't actually getting anything substantial out of the superficial dates and flings.

Not only that, but I realized I might *want* something substantial someday. When the timing is right.

My jaw clenches at his suggestion, and I have to take three deep breaths the same way I trained myself to when my temper would flare as a teenager. "Don't be an asshole. It's not like that. They're good people, and I'm just helping them out temporarily. And in case you missed the update—my rehab is ahead of schedule, and my leg is doing better every day. Ask Pierre if you don't believe me."

"Yeah, *okay*. So she's not hot, then? Your motives are completely pure?"

My silence is the only answer he needs.

"Okay, then consider this: what's going to happen when you've recovered and go back to your real life? Don't forget, Dominic; this entire situation is *temporary*. You really want to start something with a girl who sounds like she's got more baggage than an airplane, only to inevitably hurt her in the end when you go your separate ways?"

It was one thing when those thoughts were just words I could lock away in the far recesses of my mind.

It's entirely different when they're given a voice, like it somehow gives them life, too, makes them three-dimensional.

"No. That's the last thing I want to do," I finally tell him, though I'm not sure if I'm talking more to Gage or to myself.

After the conversation, I call Pierre, my physical therapist, and have him come over for an extended session, needing a distraction more than anything. But it only does so much. He spends half the session going over the timeline of where things will go once I finally ditch the crutches for good, and the walking boot comes off next week. How he makes it sound exciting that I'll get to do stationery cycling, I couldn't say.

"How long until I can actually train on court?" I ask, hoping for a different answer than last time. Initially, it takes the average person anywhere from six to nine months to return to physically demanding sports after an injury like mine.

But I've never considered myself average.

I have every intention of being at the Australian Open in January; anything else is unacceptable.

He flashes me a look of exasperation, huffing for good measure. "Let's focus first on regaining a normal gait. One step at a time, yes? You'll be ready when you're ready," he tells me in French, refusing to indulge my impatience.

Pierre has been my trainer since I was a teenager, but unlike Gage and Nash, our relationship remains mostly professional. Probably because he's a solid twenty years older than me. Also, the fact that he usually puts my body through some kind of torture makes me a little less eager to go out for drinks together. Even so, with his salt and pepper hair, stern brown eyes with lines tracing his tanned skin at the corners, and a perpetual scowl, he's grown into a second father figure in my life over the years. He's been with me through two previous surgeries and half a dozen minor injuries, and I know he won't bullshit me but also will do everything he can to get me back on the court.

"If you remain focused on the training regimen as planned without overdoing it, you'll be fine. You're ahead now, but a distraction or a setback could derail that progress."

The comment eerily echoes the sentiment of Gage's parting words, reminding me for the second time today what's at stake. As if I'd actually need a reminder about my own damn career.

I meant it when I told Tristan I'm overdue for a proper American celebration of any kind; it's probably been twenty-five years since I've been in the U.S.—Arbor Cove, in fact—for the Fourth of July. I wasn't sure exactly what to expect considering my memories of the few times we were here to celebrate are a bit hazy, but walking through the town to find its streets lined with American flags every few feet, festive decorations spilling from storefronts, smiling locals proudly sporting countless combinations of red, white, and blue filling the sidewalks, and dozens of signs and posters advertising tonight's bonfire and barbecue on the beach is definitely in line with what I remembered.

One of the flyers mentions bringing your own ingredients to make s'mores if you want, so I quickly text Tristan to ask if she'd like me to bring the ingredients.

> TRISTAN: If you can find some graham crackers, yes please! You'll be my hero; every time I've looked, that's the one thing every store seems to always be out of. :(

I luck out and walk down the cookie aisle while the graham crackers are being restocked, so I take a picture and attach it to my text.

> DOMINIC: What kind of prize does hero status earn me?

> TRISTAN: OMG! Liam and Gen will be so excited! And, hmm. You tell me—hero's choice.

> DOMINIC: Risky move. So many ideas to choose from...

TRISTAN: Oh great. That's not ominous or anything. Just so you know, I draw the line at letting you lick peanut butter off my feet.

Her text makes me burst into laughter. Not that my ideas were clean or wholesome, but the fact some part of her mind clearly went to prizes of the physical variety sends my blood rushing south.

DOMINIC: At or before? Need to know if it's on the table, or if I should consider alternative body parts.

Three dots appear and disappear twice before her text comes through; enough time for my mind to already conjure up images of some very specific alternate body parts.

TRISTAN: BEFORE! But...I'm not completely opposed to hearing these alternative body parts you come up with. Bet you're patting yourself on the back for inviting us over to swim after the bonfire. You'll really pat yourself after you see the swimsuit I'm wearing...

A second later, a selfie comes through of Tristan with blue-tinted aviator sunglasses on, her chocolate hair twisted into two messy bun pigtails, lips painted bright red, and a sliver of the top of her white bikini showing. It cuts off after just a peek of cleavage, keeping it somewhat innocent. Even so, she looks hot as fuck. I have to rub a hand over my face to snap out of the trance the photo puts me in, knowing I'm going to see the real thing in a matter of hours.

Being seen walking through a grocery store with a boner probably wouldn't do great things for my image.

TRISTAN: P.S. - Kai invited the twins over to swim, and Ellen made a batch of the world's best strawberry coconut margaritas for us. There's a very good chance I'll be drunk well before the bonfire.

TRISTAN: And just so you know, alcohol tends to loosen my tongue…and occasionally the strings of my bikini… ;)

Jesus fucking Christ. *Why didn't I think to get her drunk before now?*

DOMINIC: Oh, really? I'll have to keep that in mind…

DOMINIC: And just so YOU know, that photo just made July 4th my favorite holiday.

I've spent the last week grappling with the undeniable truth that keeping things *friendly* with Tristan is what's best—for both our sakes. But who says *friendly* can't include some harmless flirting?

An hour later, I'm the one rushing Pierre through our therapy session, for once. He doesn't seem to mind; I think he's just surprised to see me in such a decent mood. By the time he leaves, I barely have enough time to shower before I'm racing out the door to meet Tristan and the kids at Ellen's.

Only to come to a screeching halt when Nash's familiar face greets me from the driveway. He's dressed in a designer gray polo and white linen shorts, with his blonde hair in its usual gelled, groomed state. For anyone else, it's what you'd consider dressy-casual. For Nash, it's probably as casual as he'll ever be seen in public. I wouldn't be surprised if he slept in a suit.

My shock and confusion must show because Nash sighs and says, "Don't tell me you forgot. The Grants' party? Cape Cod? They personally called me last week to confirm we'd be in attendance. We have to leave, like," he glances at his Rolex, "now. It's a two-hour drive."

"Fuck!" I shout, scrubbing both hands over my face in frustration.

"I called you last night when I landed at JFK, did you listen to my voicemail?"

I shoot him a glare. "*Nobody* listens to voicemails, Nash. Maybe try sending me a fucking text like a normal person."

"I did, asshole. You didn't reply to that this morning either." He's been my agent for long enough that he's no stranger to how I get when I'm injured—hot and cold and everything in-between—so he doesn't even bat an eye at my shitty attitude and lack of enthusiasm at his arrival. He pulls down his sunglasses and makes a face at my wardrobe choice—blue swim trunks, a solid red tank top, and a sandal on my non-booted foot. Between the two of us, you'd never know he's the one who grew up in New York. "Not sure why you're dressed like you only have three figures in your savings account, but you need to go change. We're going to be late."

Without offering an explanation, I turn and head back inside and quickly change into an ensemble similar to Nash's. He barely looks up from his phone when I shove my crutches into the back seat of his rented BMW and slip into the passenger seat. Always working, just the way he prefers it.

He types an address into the car's navigation system and takes off, not wasting any time before launching into the details about the Grants' party. Michael Grant is the CEO of Linx, the third-largest sportswear/athletic apparel company in the world. They're also my biggest sponsor, thanks to Nash. I've been a part of the Linx family for almost a decade, and Nash feels pretty confident he'll be able to renew the contract when it expires in December.

Nash tells me there will be other high-ups from the company at the party, and gives me a refresher on their positions and the names of their family members who will also be there. Half an hour later, in the chaos that is Nash and his inability to stop talking about work for five minutes, I realize I forgot to text Tristan about what's going on. She's probably wondering where the hell I am by now.

I dig into my pocket only to find it empty. The other ones too.

Because the phone is in my other pair of shorts.

I mutter a string of French curses in panic, which finally gets

Nash to stop talking long enough for me to tell him we have to go back for my phone.

"No way; we're already going to be cutting it close. You know how Michael feels about punctuality. Just use mine," he offers, pulling it from the cupholder and tossing it my way.

I sigh in relief, but it's short-lived when I realize I don't know her number, or Ellen's. And trying to find and message her on social media is pointless; she deleted all of her accounts months ago. Maggie too. I'm practically clawing my way out of the window with the need to find a way to contact her. The possibility of her thinking I just bailed—especially after our last text exchange—fills my chest with lead. I feel like the world's biggest asshole.

"What's the problem?" Nash asks. "You're always bitching at me for being glued to my phone and preaching about how liberating it is to hardly use yours."

"Nothing," I mutter, forcing myself to calm down. I'd rather skinny dip in the Arctic Circle than tell Nash a word about Tristan. I have no doubt he'd figure out who she is and have an even bigger meltdown than Gage.

By the time we arrive at the Grants' mini-mansion, I've slipped into my 'Dominic the famous athlete' role and am wearing the easy—but fake—smile that role requires. It's not that I'm ungrateful to Michael or to Linx; I like Michael as a person and am proud to endorse Linx. I've just been through the dog and pony show enough to know my presence here is more for the sake of appearances than anything.

Nash pulls into the line of parked cars and turns to me with the dazzling, professional smile he usually only gets after securing a big contract. "Showtime, iron man."

I pause for a second, taking in the massive house's splendor. Surrounded by a sprawling green lawn and sitting just off the beach, it's what Nash describes as a "typical rich person Cod mansion." The early evening light paints the wooden blue exterior in a soft glow, giving it a regal feel. Everything about this place, from the wrought iron gate intricately detailed with a G on either side at the entrance to the immaculately trimmed trees and perfect garden, screams wealth. And it's probably one of a handful of homes the Grant family owns.

An attendant near the parking area directs us around the side of the house, in the direction of loud music and chatter. A stone path illuminated by soft lighting leads our way to the back, with more lights hanging along the way to highlight the entire property's elaborate landscaping. Rounding the corner into the back yard, we're immediately enveloped into the crowd of probably a hundred people. A jazz band plays in the far corner of the yard, with a modest dance floor set up in front of the stage. Waiters in solid red suits and waitresses in solid blue dresses slip through the crowd. The guests are swimming in the pool, talking, or drinking, with most sporting some kind of red, white, and blue party accessory, courtesy of Mallory Grant, I'm sure.

Nash and I weave through the crowd, offering smiles and hellos as we search for the party's host. Built like the former linebacker he is at 6'5" and pushing 300 pounds, with a shaved head and a booming voice that carries, Michael Grant is easy to spot in a crowd.

I take a few selfies with those who ask and stop to chat with the few familiar faces I actually recognize, most expressing their sympathy for my injury and wishing me well. They're well-meaning and kind, but injuries are firmly off-limits for discussion with strangers — too much opportunity for loose lips to leak information.

Nash strikes up a conversation with Logan Brooks, a wide receiver Linx also sponsors. At first, it's casual small talk, but eventually Nash shifts gears into business mode, probably trying to feel out how Brooks' relationship is with his current agent. Scanning the area, I spot Michael and Mallory across the yard, separated from the crowd and talking to Lisa, one of the VPs of Linx, so I quickly excuse myself and make my way over to them.

But when I get close, their conversation stops me cold.

"...If the rumors are true, Fitzgerald isn't faring so well in his cushy prison accommodations. Of course, I've heard everything from suicide watch to heart failure, so who knows. I still think his sentence was too light," Lisa says. Her attempt at hiding her mouth behind her wine glass does nothing to keep her comment from carrying.

Michael huffs in agreement and takes a hefty swig from his crystal tumbler. "I hope karma's a real bitch to Fitzy. It's the least of what he deserves," he replies with disdain.

"I do feel bad for their kids, though. What they've been through…" Mallory comments, shaking her head.

"The younger ones, sure, but I heard their oldest daughter knew what they were up to. She even interned there during college. I wouldn't be surprised if she was complicit."

"I don't know," Mallory disagrees, "They pretty much dissected every penny and transaction the Fitzgerald Financial Group has had over the last decade, so if she was involved, they would've charged her too. Lord knows the press tried to crucify her anyway, though," she says, voice tinged with sympathy.

"She's damaged goods, either way," Michael adds. "Fruit of the poisoned tree. It's why the nonprofit she worked for had to sever ties immediately."

Heat boils my blood, and ice-cold dread fills my chest, pushing me closer to the verge of doing something stupid with each additional comment. At the same time, I'm trying to fill in the blanks about those comments and what Michael's connection to Tristan's dad is. Clearly, they have history.

Before I can spin around to find Nash and see what he knows, Mallory spots me and waves me over, putting an end to their conversation. "Dominic! I'm so glad you could make it," she gushes, pulling me in for a warm hug like she's always done since the first time we met.

"Looking lovely as ever, Mallory," I tell her, knowing it will elicit a smile and blush as usual. It's the truth, though; for someone pushing sixty, you'd never know it by looking, with her pale skin free of wrinkles and blonde hair perfectly kept in a bob without a gray strand to be found. I've always liked Mallory

Grant, and her part in their conversation about Tristan made me like her more.

"There's my man. Glad you could make it," Michael booms, extending a hand to me, his teeth dazzling brilliantly in contrast to his dark skin. Shoving aside the unease settled in the pit of my stomach, I force an easy grin onto my lips and shake his hand. "How's the leg?" he asks, dropping his gaze to the boot.

"Getting better every day," I tell him, infusing confidence into my voice. As much as he's asking because I'm one of the faces of his brand, after a decade-long partnership, I know that's not why he's asking. At least not the *only* reason. While I have several other major endorsement deals, my partnership with Linx is the oldest one by far.

"Great. That's great. You've met Lisa Lawrence, our VP of Operations, right?" he asks, turning toward the brunette to his left.

I nod and step forward to greet her—complete with the pecks on cheeks she insisted upon the first time we met. *"You're French; it would be wrong to greet you any other way."*

Somehow I manage to stay engaged through half an hour of conversation with Lisa and the Grants, even though their earlier conversation is all I can think about. It's killing me to not have all the information, to not go off on Lisa and tell her she has no idea what she's talking about, that Tristan is nothing like her parents. That holding her accountable for the crimes her parents committed, dating back to when she was sixteen, is fucking wrong.

All I can think about as fireworks send explosions of colors bursting through the sky is how I should be watching the same scene, but with a gorgeous brunette and two smiling kids. Waiters walk around, some taking orders for dessert requests, others carrying trays of pre-made s'mores. I swallow at the sight, picturing the box of graham crackers sitting on my kitchen island and feeling like an even bigger asshole. I'll make Liam and Genevieve s'mores every day for the rest of the summer if I'm the reason they didn't get to make them tonight.

It's late by the time the party winds down, but neither of us had a single drink of alcohol, so I kindly decline Mallory's invitation to stay in one of their guest rooms. Nash doesn't seem to mind, telling her he has a conference call in the morning, anyway. I can still make out lights from the Grants' property when I bring up the question of Russell Fitzgerald's connection to Michael as casually as possible.

Nash shakes his head slowly. "It's pretty fucked up, actually. They went to college together; they were both athletes, so they kind of ran in the same circles, I guess. They didn't stay close, but Michael vouched for Russell, recommended a few of his family members—brother, nephew, and aunt, I believe—invest with Fitzgerald Financial Group. His nephew lost a moderate amount, but he recovered and works at Linx now, in the advertising department. But his brother lost a small fortune, then in the middle of it all, Michael's niece was diagnosed with cancer." He glances over and sees my shocked expression, and he shakes his head again. "Told you it was fucked up. Pretty sure the Grants even attended and testified at the trial."

My head swims with all the new information for the rest of the drive back. I can't say I blame Michael for hating the Fitzgeralds; I don't know what I'd do if it had been my family. Later, as I'm finally drifting off to sleep, Michael's words from the party dance through my dreams, embedding themselves into my head.

"She's damaged goods either way. Fruit of the poisoned tree."

And it's that moment that my eyes pop open, and I realize how fucked everything is.

9

TRISTAN

"Shh, you'll wake Josie up," I tell Genevieve and Kai, whose giggles only grow louder. They're completely absorbed in the app they discovered yesterday, where they start out with a theme for a drawing, then take turns adding to and creating a digital drawing of their own design. It's pretty cute to watch them strategize and get excited about what they want to make.

"It's...just...so...funny," Gen says between persistent giggles. "Kai gave the unicorn two butts!"

I turn down the griddle's heat to avoid burning the pancakes, go close my bedroom door, where Josie is still snoring away, and go peek over their heads from behind the couch. "Oh wow, you two make quite the artistic duo," I tease, ruffling their hair. Kai smiles, the deep tan of his dimpled cheeks grows red.

It's as close as I've gotten to getting actual words out of that kid. Usually, Liam and Gen do more than enough talking for him, though I have seen him come out of his shell more and more each time the three of them get together.

Leaving them to their shenanigans, I go back to making pancakes, eggs, and bacon, purposefully avoiding the temptation to go to my phone. When it became clear Dominic wasn't coming yesterday, I swore to myself I wouldn't let it bother me—for *my* sake, at least. Gen and Liam were crushed when I finally told them he couldn't come anymore, though, and seeing them get so disappointed broke my heart. For their sakes, I'm furious with Dominic. Whatever reason he had for flaking at the last minute, I don't care. Who can't *at least* send a text? Who just totally blows off kids who practically worship you?

Especially when he knows what they've already been through with our parents.

Thank God Josie saved the day and borrowed a classmate's car to drive out at the last minute. Between Josie, who was able to pick up graham crackers on the way, the magic of fireworks, extra dessert, and having Kai sleepover, Liam's disappointment about Dominic all but disappeared. Gen was upset, but she pretty much got over it the instant Josie showed up.

And it annoys me that I can't say the same for myself.

I think it's because a part of me knows there's a chance his unexpected flakiness was a direct result of the direction our text exchange took. Josie says that's absurd. But I'm not so sure. A week ago, Dominic and I were on the same page—things were fine. Easy. We were just two people who shared a little harmless, innocent flirting here and there.

Then Ellen's margaritas happened, and Tispy Tristan came out, emboldened by too much sun, *way* too much tequila, and the excitement of the holiday. The upside of drinking early meant I was able to go to bed with a somewhat clear head, and I gave Josie my phone for safekeeping, so I wouldn't be tempted to obsess and reread the text exchange again. Sending him multiple angry texts was a mistake, but his continued silence only served to further piss me off. But eventually, Josie stole my phone and pointed out how much fun the kids were having, and that this was my only shot at creating new Fourth of July traditions and memories with them—ones completely our own. So I let her hold onto my phone and spent the rest of the night laughing, making s'mores, and enjoying the fact my siblings were having a great time—even Maggie, who managed to stay off her phone long enough to join in on the fun.

It turned out to be one of the best nights we've had in a while.

"Good Lord," Josie says, drawing me out of my thoughts. "Please take your phone back. Pretty sure it's been vibrating for ten minutes straight." She slides it over to me and slips onto a stool at the island, flipping her wild locks—now an icy blue shade —out of her face and over her shoulder.

Our eyes lock, and she nods before I even have to ask. "Yeah, it's him. There are probably half a dozen texts too. I didn't read them all, but you should."

Before I can pull up the messages, it starts buzzing again, his name flashing across my screen.

"Here," Josie says, coming to the stove and taking the spatula from me. "I'll finish this; you deal with that."

I swipe to answer once I'm in the back yard and out of listening range of small ears.

"God, I am so, *so* sorry," he immediately rushes out, like he's afraid I might have answered only to hang up on him. "My agent showed up as I was about to leave the house, and reminded me I had a prior commitment with one of my sponsors all the way out in Cape Cod. We were going to be late, and in my haste, I accidentally left my phone behind. By the time I realized it wasn't in the car, we were already too far to come back. I really am sorry, Tristan."

His explanation catches me off guard, and I have to let it sink in for a second. In all the scenarios I'd run through in my head, one as simple as him forgetting his phone wasn't one of them.

"It's Gen and Liam you should apologize to, not me. They were really excited to help you have a proper Fourth of July celebration," I finally settle on. It's the truth, but it's not the *whole* truth. It's just easier if I keep things about the kids.

"Fuck. You're right. I hate that I missed it. Can I come over? Apologize to them in person?"

The thought of seeing him makes me want to dissolve into the grass. I can't face him, not after basically telling him he can lick peanut butter off my body, followed by informing him that alcohol makes my clothes come off. *God, I'm a mess.*

"I don't think so. We'll be gone most of the day. Hiking."

"Oh? I didn't realize you all had plans today."

That's because we didn't…until ten seconds ago. I have no clue why hiking, of all things, came to mind, but it's happening now. Even if it's just hiking across the mall.

"Yeah, well, Josie was able to drive out at the last minute, and they're really looking forward to spending the day with her." Not a lie. "Look, Dominic, I can tell you genuinely feel bad, and I get it; these things happen. But the kids were pretty upset, and having Josie come was the day's saving grace. Bringing it back to their attention right now isn't the best idea. How about Gen comes with Liam to your house on Tuesday, and you can apologize and make it up to them then?"

"Yeah," he says slowly, the sincerity in his voice almost making me change my mind to let him come over. "I'd like that."

"Great, Tuesday it is."

The silence stretches between us, and I hate that it feels heavy. Awkward. Like it's filled with too many unspoken words on both our parts. The longer it lasts, the harder it gets for me not to say something about our texts from yesterday. But then the thought occurs to me that it's entirely possible I just read too much into the whole exchange. The texts were mild. Practically nothing. He probably hasn't even given them another thought, for all I know.

As if he can read my mind, he finally breaks the silence. "I'm sorry I messed up the graham cracker situation; guess I'm not a s'mores hero after all."

What? Does he seriously think that *is what I care about?* I guess I have my answer about whether he's thought about our texts.

"Josie managed to find them, so no worries. Crisis averted."

"Ah, good, Josie to the rescue. So, you and me; are we good?"

I don't know that I've ever experienced anything more painfully awkward than the last few minutes, and I'm crawling out of my skin with desperation to erase whatever this new version of us is becoming. Thankfully, Josie waves at me through the window to signal that breakfast is ready. Bless her and her perfect timing.

"Uh-huh. Just peachy. I better go, or Gen and Kai will probably eat all my pancakes."

He chuckles like it doesn't surprise him, and I hate that the sound of his voice slides over me like warm honey, even over the phone. "Okay, yeah, can't have that." He pauses for a second, a soft sigh leaving his lips. "Tristan, I…"

"Yeah?" I prompt when he doesn't finish the thought.

Maybe he's going to fix this. Maybe he sees through my weak words. Maybe—

"I'll see you next week. Have fun hiking."

Maybe I'm a bigger idiot than I thought.

The gallery's door swings open, letting in a blast of warm air and sunshine with it. I flash my sister a smile and quickly close the email from my parents' attorney, reminding me of our upcoming meeting.

"Have you noticed that Dominic has been kind of…grumpy lately?" Maggie asks, strolling into the gallery on our shared lunch break. The dance studio where she works is only a couple blocks away, so we've been eating together on days when our schedules allow it. I was shocked when she suggested it, but also really happy she did. It's become a kind of gateway for us to find a middle ground as far as balancing our new sister-slash-stand-in-parent relationship.

I frown. "He has? I hadn't noticed." *Because I've been avoiding him,* is the part I don't tell her. Over the last week and a half, I've only been to pick Liam up from his house once, and I faked a call from Josie before our conversation could go beyond superficial topics.

She leans up against the front desk and steals a grape out of my bag, tossing it up and catching it. "It's weird. Sometimes I swear it's like my very presence irritates him or something. Other days, he's his usual, charming self. Gives me serious Jekyll and

Hyde vibes. Liam doesn't seem to notice anything, though, so that's good, I guess."

"It probably has to do with his recovery," I offer on a shrug. "I think he's under a lot of pressure to make a strong comeback."

"I don't know. I get the feeling it's more personal than that. I overheard two of the other teachers at the studio talking about him, saying something about him being photographed having lunch with some redhead chick in Manhattan last week. Apparently, there were several pics of them at the restaurant *and* leaving together. Maybe it's related to that."

"Oh? That's...good for him."

Maggie's green eyes narrow on me as she tosses her blonde locks over her shoulder. "Is it? Because the way you said that is how you'd react to finding out someone has syphilis instead of a brain tumor. Not to finding out about someone's relationship status."

I take a deliberate bite of my sandwich to buy time, chewing slowly. I finally choke it down and meet her scrutinizing gaze with my poker face ready. "What do you mean? Why wouldn't I think it's good for him to be seeing someone?"

"I just thought..." She shakes her head and shrugs after a beat. "It kind of seemed like there was something between you two. Or, at least, that there could've been. I wouldn't blame you, you know. Who could? He's hot; you're hot. He's obviously a good guy. It would make sense. I'd 'ship it."

My brows pinch together at her teenage logic. "He's a wildly successful professional athlete with the world practically at his fingertips. I'm not even sure I'd qualify for a mortgage. Plus, he's only here for the summer. Nothing about any of that makes sense."

"Hey, don't sell yourself short." She sets her salad bowl down and covers my hand with hers, holding my gaze. "I know I've been a pain in the ass over the last six months. But you know, you're kinda incredible, right? I mean it, Tris; I don't know how I would've made it through everything with Mom and Dad without you, and I'm sorry I haven't exactly treated you like I should. I don't care how many millions of followers or dollars he has; he'd be lucky to have you."

I squeeze her hand back, temporarily unable to respond without turning into a blubbering mess. "How'd I get such awesome siblings?"

"God knew it'd be cruel to saddle you with our parents by yourself?" she poses, stabbing at her salad with a little extra aggression than necessary.

It's the perfect segue into a conversation about our parents that I've been putting off. "Speaking of our lovely parents... there's something I need to talk to you about."

A tick in her jaw is the only indication of where her emotions are. When I've tried to sit all three of my siblings down to talk about matters related to our parents, she and Liam practically shut down. It's gotten better—I think the therapy has helped—but I have no idea how she's going to react to this news.

Loud laughter and splashing emanate from Dominic's back yard when I arrive to pick up Liam and Gen. Bypassing the front door, I follow the stone path around to the back, but stop short before they can spot me. The three of them are in the pool. Genevieve and Liam hang around Dominic's neck like monkeys as he tries to wriggle free from their grips. He plucks Liam off, tosses him toward the deep end with ease, which makes Gen panic-giggle, knowing she's next.

As usual, seeing how genuinely happy my siblings are fills my chest with warmth. Whether they're playing an ultra-competitive game of Wii Tennis (hilarious), or Liam is giving Dominic a cooking lesson (adorable), or they're goofing around in the pool like they are now (hilarious *and* adorable), I'm never sure who's having more fun: the kids or Dominic.

My eyes zero in on Dominic's broad, muscular shoulders and the way they flex and strain as he tosses Gen in the same way he did Liam. Her head breaks the surface; her ever-present smile grows even bigger. "We should play Marco Polo," she calls, bobbing up and down in the water.

Liam gleefully agrees before cannon-balling back into the pool from the diving board.

"Maybe in a few. I'm old and injured; I need to catch my breath," Dominic tells them, pushing himself up to sit on the edge of the pool. The angle gives me a profile view of him, and I'm not even remotely apologetic for giving myself a second to take him in. Long summer days in the sun combined with his predominantly sleeveless wardrobe have erased the faint tan lines he used to have from sleeves. He laughs at something Liam says, the bright white flash of his teeth popping against his tan skin. Water drips from the ends of his hair down his forehead, causing him to shake his head and send droplets in all directions. A couple of tattoos decorate the side of his ribcage, begging to be touched. *What would it be like to trace that ink? To feel the heat of his skin under my fingertips?*

"Tristan!" Gen wails, jerking me out of my Dominic ogling-induced fog.

Dominic's head whips around to find me, and I try to ignore the heat creeping into my cheeks under his gaze. I might have taken a few minutes to fix my makeup and hair before I left the gallery.

"Looks like you guys are having fun," I comment, coming to a stop a few feet from the pool. "Sorry to break up the party."

"Aw, can't we stay a little longer?" Liam pleads. He flashes me a look of desperation, sticking out his bottom lip.

"Yeah, can't we?" Gen asks, following her twin's lead. She spins around to face Dominic, turning her hazel puppy-dog eyes on him. "You don't mind, right, Dominic?"

"Genevieve, it's not polite to put him in that position," I chastise, but he's already shaking his head.

"Not at all. You little fishes are welcome to stay as long as you'd like," he tells her before looking up to me. "You're welcome to hop in too, if you'd like."

"Yeah, Tristan! Join us! You can play Marco Polo with us since

Dominic is *too old*," Liam taunts, waggling his eyebrows and making us laugh.

"Thanks, but, uh, I don't generally travel with a swimsuit in my purse, so this fish will be staying out of water. Maybe next time. Fifteen minutes, guys," I tell my siblings. I add on a stern look that leaves no room for negotiation, but they're already splashing away and not paying me any attention.

I slide into a patio chair in the shade and pull out my phone to set a timer; at the same time, an email from Frank Belford pops up.

Ms. Fitzgerald,

I'm pleased to hear you've made a decision regarding the funds. I'll have my assistant phone you tomorrow to get an appointment on my calendar. I'm going to speak with your father tomorrow, have you given any more thought to—

At that, I close out of Mail and click my phone's screen off. I don't need to read the rest to know where it's going.

"Rough day?" Dominic asks, studying me as he slips into the seat across the table from me.

"Not really. Just a thing with my parents' attorney that I have to deal with."

"Ah." He winces sympathetically. "He's the same guy you said has been pressuring you to see your parents?"

I forgot I even told him about that, but then, we talked about a lot of things that night when he offered to help me out with Liam.

That night feels like forever ago.

I nod. "Yep. But it's fine. Nothing I can't handle." I tear my gaze from watching Liam blindly fumble around the pool, trying to find Gen, and meet Dominic's penetrating gaze. Realizing it was already on me brings goosebumps to life along my neck. "How's the therapy going? Liam told me you're completely free of the boot and crutches? That's great. You'll be hitting aces and chasing down balls in no time."

He grins, lacing his fingers behind his head and nodding. The move puts the inside of his biceps on full display, and I suck in a breath at the sight. "It's going well. Really well, actually. Pierre and my doctor think I'll be ready for a progress test after Max's wedding. It's still a ways off, though, so I'm trying not to get ahead of myself. But if that goes well, I'm hoping to get back into a revised training regimen by late October or November. Pierre says that would be pushing it, but we'll see."

"Wow. That seems so soon," I sputter, suddenly feeling like all of the air has been sucked from my lungs. "I mean, considering you *just* got out of the walking boot."

The realization slams into me that once he's healed enough to get back to normal, or normal-ish, workouts, it'll probably signal the end of his time in Arbor Cove. Hell, if he even stays beyond the summer. How much peace and relaxation can someone who's used to being surrounded by people and family and friends handle before they go crazy?

"I've dealt with enough injuries over the years to know nothing is guaranteed with a recovery window," he says, shrugging and letting his gaze land beyond the yard, somewhere in the waves. For some reason, the sentiment feels deeper than passing skepticism, like he's genuinely worried about it, even though he was trying to sound casual.

"Dominic Moreau," I say, the use of his full name doing the trick to get his attention. With his eyes on me, I pull my sunglasses up to rest on top of my head, so our eyes lock. "I know enough about you to know that if you're determined to be back on the court by October or November, it's going to take an army to stop you. Forget whatever the skeptics or doubters say and think; they don't see you putting in the effort day in and day out. I have. And it's nothing short of inspiring."

"It's funny you say that. I've never thought of my absolute dedication as something admirable. I'm an all-in kind of guy when it comes to something I love, which is pretty much why tennis is my life. It's all I've ever wanted—the only thing I've ever loved enough to sacrifice a normal life to have. I wouldn't know who to be without it."

"That kind of passion..." My head shakes slowly, incredulously. "*That* is exactly why you'll be back to wiping the court with opponents in no time. They don't call you 'iron man' for nothing."

The corner of his mouth tilts up, and I feel my own twist with satisfaction because it's exactly what I was hoping for with the comment.

Silence falls over us, and for once, I don't mind. It's light and easy and comfortable, letting us exist in peace. Just two people staring out at the same golden sunset set against a purple and orange explosion in the sky. It's a beautiful reminder to take the time to appreciate the small things. I spend so much of my time rushing around for Lorraine at the gallery, or carting the kids around, or worrying if I'm doing enough for them that I forget to just stop. Take a minute to breathe. Catch a sunset. Smile at a stranger. Savor a dessert.

With a silent promise to myself to be better about carving a little time out for me, I sigh and soak in the warm breeze.

"This view," I say after a minute, gesturing toward the sunset. "It's spectacular."

"It really is," Dominic says, looking right at me.

A thousand unspoken words swim in his eyes, and I'm torn between wanting to hear them all and hoping he never sets them free.

His lips part, but before he can speak, my phone's timer goes off, cutting through the air.

A beat passes between us, but his lips seal again, his jaw setting and brows pulling low.

"Liam! Gen! Time to get out and dry off," I call.

To my surprise, neither argues or asks for extra time. It's either a miracle or they're angling to get me to agree to something they want. They even go inside to change and get their bags without me having to ask. I'm frowning at the door, trying to figure out what they could ask for, when Dominic interrupts my thoughts.

"Are you free this Saturday? And your siblings? Liam says I can't be here a whole summer and not become a barbecue master. I thought maybe you and Maggie and the twins could come over for grilling and swimming. And s'mores," he adds, his smile a little lopsided and a lot sexy.

"Yes. They'd love that—we'd love to come," I amend, a little surprised at how quickly the words tumble out of me. This morning, I wasn't sure we'd ever find our way back to something resembling a sort of friendship. But now...things feel different. Better.

And I'm not going to question it.

10

DOMINIC

I might've gone a little overboard with supplies for today.

A new, giant inflatable slide perches on the side of the pool, new floats and dive toys litter the pool, a couple of yard games wait to be unboxed on the back patio, water balloons sit filled and wait in buckets, there are three kinds of frozen popsicles in my freezer, and enough food—s'mores ingredients included— is scattered around the kitchen island to feed an army.

Liam and Genevieve were all smiles when they came over the week after the Fourth of July, but every time they mentioned something they did or saw at the bonfire, a little more guilt seared into my chest. I'd been beyond tempted to fish for information about Tristan, but each time the words crawled up my throat, I swallowed them back. Just like I did every time the urge to text her burned the tips of my fingers. By the third time Maggie showed up to pick the twins up instead of Tristan, I knew she was avoiding me. I couldn't even blame her. But that didn't stop me from missing the sight of her smile or the sound of her laugh. Having effortless, meaningful conversations with her, even by text. Being on the receiving end of her teasing jokes.

Everything Gage said remains true, and it probably would make more sense to keep things shallow and light with Tristan for the duration of my stay in Arbor Cove.

But that's the last thing I want things between us to be.

I want the Tristan who wasn't intimidated or even overly impressed by my fame.

I want the Tristan who was bold enough to storm into my house and unleash her rage on me when I fucked up.

And I definitely want the Tristan who didn't shy away from sending flirty texts when I took things that direction.

I'm hoping today will bring *that* Tristan back. Or at least start to bridge the gap between the way things between us were going and this new, awkward version of whatever it is we've become. And it seems Mother Nature is on my side because the weather is perfect—warm but not melt-your-skin-off hot, a few wispy clouds fill the sky, a soft breeze blows. With some luck, it'll stay this nice and be the perfect pool day.

"Dominic, what on earth did you do? Buy out the nearest Academy?" Ellen asks, later, walking through the side gate into the back yard.

Kai's jaw hinges open in wonder as he takes in all the new additions.

I shrug, suddenly unsure of it all. "Too much?"

"No way! This is *awesome!*" Kai exclaims before hugging my waist. "Can I go set up the washers game before Liam and Gen get here?"

Just like that, a toothy grin from an over-the-moon nine-year-old erases my doubts.

"Of course, buddy. You can set any of them up that you want," I reply, gesturing toward the rest of the stack over his shoulder.

"Thanks, Dominic!" he shouts, already off and running.

Ellen chuckles and shakes her head. "You sure are going to make several people very happy today."

"That's the plan. I just thought, why not go all out and make today one of those days the kids still remember and talk about down the road? Some of my favorite childhood memories are from days like this when you and Dan and my parents would surprise us with pool toys and let us just run wild all afternoon."

"Uh-huh," she says slowly, suspiciously. "This wouldn't have anything to do with making a certain blue-eyed brunette who's also coming over happy too, would it?"

"No more so than it does with making *everyone* happy. Come on, Ellen," I say with a sigh. "It's not like that with Tristan. You know that."

"But you'd like it to be," she muses, sitting on the lounge chair next to mine, studying me.

I release another sigh and adjust my cap to stall for time. She's been around and seen enough of my exchanges with Tristan to know if I tried to bullshit her right now.

"I don't *not* want it to be like that," I finally offer vaguely. *Even though it's probably a terrible idea.*

An *ah-ha* smile stretches across her face, and I'm bracing myself for her 'I knew it!' speech, but she just reaches over and pats my leg. "Then make it happen, Dominic. I've seen the way she looks at you. *And* the way you look at her. It's not rocket science, my dear."

"It's also not that simple," I counter. "My life here is temporary. You know that. She knows that. *Temporary* is all I have to offer, and I'm not sure that's fair to her. No matter how great or how much fun it could be."

"Honey, I'm not sure you've noticed, but the girl could definitely use some fun—even if it's only temporary. So could you. What's wrong with that, anyway? Who says that's not enough? You'll never know if you don't try. Or at least do *something*. Because seeing you mope around more and more irritable than ever isn't going to work for me. And don't insult me by trying to say it's not because of her."

She's right, of course. I could lie—to her and to myself—and insist my frustration is related to my career, but I don't want to. Not anymore.

"I just…hate that things have become so awkward between us. And it's one-hundred percent my fault."

"Well, I'd say this is a pretty solid step in the right direction of mending things."

"You think? That's what I'm hoping for, but with her, I just don't know, sometimes. She's not like the women I'm used to meeting."

"I would imagine not. Otherwise, you wouldn't have gotten yourself into this pickle." She chuckles, pushing up from the chair and patting my cheek. "On that note, I'm off to the kitchen to make the margaritas. Give me a shout if you need something! Kai, listen to Dominic, and do what he says."

"Yes, ma'am," Kai acknowledges, looking up from the lawn dart game he's setting up.

I'm about to go see if Kai wants to break in one of the games when my phone pings with a text.

NASH:Don't forget about the fundraiser photoshoot in Manhattan next week.

DOMINIC:Thanks for the reminder, Dad. I won't forget.

I don't even bother reading his response when the sound of Tristan's voice carries from the front, indicating their arrival. I'm already smiling by the time they walk into the back yard, but my jaw practically hits the ground when Tristan rounds the corner... looking like she should be on her way to a Sports Illustrated swimsuit edition cover shoot. Her sheer black cover-up does nothing to actually conceal her body; Instead, it ensures every curve and muscle is on display. It also answers my question of whether she'd wear the same bikini she sent me the selfie in. The angle of the photo was deceiving; the top looks like it's struggling to contain her breasts.

I need to force my gaze back to her face, or things are about to sail right past PG-13 and land dangerously close to R-rated.

Not that this sight is any less of a kick to the chest. Wild choco-late-brown waves frame her heart-shaped face, identical lines along her eyelids draw attention to her big, sky blue eyes, and bright red lipstick highlights her smile. A single dimple I've never noticed before pops in her left cheek, along with the light blush I've become accustomed to seeing from her only when she knows I've been checking her out.

It's cute as hell.

"Sorry we're a little late; just one of those days when we couldn't get our act together," she offers, pointing at Gen and Liam from above the tops of their heads so they can't see.

"Not a problem," I manage to respond, though I'm still too caught up in how fucking incredible she looks.

Something between a smile and a smirk pulls at my features when I realize she's giving my appearance the same perusal I gave hers. Her eyes trail lazily over my body before she swallows and brings her gaze back up, her eyes catching on my backward cap. I realized a while back it always seems to catch her eye. And if I catch her staring, it'll make her blush.

So, now I'm never not wearing my cap backward.

"Is this *all* for us?" Genevieve asks, her voice full of shock as she looks around.

"Holy sh—" Liam cuts himself off quickly, going with, "cow!" to finish that thought instead.

Their surprise pulls Tristan's attention off of me, and her reaction is the exact one Liam almost had.

She spins around, taking it all in, before turning to me. "Dominic, what did you do? This is….insane," she finally finishes, but her laugh is light and happy—exactly what I was hoping for.

"Yep, it's all for you guys!" I tell Liam, gesturing for him to go explore. "Kai was around her a minute ago; I think he went inside, though."

Gen and Liam take off at that news, and only then do I register Maggie's presence. She's looking across the yard with a similar look of shock as Tristan, and I think it might be the longest I've ever seen her go without looking at her phone.

"Well done, D-Mo," she says, dropping her shoulder bag and stepping right into the pool. "Dibs on the flamingo float!"

The nickname makes me smile. Of all the Fitzgerald siblings, she's been the toughest one to crack, at least in some ways. But I guess that's par for the course when it comes to teenagers.

I give Tristan a rundown of my rough plans for the day—hang out, swim, let the kids use the slide, play the lawn games for a while, and then a friendly pool volleyball competition before throwing some burgers and hot dogs on the grill.

She's on board with everything, but then her eyes fall to my leg, and she arches a brow. "But, you're basically a handicap for whichever team has you for volleyball."

"Ah. Actually," I say, looking down at her with a cheeky grin. "I have a solution for that: all-time server, and I'll sit on the edge."

Her mouth falls open. "But *that* isn't fair, either! You're a friggin' professional athlete! And probably have some annoying secret talent for serving."

"Better hope you're on my team, then," I counter, giving her a wink.

Her arms fold across her chest, and it takes every ounce of willpower I can summon to keep my eyes from doing more than a quick drop. "That sounds like a challenge. Makes me think you might be bluffing."

I fold my arms and turn to face her, mirroring her stance. "One way to find out."

"Works for me. I'll even let you have the advantage of an extra player since there are seven of us."

I lift a brow at her and try desperately to contain a grin. Seeing her feisty and competitive would probably be adorable to a regular guy. But for me, it's more along the lines of the biggest turn-on possible. "Maybe *I'm* the one who should be asking if you're some kind of pool volleyball superstar."

"I'll never tell," she says before making a zipping gesture over her lips.

"Uh-oh," Ellen calls from the patio doorway, a pitcher of margaritas in one hand and cups in the other as she watches our exchange. "This looks like a situation that could benefit from some margaritas."

"That depends," Tristan replies warily. "Exactly how much

tequila is in this batch? I need to be firing on all cylinders for this pool volleyball match."

"Sure you don't want to have the excuse of having one too many margaritas lined up?" I tease, knowing I'm stoking her competitive fire.

"Oh, big talk for a guy who's probably going to fall back on the, 'well it's hardly fair; all I'm doing is serving' excuse. Don't think I haven't already realized that," she says, eyes narrowed, even as a smile cracks despite her best efforts to contain it.

We fill Ellen in on our friendly volleyball competition over margaritas that are thankfully less lethal than the ones she made previously. To make things fair, Ellen suggests drawing names from a hat for the teams, which we both agree is the best option. For a while, the three of us make small talk and watch Kai, Liam, and Gen take turns flying down the slide. The fun eventually turns into a diving and 'best jumps' competition. Tristan accuses me of turning her siblings into competitive maniacs, but I point out she's *slightly* competitive herself, so maybe it wasn't all my doing.

We go back and forth about it, keeping things light and teasing before Maggie shouts at us that we're *both* partially responsible for their competitiveness. *"You, Mister 'takes every game seriously even if it's just foosball' are just as guilty as Miss 'let's see who can clean their room faster,' so let's call it a tie."*

Ellen applauds Maggie's assessment, and we both realize there *might* be some merit behind it.

"Eight point five," she shouts after Kai breaks the surface from a wild front flip.

We all play along and indulge their competition by calling out scores, aside from Maggie, who's back to staring at her phone while floating on the opposite side, until Liam and Genevieve get into a rare, heated argument over whose dive was better. Tristan leaps into action when Liam splashes Gen in the face. I'm too stunned to react. I've seen them bicker, but this is new.

Tristan summons them out of the pool and pulls them aside, and I watch the whole thing feeling a mixture of shock at how quickly things escalated between them and awe at how well and seemingly easily Tristan handles the situation.

"I seem to recall similar incidents between you and Max," Ellen muses. "You would terrorize each other over the most insignificant issues. I remember telling Dan we should be glad we stopped at one kid." She smiles, tucking her blonde hair behind her ear. "But then, by the last summer you guys were here, I could see the shift. You still bickered and were insanely competitive, but the sibling love was stronger than any argument you had."

I nod slowly, recollecting a few bits and pieces from that summer. "And now he's getting married. Can you believe it? Sometimes I still feel like he shouldn't possibly be old enough to settle down. But then something happens to remind me I'm old now."

"Hey," she chastises, giving me a light punch to the arm, "you can't be old. What would that make me? Speaking of the wedding, though; have you thought about what you'll do after it? Your mom mentioned she's trying to convince you to just stay in France."

"I don't know yet," I tell her honestly. My mom has not been shy in suggesting I spend the rest of my rehab and recovery time back at home, and every time she brings it up, I put off giving her a real answer. Instead, I make some kind of excuse about not wanting to mess up the rhythm I've found here. The truth, though, has less to do with my recovery and more to do with the woman and her siblings across the yard.

"Can't say I blame you. September will be here before we know it."

Before I can let myself think too much about it, Tristan reappears. "Well, that was fun."

"They okay?" I ask, watching them both go to different lawn games. Kai looks torn but ultimately opts for washers with Liam.

"Think we can start the food soon? Think they're getting a little hangry."

"I can do that."

"Need any help?" she asks, shielding her eyes from the sun to look up at me.

Pretty sure having to focus on not burning food with you standing next to me, in what amounts to almost zero clothing, wouldn't exactly be helpful.

"Nah, I've got this. You ladies relax. Take a dip if you want. I've got food covered."

Even though I didn't want her help, I still manage to sneak looks at her while working the grill. She spends a few minutes talking to Ellen, their conversation looking serious, before making her way over to Kai, who's playing lawn darts by himself. He smiles when she asks if she can join him, and she smiles back.

Yeah, I think, *she has that effect on me too, bud.*

With what I hope is an edible meal of burgers, hot dogs, potato salad, and roasted corn, I call everyone to the table. Liam was the one who chose the spread, so I have no doubt he'll be the first to let me know if I screwed up. After a few minutes of mostly silent eating, I take it as a good sign and release a sigh of relief. Sure, I'm a pro under the pressure of having a Grand Slam final on the line, but when it comes to having a nine-year-old scrutinize my cooking, I'm apparently not so cool under pressure.

"So, how do you guys feel about a volleyball match?" Tristan asks, directing the question to the younger kids. "The teams are Maggie, Gen, and me, versus Dominic, Liam, Kai, and Ellen."

"Hell yeah!" Liam exclaims. "I mean—*heck* yeah," he corrects before Tristan can say anything. It doesn't stop her from giving him a warning look, though.

With everyone in agreement and excited about the competition, we give our food a while to settle before getting the match underway.

"It's okay if you need a few warmup shots, you know," Tristan calls from across the net, a taunting smirk in place.

Fuck, she's hot when she's giving me shit.

"Nah, I think I'm good," I say, pulling back and striking the perfect serve at her. She wasn't expecting it but still manages to get it back over.

"Suit yourself. We're ready. Right, ladies?" she says, turning to her sisters.

They nod enthusiastically, and it's all the indication I need to launch an actual serve. It flies into Maggie's area, and she dives to keep it from hitting the water with Tristan right behind her. She pushes off the bottom and spikes the ball directly into an open area, smacking the water before Liam or Kai can make it there. The girls cheer and give each other high fives, and I should be motivating my team with some kind of line like *that's all right, we'll get 'em this time*, but my eyes won't leave Tristan. Having her on the opposite side of the net, *bouncing up and down*, was a huge mistake. The water hits right at her waist, putting entirely too much of her tan, taut skin on display.

It's going to be one long-ass game.

Either Ellen notices where my head is or is genuinely trying to motivate the troops because she sends a splash my way and claps. "Let's go! Focus! Liam, take two steps to your left, away from Kai," she instructs, adjusting her own position to cover more of the pool.

The first few points of the game pass in a similar fashion before Kai and Liam huddle together, exchanging words with stern looks given across the net. After that, it's a lot closer as they find their groove and realize Maggie is their weak link. She's tall but has the coordination of a baby giraffe, and they take relentless advantage of that fact.

We're tied at one set apiece, with Tristan up to serve for the match. She calls her sisters into a huddle, looking up and over here a couple of times before she leans in to whisper something to Maggie. Maggie whips her head around to our side before turning back and whispering something in return. I have no idea what the exchange was about, but whatever it was put a fierce look of determination in Tristan's eyes and a confident grin on her lips. She rolls her shoulders and adjusts her bikini top—a move I'm certain was meant to torture me—before pulling back and striking the ball in one swift motion. Kai lunges forward and saves it, setting Liam up to spike it at Gen, who was braced and ready.

Maggie manages to reach it in time and sets Tristan up for the perfect spike just out of Liam's reach.

The ball bounces onto our side with a final splash, and all three girls across the net cheer in unison. Liam smacks the water in frustration, and Kai's head falls, his hands pulling at his hair, but Ellen's quick to squash their sour attitudes by reminding them it's *just a game*, and there are plenty worse things in life than losing some silly volleyball competition.

Liam looks less than convinced, though I'm the only one who catches his eye-roll.

"She's right," I agree, sliding into the pool from the edge to go shake hands at the net. "Losing is never fun, but without the losses, victory wouldn't be as sweet."

Liam arches a brow. "You read that in a fortune cookie or what?"

"Liam!" Maggie admonishes, giving him a reproachful look. "Don't be a sore loser. Take a lesson from Dominic. Just think about how many times he's had to handle big losses with grace. Yet you don't see him being a baby, do you?"

Clearly, she's never seen me in a locker room after losing a marathon five-setter.

The afternoon bleeds into the evening, with more slide and pool time for the kids, a few friendly games of washers between Ellen, Maggie, Tristan, and me, and another round of Ellen's margaritas. Eventually, Ellen disappears inside, insisting on preparing snacks since I grilled earlier, and Maggie pulls Tristan into the yard to teach her a new dance she's been working on. I stick close to the pool to keep an eye on the trio's handstand competition; only, I can't stop stealing glances at Tristan, shaking her hips and laughing at herself when Maggie corrects her steps. Seeing Tristan like this—relaxed, happy, and free of any kind of stress—makes me never want the day to end. Makes me want crazy things, like a thousand more days like today.

Two trays of nachos, one bowl of fruit, an entire box of popsicles, and a dozen s'mores later, we're all settled into the theater room with an animated movie on, even though all three kids fell asleep within a few minutes. Ellen too. Maggie's sprawled out in the back row with headphones in and not paying any attention to the world beyond her screen.

"Psst," Tristan whispers, nudging me. "Wanna go for a walk down to the beach?"

"Let's do it," I agree with an eager nod, already grabbing the blanket off the empty seat to my left.

Guided by the last rays of sunshine clinging to the horizon, she leads the way down the sandy path to the beach, her hair whipping around in the warm breeze. I can tell she's walking slowly for my benefit, which is both thoughtful and cruel; the view of her from behind in cutoff jean shorts that make her legs look a mile long is pushing me to the verge of asking her to let me lead. But she's either blissfully unaware of what she does to me or is intent on inflicting as much torture as possible before finding a suitable area to sit.

Mercifully, she comes to a stop, twirling her hair into a knot around her hand and flashing me a smile. "This spot okay?"

"Perfect," I say without even looking as I unfold the blanket and lay it out.

For a couple of minutes, we sit in silence; she's staring out at the ocean, watching the waves, and lost somewhere in her thoughts. And I'm watching her. Because it's all I seem to want to do today, whether we're in the pool or eating lunch or walking to the beach. Each second my eyes stayed on her in the pool was both torment and bliss—having her so close, only to still feel like she was just out of reach.

But I've never known a sweeter torture than the sight of Tristan at twilight.

Her skin—still smelling faintly of chlorine and sunscreen—glows against the backdrop of sea and sand. A dimple appears in her cheek as she catches me watching her from the corner of her eye, turning to face me. "What?" she asks, lifting a hand to her hair like she thinks I'm staring because there's something in it. The dim light softens her features and makes the blue shade of her eyes match the ocean, drawing me into their depths.

I break the silence by setting free the words I've wanted to say to her all day. "I'm sorry about the Fourth. For letting not just the kids down, but you too. You have to know; you're the last person I want to disappoint or hurt."

Brows pulled down and lips set in a frown, she shakes her head, turning back to the ocean before speaking. "I just thought..." But then she just shakes her head again, sighing.

And it makes my heart thump inside my chest, whatever it is she isn't saying.

"Thought what?" I prompt.

"I don't know." She finally turns back to me, biting her lip. "I wasn't sure if maybe...my drunk texts made things too weird for you?" she says, posing it like a question.

"Weird?" I frown. "Weird isn't even in the realm of how I felt about those texts. Not even *close*. I had to leave like the store was on fire to avoid being the star of a very inappropriate scene in the middle of the cookie aisle."

"Really?" She laughs, and I can hear the relief in it.

"Swear." I mark an X over my chest for good measure, hoping she can read the sincerity in my eyes.

"Okay."

"So...are we good? Now that we've cleared the air, can we, I don't know, pick up where we left off? Before I was an idiot?"

"I'd like that. You know, this kinda makes me wish I could retroactively make a wager on the volleyball game."

"I can get on board with this," I acquiesce. A thousand filthy possibilities are already flitting through my mind, and I know I should rein them in. But it doesn't stop me from hoping she's on the same wavelength. "What would I owe you for losing this wager?"

She hums in contemplation for a beat. "I don't know; so many ideas to choose from..."

Her answer—turning my own words against me—makes me laugh. "Touché."

Silence falls between us, but this time it's comfortable and easy, as we watch the last rays of light slip from the sky.

And when we do break the silence, our efforts are simultaneous.

"I don't—"

"So how's—"

We both stop with a laugh, and I shake my head. "You first."

"I was just going to say that I don't know if there's a better recipe to make kids conk out faster than a day in the pool followed by a food coma and a movie they've seen at least a dozen times. I'll have to remember this trick."

"Feel free to use the pool at my place anytime."

"You're just hoping my white bikini makes another appearance."

"Oh, were you wearing that one today? I hadn't noticed," I tease, knowing she'll call me on it.

She laughs and shoves my shoulder. "You're a terrible liar, Dominic Moreau."

"Guilty. But, for the record, please tell me you weren't wearing that bikini to play pool volleyball on the Fourth?"

"Nah," she says, shaking her head. "Just beach volleyball. Why?"

Her words make me do a double-take, only vaguely aware of my jaw hinging open. Tristan carefully watches me before a smile slowly breaks free.

"You should have seen your face!" She laughs again, the sound sending a shockwave through my system.

"Yeah?" I ask, a split second before wrapping my arms around her from the side, catching her off guard and pulling her down to the ground. My fingers run loose over her torso, tickling her relentlessly. She giggles and puts up a weak attempt to wiggle free that somehow ends with my body covering hers, effectively pinning her against the blanket.

In a blink, the mood shifts from playful to something entirely different.

Her hands freeze on my chest, her touch seeping through my shirt and branding me.

The sounds of labored breathing replaces our laughter, the heaving of our chests, causing them to brush together.

My eyes fall to her lips that are now their natural pink color, every last trace of her signature red lipstick long gone.

Erasing the distance between us and finding out what those lips feel like against mine is all I want at this moment. Showing her how much she affects me, how *not* weird I felt about our text exchange is the only thing going through my mind.

Until it isn't, when fucking Gage and his bullshit reminders bulldoze their way into my thoughts. *"Don't forget, Dominic, this entire situation is temporary. You really want to start something with a girl who sounds like she's got more baggage than an airplane, only to inevitably hurt her in the end when you go your separate ways?"*

I lean my head back enough to think straight and notice Tristan's expression is filled with the same conflicting emotions I'm feeling.

"Who were you eating lunch with in Manhattan?" she asks, throwing me for a serious loop.

I pull back even further, more so out of surprise than anything. "What?"

"Last week, Maggie said there were pictures of you with some redhead at a restaurant in Manhattan, having lunch. Looking cozy."

Frowning, I lift myself off of her. I'm lying on my side, wracking my brain trying to put the pieces together. "Oh. You mean Monica? She's my main liaison for Rolex. They're one of my sponsors. We were meeting to discuss the details of a fundraiser I'm helping them with."

"Oh. That's…good to know."

"I'm not seeing anyone, Tristan. I want to make that clear. Each time I happen to be photographed out with a female, gossip inevitably follows. There's almost never any truth in what gets written or speculated about my love life. It's just the way my life is. I can be playing the greatest tennis of my life, heading into the finals of a major, and some reporter will still ask if rumors about whom I'm dating are true. Usually, I'm able to fly under the radar as far as my personal life, but occasionally…shit happens," I finish with a shrug.

"I see," she says, nodding in understanding—or at least what I *hope* is understanding.

And knowing her rocky track record with reporters and history of being the subject of brutal tabloid headlines, I also hope I didn't just destroy the progress we made today.

11

DOMINIC

*T*he Tuesday after our pool day, when Tristan came to pick Liam up after work, things were definitely different between us. Distracted and quiet, I could tell something was off. We'd made so much progress that day, and I was trying to accept the fact that I had fucked everything up by bringing the media bullshit into the picture. But then, while Liam was taking full advantage of his "ten more minutes," and out of earshot, she told me her parents' attorney wanted to meet with her in New York at the end of the week. She'd been putting it off for weeks, but finally couldn't any longer—a reality she hated.

I would've done anything at that moment to alleviate her fears and ease her stress. Luckily, I happened to already be going to New York on Friday as well, and the suggestion that we make the trip together occurred before I even had to think about it. When she joked that the only reason she accepted my offer was that I had a private car service driving me there and back, I knew things between us were okay.

"I used to think I'd never want to live anywhere other than Manhattan," Tristan says, eyes glued on the skyscrapers closing in on us as we approach the city. "Now I don't even want to spend another night there. It's crazy how much your life can change in just a year."

Originally, my plan was to check into a hotel after the photo-shoot and a lunch meeting with Nash, maybe see some of the sights I've missed out on during my stays here for the U.S. Open, and spend the night to avoid sitting in horrible traffic. That plan dissolved the second Tristan agreed to come with me instead of driving separately. I'll sit in an entire day's worth of traffic if it means she's in the car too.

I reach across the seat between us and pull her hand into mine. "You can do this," I tell her. And I mean it. She's the picture of strength in a storm of adversity.

She nods and squeezes my hand. "You're right; I can. I'm just glad I had you to keep my mind occupied during the trip. Even if your music taste is questionable," she jokes.

She's not wrong, though; I purposefully searched for awful songs, spanning from early 2000s pop to 80s rock and 90s French rap, and everything in-between, just because I wanted to make her laugh. Distract her from the nerves I knew she felt.

"All right, fine, you can be in total control on the ride back."

Her eyes light up. "Great! Hope you like Britney and Christina!"

"Are you trying to make me regret the offer already?"

Her answer comes in the form of the chorus from "Genie in a Bottle," and I weirdly find it sexy *and* hilarious.

"I believe we're here, Mr. Moreau," Isaac, our driver calls, bringing the car to a stop a few minutes later.

The smile fades from Tristan's lips, and I suddenly hate that I can't go with her, or even meet her down here after the meeting is over.

"Guess that's my cue," she says, flashing me a forced smile and picking at imaginary lint on her dress.

"You sure you don't want Isaac here to come pick you up after you're done? Bring you to the photoshoot?"

"No, I'll be fine meeting Josie. And don't you have a lunch meeting after, anyway?"

"Yeah, but I'm always happy to cancel on Nash. Make him work a little harder for his money."

That gets a chuckle, but she shakes her head and pushes her door open. "Don't do that on my account. I'll just text you after Josie and I finish. I'll either come to you at the restaurant or find something to do until you're done."

I agree and wish her luck, to which she smiles and offers me the same, along with, "try not to break any hearts with that blue steel look you're *so* good at."

I shift over to her now-vacant seat and roll the window down to give her one last look at my *perfect* blue steel impression as the car pulls into traffic.

"These last shots are perfect! You two nailed it," Monica calls from behind the photographer's shoulder, eyes glued to his camera's screen as he flips through the 47,000 photos he took. Or maybe it just *felt* like 47,000.

Either way, I'm ready to get out of the ridiculous tuxedo I've worn for the last hour. *When would anyone ever wear a fucking tux to play tennis anyway?* But when one of your sponsors wants you to wear a tuxedo and a half-million-dollar watch and pose mid-serving motion, you do so without complaint. Plus, these photos are for their annual fundraiser gala where the money raised goes to various non-profits and charitable organizations, so knowing it's for a good cause makes it easier to be moved and posed like a puppet.

I grab my phone and make a beeline for the changing rooms, ignoring Nash's attempts to get my attention while he talks to two models from the shoot. *Not the first time he's crashed a photoshoot for the sake of a private meet and greet with models.*

TRISTAN: Just left the lawyer's office. On my way to meet Josie now :)

DOMINIC: How did it go?

TRISTAN: It went…about as well as I expected. How was the photoshoot? Did all the ladies swoon over your blue steel pose?

DOMINIC: You know it. Still trying to beat them off with a stick.

DOMINIC: The shoot was long and tedious, but went well, I think. Heading to lunch with Nash as soon as I ditch the penguin suit they had me wear.

TRISTAN: If you were in a tuxedo, I hate to break it to you, but the swarm of ladies probably isn't after you for the godawful Zoolander impression.

I'm about to reply when Nash walks out of the building with a model hanging on each of his arms.

Bri, the brunette on his left arm, shoots me a wink and leans in to whisper something into Nash's ear before releasing his arm and heading back inside.

"Looking forward to seeing you later, Nash," Talia, the blonde one on his right purrs, fluttering her artificially long lashes at him.

I just shake my head and walk to the car without bothering to ask.

"What?" he asks, sliding onto the leather seat on the other side.

"I didn't say anything."

"Your judgmental eyes did." He frowns and crosses his arms. "Thought you'd be up for a night out. Bri seems like your type."

"I told you, I had a change of plans, so I won't be staying tonight. Should make you happy; the girls are all yours."

The car jolts to a stop as Isaac slams on the break to avoid a jaywalking couple, smacking the dashboard and muttering curses at them before offering apologies to us.

"No worries, my man," Nash assures him, smoothing a hand over his tie and Tom Ford suit pants. "Fucking New York. And you wonder why I prefer Paris. Wait, what were you saying about not staying tonight?"

"Exactly that—I'm not staying. Something came up, and I need to get back to Arbor Cove tonight."

He rears back like I've deeply offended him. "You're passing on a night with a couple of *very* hot models, in a city you're always saying you wish you had more time to explore because *something came up* in a town whose most exciting nightlife is a bar on the beach? Unless this 'something' has tits and a killer ass, I'm calling bullshit."

"And *you* wonder why women want nothing to do with you after a couple of dates."

He shrugs. "I don't wonder; I'm aware I'm an asshole, and I don't try to hide it. By the way, that little attempt to change the subject was a dead giveaway. Nice try, though." He leans over and punches me in the arm. "I think it's great you're getting some. Might as well; what else is there to do in that town?"

A heavy sigh and head shake is my only response. Pretty sure he wouldn't think it's "great" if he knew the whole story. But I have no intention of letting that happen. Luckily for me, we're meeting one of his bosses at the restaurant, so he'll be in professional mode for the duration of our lunch.

He spends the rest of our car ride on the phone with his assistant, going over his itinerary for the rest of his time in New York, and I spend it ignoring my mom's eighth text this week, asking what my plan is for Max's wedding and beyond. Max already warned me she's mentioned that a couple of friends' daughters will also be at the wedding, and maybe I'd like to be seated near them at the rehearsal.

The lunch meeting with Nash's boss, Jack, seems to last forever, though, in reality, it's no longer than any other lunch I've had with the two of them. Jack has never been my favorite person for multiple reasons. He's about ten years older than me but acts at least ten years younger. The first time I met Jack, he made a tasteless and wildly inappropriate joke about my mom being "totally bangable." If I hadn't already met and gotten along really well with Nash, I never would've signed with their agency. Nash pushes boundaries and isn't exactly the poster boy for maturity, but he at least knows there's a time and place for that kind of behavior. I've always wondered how he puts up with Jack, but I guess it helps that they're based in different countries.

Thankfully, one thing Jack and Nash have in common is that they're both workaholics, so it never takes long for them to steer the conversation in that direction. Nash reviews the latest information on my current endorsement deals and prospective ones, and they go back and forth about what strategy is best in negotiations considering my injury. Usually, I'm focused and engaged during this part of the meetings, but right now, all I can think about is wrapping things up to meet Tristan.

As if she's reading my thoughts, my phone buzzes against the table with her name popping up in a text.

TRISTAN: You didn't have to send Isaac to get me, but thank you. We're on the way back to you now.

DOMINIC: Perfect, I think we're almost done here. Let me know when you get here and I'll meet you out front.

Jack finally settles the bill, asking Nash if we've made plans for tonight yet, and if not, he says we should come to a rooftop pool party his friend is throwing.

"I'm afraid I'll have to pass," I respond, offering no further explanation.

"Well, I'm in," Nash replies. "What's the policy on party crashers like myself bringing more party crashers? Say, a couple of models?"

They launch into a conversation about the models from earlier, and I glance at my phone to see Tristan texted she's popping into the restaurant to use the restroom before we leave. My chest tightens with the need to see her, and I'm about to text her that I'm wrapping up when our waiter clears his throat from behind me.

"Um, sir?" he asks, shifting uncomfortably. "I apologize for the interruption, but I thought you might want a heads up that there is a group gathering in front of the restaurant, apparently fans of yours. How would you like to handle the situation?"

My head falls back on a groan, and I immediately look between Jack and Nash. "What the hell?"

"Oh shit," Jack says. "I wasn't thinking and posted that photo from earlier…and tagged our location," he says.

The urge to punch him has always simmered, just low enough to contain, but right now, it's a blazing inferno.

I glare at him in disbelief. It's their company's unwritten policy to not post photos with their clients until *after* they've left a location, and I'm having a hard time believing that fact slipped his mind. Usually, I try to be accommodating and don't mind taking selfies and signing autographs for fans, but not when I'm trying to make a quick exit.

"Jack, what the fuck? That's unacceptable," I snap, ready to rip him apart when a flash of dark hair catches my eye from over Nash's shoulder.

Shit. Tristan. She might've slipped past the crowd on her way in, but there's no way she'll go unnoticed if she's seen getting into the same car as me.

"Nash, I'll be going out the back. Let Isaac know to circle around and pick me up in the alley," I call, already shoving the chair back to dash after her as quickly as my leg will allow.

A couple of restaurant patrons glance my way, but I'm too focused to care. "Tristan, wait," I call out, finally close enough not to draw the entire restaurant's attention.

She whirls around with wide eyes and arched brows. "Uh…"

"This way. I'll explain in a second," I quickly whisper, grabbing her hand to lead her in the opposite direction, through the back of the restaurant until we reach a door with a glowing red 'EXIT' sign hanging above it. I push the door open and pull her into the alley along the side of the building, finally coming to a stop when we're more than a couple of feet from bags of trash and partially hidden from view of the street by a dumpster.

"Why the detour?" she asks, following the path my eyes are taking as I scan the area.

"Did you notice a group of people out front when you came in?"

"Yeah, but I didn't really stop to see what it was for..."

"My agent's idiot boss shared a photo on social media of the three of us and tagged the restaurant. It might've been okay if you were still in the car, but when I realized you were inside, and I was about to leave...there's no way some kind of photo of you wouldn't have made its way into the Twitter-verse if we were seen getting into the same car. I just couldn't let you be caught off guard like that."

Her face morphs from initial panic to relief, and she squeezes the hand that I didn't realize still held hers. "Thank you. And I'm sorry for complicating things. I would've dealt with it no matter the situation, but..." she trails off, shaking her head and shifting her gaze to the end of the alley. "Am I being completely crazy? My family is old news; it's not like I'd get recognized walking down the street. Well, I don't *think* I would—not now, anyway. But after you've had eggs and rotten fruit thrown at you as soon as you step foot outside, it's not exactly an experience you forget easily."

"Hey," I say, lifting her chin to bring her eyes back to me. "You're not crazy. I can't even begin to imagine what it was like for you those months you dealt with that shit while you were here *while* taking care of your siblings. I'd be a little shocked if you *weren't* wary of situations like this one."

Suddenly, the door to the restaurant opens, its hinges screaming to let us know, and I instinctively back Tristan up, bracing my hands against the wall on either side of her and using my body to shield her from view. She sucks in a breath at the contact of our bodies and looks up to lock eyes with me. For one electric second, the spark between us crackles; the need I feel for her burns a little brighter. One tilt of my head is all it would take for our lips to brush. One tilt of hers is all it would take to obliterate my last sliver of self-control.

I want this so much, I don't tell her.

"Dominic?" Nash calls, effectively breaking the spell.

"Yeah?' I croak, slowly pushing against the wall.

His eyes flit from me to Tristan and back, but he thankfully knows better than to ask right now. "Y'all can go down that way and meet Isaac. Jack went out front to try and distract them, and if that doesn't work, I'll wait until you're out of sight and then yell something about seeing you go the other way."

"Thanks," I tell him with a nod.

I grab Tristan's hand and tug her in the opposite direction of Nash until we're safely out of the alley and spot the town car waiting down the block.

"So, do you deal with this kind of situation often?" Tristan asks once we're settled into the back seat.

"It depends on the city and the occasion, but not really. It's usually more like getting recognized at meals or stopped on the street occasionally, but it's not usually a crowd of people waiting, no."

"Before everything fell apart," she says quietly, keeping her head turned toward the window, "I would have the occasional run-in with paparazzi or journalists, and I never had a problem with it. I never even thought much about it. My parents were friends with some really important people in this city, and by association, we'd sometimes be photographed and recognized when we were coming or going from a big event. I used to secretly love it. Sometimes, I wonder…how different things would be right now, or at least in situations like that, if things hadn't imploded so spectacularly. And the irony is, I could probably walk naked into Times Square, and people wouldn't recognize me as Tristan Fitzgerald, daughter of disgraced hedge fund managers. I highly doubt anyone would care. But it's *me*, you know? *I'm* the one that can't get past what happened, how horrible it felt to be in the spotlight for the *wrong* reasons—for things completely beyond my control."

It takes me a few seconds to process her words, to truly try and put myself in her shoes. "I don't think anyone could blame you for that. You've suffered for sins you didn't commit, and nothing makes that okay."

We ride in silence after the exchange. Something tells me that after everything she's dealt with today, she needs time and space to process. So I give it to her, flipping through some emails, texting my brother, and checking in with Nash, who assures me the situation was handled and there wasn't anything else on social media about it.

With that knowledge putting my mind at ease, I turn my attention to the passing scenery, a blur of greenery, a cloudless blue sky. During the year, regardless if the tournament is in Beijing, Brazil, California, or Turkey, I spend so much of my time traveling, but I don't ever take the time to slow down and appreciate the views. My determination to get back to full strength on my leg is unwavering, but I can't deny that I'm enjoying the downtime more than I ever would've thought possible.

Tristan's phone pings with a text, and whatever it is makes her laugh, drawing me out of my thoughts.

"What's so funny over there?" I ask, smiling along because *fuck* if it's not doing something to my heart to hear her laugh.

"Maggie sent me a picture of the practice pizzas Liam and Gen and Kai made, getting ready for our pizza competition on Sunday. So. Much. Flour," she says with emphasis before turning her phone screen to me.

"Jesus," I chuckle, shaking my head at the photo of three kids with similar amounts of white flour in their hair. "What are the odds the kitchen is in any better shape by the time you get home?"

"Slim," she says immediately, giving me another laugh. "But that's okay because I'll be leaving it that way until *they* can follow the rules and clean up after themselves. I refuse to provide maid services for my able-bodied siblings in addition to taxi services."

"Seems fair to me. Hey, I've been meaning to ask, how is Maggie?"

"She's good. Really good. As far as I can tell, at least. Which could be off, because…teenagers. But she seems happy and is loving her classes at the dance studio. She told me Shane showed up at the studio one day, but she slammed the door in his face before he could even finish spewing whatever lies or bullshit he had up his sleeve."

"Wow, that's great. Aside from the Shane part."

"You know, I don't think I ever did thank you for that. The Shane thing, I mean. For helping with it. In a roundabout way, it feels like you gave me my sister back. And while we're on the subject," she says, pausing to angle her body toward mine. I curse the seat between us for keeping me from feeling the warmth of her thighs brushing against mine. "I owe you...I don't even know *what* I could possibly do or give you that comes close to expressing my appreciation for how far Liam has come. Gen too, but she was never as difficult to get to open up as our brother. But Liam is almost like a different kid. He asked me if he could start going to therapy like Gen. Swear to God; I almost cried when he asked. And I'm ninety-nine percent sure it has to do with spending time with you. So, again, thank you."

She reaches across the middle seat and twines her fingers through mine, squeezing.

"That's incredible. I'm glad to hear he's making progress. Honestly, I'm just building on the foundation you've already given him. It might not feel like it, but I promise that kid loves and looks up to you more than you know. He's a great kid, and I think with the right tools from a therapist, he'll be able to work through things and be just fine."

"I hope so."

The partition separating us from the front seats slides down. "Sorry to interrupt," Isaac says, "The car's check engine light came on, and it's company policy to ensure there's not a serious safety concern. I'm going to have to pull off the interstate and check things out. Shouldn't take too long, but I do apologize for the delay."

He pulls into the parking lot of a 24-hour diner with a sign that boasts they serve the best pie in Connecticut, so we quickly decide it's worth checking out. Stepping into the diner feels like I'm stepping into every stereotypical small-town diner you see in American movies—booths with cracked blue vinyl benches, black and white checkered tiles, bar stools lined up at the counter with locals chatting over pie and coffee, a waitress sporting an old school apron who tells us to have a seat wherever we'd like.

"You know," Tristan says, sliding into one side of a booth. "I've seen this town in various brochures for the best places to explore in Connecticut. It has a really cute little downtown area with a bunch of shops and restaurants. A couple of B&Bs. Nice hiking trails. Sometimes, when the kids or Maggie drive me insane, or I have any other self-pitying thoughts, I daydream about getting in my car to drive up here for a weekend by myself. Then I feel guilty and drop it."

"Why? You shouldn't feel guilty for wanting a break." I pause and wait for her to look up from her menu to catch her eyes. "When was the last time you did something just for fun for yourself?"

"Honestly?" She exhales a breath, taking a second to think before shaking her head. "I don't know. It's not that I don't have fun—don't get me wrong, I've come to love having this time with my siblings, despite the circumstances. My life in New York was focused mostly on my job and social life, and I rarely made the effort to come home for more than the occasional dinner, even though they were only a subway ride away. I took so much for granted. And now that it feels like we're finding our groove in Arbor Cove, I promised myself I wouldn't do that anymore."

"I get that. But you're allowed to have a life for yourself too, you know."

"I could say the same thing to you," she counters, closing her menu. "Before your injury, when was the last time you did something for fun? Took a day off—a *real* day off—without a single obligation?"

I frown, searching for an example or a specific day that I can recall. Even on the off-season, which is only from mid-November until the New Year, I still train and tend to obligations with the foundation or with sponsors. A true day off is a novel concept for me. I'm still thinking it over a minute later when our pies arrive;

their famous peanut butter pie for Tristan and cinnamon apple for me.

She lets out a soft little "mmm" after the first bite, and I snap my eyes up at the sound. But she just goes back for bite after bite, blissfully unaware her sounds of enjoyment are summoning every dirty thought I've had about her.

"Oh. My. God. You *have* to try this, Dominic. It seriously might be the single most amazing thing I've ever put in my mouth."

Jesus.

I think this girl might just ruin me.

"Clearly, you've never put anything French in your mouth before, then," I tell her, waiting for the blush I know it'll evoke.

Her eyes narrow at me while her lips pull into a teasing smile, twisting up on one side, and I'm already wondering if it was a mistake to play with fire while we're in public.

"Er, excuse me, Mr. Moreau," Isaac says, walking up with a light sheen of sweat on his brow and an apologetic look on his face. "I'm afraid I have some bad news. There's a major issue with the radiator, and it's going to require immediate attention. Probably won't be finished until sometime tomorrow. I've called the main office to see about getting another car out to get you both back to Arbor Cove, but the closest one is about three hours away. And unfortunately, the closest taxi service is, well, in Arbor Cove. So I'd be happy to call them on your behalf, but it would probably be a couple of hours before they could get a cab here."

Tristan shakes her head in casual dismissal. "Oh, that's okay. I can just call Maggie to come get us. She took the kids to Ellen's for the rest of today and tonight, anyway."

"Or," I say, the turning wheels in my head picking up steam. "We could just stay."

12

TRISTAN

"Stay?" I repeat like I'm not familiar with the word. "You mean stay...overnight?"

He nods. "That's exactly what I mean. You said you've always wanted to have a weekend away here; why not a night? Since we're already here, it only makes sense to stay. Plus, you just said the twins are with Ellen for the night, so there's nothing forcing you to get back tonight."

"I don't know..." I bite my lip, contemplating his argument. He's not wrong. But the truth is, of the hundred and one reasons this is a bad idea, needing to get back to my siblings surprisingly isn't even in the top five. I'm more concerned about the idea of spending an entire twenty-four hour period with Dominic. Alone. Especially considering the direction our conversation was taking before Isaac interrupted. And *definitely* after what happened in the alley.

I've never wanted him more than I did at that moment.

The way he took my hand and pulled me through the restaurant.

The apology in his eyes for something that wasn't even his fault.

The way his body fit with mine, caging me in against the wall to act as a shield.

The desire I saw in his eyes that matched mine.

Seconds of being in his presence, and I felt like I'd go insane if he didn't kiss me. As illogical as it was given the circumstances, it's all I wanted. *That* is what he does to me, though; his touch melts away reason, his smile rewrites logic, and his heart...it gives me crazy, reckless ideas.

Crazy because if the restaurant incident proved anything, it's that indulging in anything more than easy flirting isn't a good idea. Reckless because, even knowing that, a big part of me wants to pursue something more anyway.

So staying the night in Rockdale is asking for trouble.

I wrestle with indecision for another few seconds, until a text from Maggie comes through and all but makes the decision for me.

MAGGIE: Is it okay if I spend the night with Meredith? You could have the house to yourself...or NOT to yourself, if you know what I mean ;)

"Let's do it," I say, almost not even realizing I spoke the words until Dominic's face lights up like I've just given him the keys to a candy store.

I'm pretty sure the universe wants me to sleep with Dominic.

How else do you explain having the luck of getting the only available room in the last B&B on the list, only to find that it's a single, not a double as the sweet lady at the front desk thought? *"You're in luck! With the carnival going on this weekend, we've been booked solid for months, but we just had a cancellation!"*

I had seen posters and heard locals talking about their annual carnival starting tonight, but hadn't given it much thought.

"So," Dominic says, eyeing the queen-sized bed then looking back to me. "Is this what you had in mind when you said it was a sign that we got the last available room in the entire town?"

The B&B is a picturesque early 1900s home with a baby blue exterior, wrap-around porch, and the cutest garden I've ever seen. It's in the best location of the three we'd called, a block off the main downtown Rockdale area, and the owners are an adorable couple in their seventies. When they mentioned their breakfast is prepared by their daughter, a Le Cordon Bleu graduate, that was it; I was prepared to sleep on their tiny couch in the lobby if that's what it took to stay at this place.

"Not exactly." I scan his body, look back at the bed, and make a show of looking around the modest room. "But I'll sleep on the floor if it means I get breakfast here tomorrow."

His arms cross as he flashes me a knowing smirk. "That so? Scared to share a bed with me?"

"Scared you'd hog the entire mattress? Yes, definitely."

"We could always...cuddle," he quips.

My eyes drift to his chest, imagining what it would feel like to actually *cuddle* with him. He's a brick wall of muscle, but something about his chest makes me want to crawl into his embrace and just have him hold me. The desperation I felt for him in the alley is still there, sitting at a low simmer, but this new kind of desire is also there. One that goes beyond just the physical aspect.

"I'm sure we can figure something out," I reply, pulling out the tie holding my hair up on my way to the room's shoebox-sized bathroom. "I'm just going to freshen up, and then I say we go check out the main square area, maybe find this carnival everyone's talking about if you think the leg is up for some walking?"

"Sounds good. Walking should be good, and if not, you can always give me a piggyback ride back, right?"

"Yep, definitely. That way, you can have a torn Achilles, and I'll have a broken back," I call from the other side of the bathroom door.

His laughter carries through the door, and it makes my smile grow even wider.

Half an hour later, we're walking through the heart of Rockdale, a cute cobblestone street lined with shops for everything from handmade soaps to antiques to boutique clothing and accessories. Twinkle lights hang above the sidewalks, combining soft lighting with the fading evening sunlight. The street is alive with locals and tourists alike; nobody seems to be in too big of a hurry. It's such a stark contrast to the vibe and feel I had walking through Manhattan earlier today that it makes my head spin. It's hard to believe I ever found the New York hustle and bustle more appealing than this.

It feels like a different lifetime.

"You sure you don't want to do any shopping?" Dominic asks, pulling me out of my thoughts.

I shake my head. "I'm sure. I'm perfectly fine just window shopping for now. I can come back in the morning for real shopping, so I'm not dragging you around, boring you to tears."

"Pretty sure I saw a shop with swimsuits back there; I would most definitely not be bored if that's the kind of shopping you happened to want to do."

"You and this bikini obsession," I tease, shoving him. Except the gesture does nothing to shake his balance.

"You're the one who sent me the picture in the first place!"

I shrug, holding my hands up like I'm completely innocent. "Hey, maybe you should just consider it payback for all the times I had to come over and see you working out without a shirt on."

"Was the volleyball game part of that payback?"

"No idea what you're referring to." I clear my throat and dart my eyes away, and when I do, a sign pointing the way to the carnival catches my attention. "Oh, look! The carnival's just ahead."

He frowns. "You know, a true *carnival*," he says, emphasizing the last syllable, "experience is more than a bunch of rides and silly games. You should see the one in Nice. It's got a huge bonfire and fireworks show on the last day. Parades every day, and more flowers than you've ever seen in your life."

"I bet. Josie and I went to New Orleans for Mardi Gras when we were twenty-one, and that was crazy enough. I can't imagine a true carnival experience in another country."

"There's nothing like it; that's for sure." He grins, gesturing the carnival entrance ahead. "But, by all means, show me what an American 'carnival' is like."

I gladly oblige and launch right into explaining how the tickets work, what each ride is, and which games I used to be obsessed with as a kid (ring toss and darts) before we finally get to an aisle where all the typical carnival foods are.

"And what's this, Heart Attack Way?" he asks, his jaw practically falling to the ground. "Fried Oreos. Fried cheesecake. Fried Snickers. Funnel cakes. Foot-long hot dogs and corn dogs. Turkey legs. Cotton candy," he lists off as he reads the signs above each vendor. "You people can't be serious!"

"Come on," I say, pulling his hand into mine and leading him toward the line at the corn dog stand. "You can't not try *something*."

He groans, but lets me pull him along. "Okay...but can we avoid the ones that are so ridiculously phallic in nature?"

"And miss out on inflicting that kind of torture on you? Not a chance."

Once we're at the front of the line, I order both a corn dog and a hot dog, just to cover both bases. And maybe a little bit to torture him. Squeezing through the crowd comprised mostly of squealing kids and giggling teenagers, we find an open bench and plop down. I snap a photo right before his first bite, capturing a priceless look of equal parts horror and resignation.

"Mmm," he says, after a second bite. "Okay, so it's not completely awful. But I can practically feel my arteries clogging. Trade?"

"See? Told you it's fried goodness." I laugh and offer him the swap.

He eats a few bites of the hot dog before shaking his head and tapping out of the food experience.

I just shrug and finish the rest of the corn dog.

"So," I say, tossing the trash from our food into a nearby bin. "Which rides do you want to go on? I'm thinking maybe the Zipper?"

"Oh, no. I'm not going on *that*," he says, eyeing the Zipper as it flips and spins in loops. "It looks like it hasn't been seen by a mechanic in at least a decade. And I'm certainly not willing to see the food I just ate for a second time. You're certifiable if you think going on that thing is in any way a good idea."

He turns back to find me burying my laughter behind a hand.

"You had no intention of going on that death trap, did you? Just wanted to get a kick out of giving me a mini heart attack?"

I nod, still trying to reel in my laughter.

"I see. Well, just for that, you're getting a face painting of my choosing," he says, gesturing behind me. I swivel my head around and see there is indeed a booth advertising face painting for five dollars. Before I can protest, he has my hand wrapped in his and pulls me up to the tent.

He takes a minute to peruse the options before finally looking at me with a devilish grin. Whispering to the woman working the booth, he nods enthusiastically at whatever she asks him in return. Giving him one last look that he hopefully reads as, *"I can't believe you're really making me do this,"* I sit in her chair and close my eyes, awaiting his payback by face paint.

To my surprise, the torture only lasts a few minutes, and I'm pretty sure I don't have much paint on my face at all.

"Ta-da," she says, holding up a mirror when I peel my eyes open.

My first reaction is to laugh out loud at my forehead—painted to look like a tennis ball. The second is to groan at my left cheek —"#Tennis4Ever" written in black paint.

"You're pretty proud of yourself, huh?" I ask, turning my narrowed gaze at him. But his grin makes it hard to hold onto my fake annoyance.

"Yeah, I'd say so. I'm starting to come around to this kind of carnival. Thanks for making me come," he says, lips twisting in satisfaction.

"Yeah, well, you're *not* welcome."

"Oh, come on; you don't think it's cute? I thought about having her write 'DM #1 FAN' but didn't want to be presumptuous."

"Well, I *was* your number one fan. Then you had my face marred with bright yellow paint! Not only that, but it really itches. You have no idea how tempted I am to scratch my face and mess it all up."

"Wait, back up to that first part. What was that?"

"Oh my god, you really *are* one of those athletes with a huge ego!" I groan, rolling my eyes to the sky.

He laughs and shakes his head. "You're the one who said it. I was just seeking confirmation I didn't mishear you."

I sigh, tugging him toward the Ferris wheel. "Sure you were. Come on, big head. I bet the view from up there is incredible. Ferris wheels used to be my favorite thing about carnivals, as lame as that sounds. And not just because it meant I could sneak away for a few minutes with a boy. Though, it was *the* thing to do with your crush as a teenager," I quip with a wink.

He eyes the Ferris wheel then looks back at me, a smirk pulling at the corner of his mouth. "Yeah? And what about as an adult?"

"Well, my actual celebrity crush—Chris Evans—isn't around, so I guess you'll do."

He comes to an abrupt stop with his mouth hanging open.

"You seriously make it way too easy, Dominic," I tease with a laugh, looping my arm through his again to drag him the rest of the way.

We wait in a comfortable silence until I look over and notice a vein in his neck is popping out and his brows are pulled down, leaving lines imprinted on his forehead.

"You okay?"

"What?" he asks, looking at me after looking at the ride for the twelfth time. "Oh, yeah, I'm good."

"Oh…kay," I reply slowly, not really believing him.

I had the attendant six tickets, and he ushers us into the pod, pulling the railing down and reminding us to keep our hands and bodies inside at all times. Dominic nods once and tugs on the rail before our pod lurches forward.

"You sure you're okay?" I ask, watching his pulse jump in his neck. "You don't look too hot."

"Uh-huh. I'm fine. Just…not a huge fan of heights," he admits, swallowing thickly.

My body jerks away from him at the admission, and I immediately look behind us to flag the attendant and tell him to stop. But we're already lifting up and too far gone to get his attention.

"Why didn't you tell me? I feel terrible! You're not going to, like, pass out on me or something, are you?" I ask, horrified at the thought.

"No, I'm not going to pass out. But I do need a distraction. Something to focus on," he says, his chest heaving with his deep breaths.

"Okay. A distraction," I repeat, searching my brain for something to talk about that would be enough to distract him from the world outside our pod. "When I was in college, I used to volunteer at a pediatric hospital." He angles his body toward mine, eyes focused completely on me like he wants to absorb every word I give him. "My parents insisted I needed a serious internship during the summers, so the volunteering was on my 'free' time. I didn't mind, though. I never really wanted to intern at The Fitzgerald Financial Group, but I did it because it's what they wanted. But after just a week of volunteering at the hospital, I knew I'd never be happy following in their footsteps in the world of finance and money management. I met kids who were battling cancer, coping with chronic illnesses, waiting on organ transplants, recovering from horrible car accidents. You name it; I saw it. Each and every volunteer session, it felt like little pieces of my heart were broken off and given to the kids I met. But their resilience and their unbelievable will to overcome any obstacle was incredible. Inspiring. It's why I was willing to risk my parents' disappointment to accept a job at a non-profit for kids with cancer right out of college despite the fact it didn't even pay as much as my internship at FFG. Because I was making a difference. And I was *good* at my job, dammit. I never regretted it, even though it did cause a rift."

"Tristan, I can't even imagine," he croaks, his voice thick as he shakes his head slowly.

"Aside from all the media bullshit affecting my siblings, I think *that* was what I hated the most about having my name slandered by obnoxious reporters trying to create click-bait worthy headlines. They probably had no idea, or if they did know, they didn't give a damn that my job was helping kids with terminal fucking cancer. Sometimes, I wonder what those kids thought when I stopped coming. Did they know? Did they think I just up and left? Did their parents tell them I'm a bad person? Do they hate me? I don't even know that I could blame them if they did."

"No. No way," he says, scooting over to close the gap between us and locking his eyes on mine. My heart beats in triple time. "Those kids knew you cared about them. They don't hate you. Anyone who knows the real you could see that's just not possible. Don't even think it."

He moves the arm that's slung over my shoulders and brushes the hair back from my shoulder before bringing his hand up to cup my neck, his thumb caressing the space between my jaw and ear.

"Promise me you won't go down that path, thinking those things."

I nod, leaning ever so slightly into his touch, and he brings his free hand up to cup the other side of my face.

"Because you, Tristan Fitzgerald, are extraordinary."

My stomach dips, and I don't have the chance to assess if it's from the motion of the Ferris wheel or his words because the second he leans in and brings his lips down on mine, everything else ceases to matter.

Not the view I was looking forward to seeing five minutes ago.

Not the possibility that this might be a mistake.

Nothing but this moment—this kiss—exists.

I move my hands to his chest, gripping his t-shirt like it's the only thing keeping me from floating away. Right now, that's exactly how it feels. His grip is rough, both because of the permanent callouses on his palm from his racket, and in the way he holds me close like he's as desperate to hold on to the moment as I am.

Only when the Ferris wheel jerks and slows to a stop at the top do we pull apart.

He rests his forehead against mine, and I feel his smile without having to see it. "I'm sorry; I just couldn't spend another minute not knowing what it felt like to kiss you."

His confession makes my heart soar. "Don't apologize; the feeling was mutual."

"Oh yeah?" His eyebrows jump up and down. "Was it on par with the experiences of your teenage Ferris wheel riding days?"

"Eh. It was...okay," I tease with a shrug.

"*Okay?*" he echoes, wrapping an arm around me until he can reach to tickle-poke my ribs. "*Just* okay?"

I laugh and try to wriggle free from his relentless hold on me, but it's no use.

"Whoa, look," I say, freeing a hand to point behind him. "A shooting star."

He whips his head around and searches the starry sky, letting his grip slip.

I try to hold it in, but my body still shakes with silent laughter. "God, men can be distracted so easily. It's almost unfair."

"I'd argue against that if there wasn't a tiny bit of truth to it."

"But hey, look," I say, looking down, where we're quickly approaching the platform to exit. "It worked. You survived the big bad Ferris wheel."

The attendant disengages the safety bar, and Dominic steps out, offering me his hand to help me down. "You're right. That wasn't terrible. I think teenage Tristan might've actually had the right idea about Ferris wheels," he says with a subtle bump of my shoulder.

I chuckle, shaking my head at that. "One of the few things teenage Tristan got right."

"Is there any teenager who gets things right most of the time?" he asks, putting an arm around my shoulders as we walk through the crowd that consists, coincidentally, mostly of laughing and carefree teenagers. "I certainly didn't. Arguments with the umpires and my coach, fights with Max, giving my parents grief...I was a pain in the ass all around."

"What changed? I mean, obviously you haven't been a teenager for a while, but did something spark a change? I can't imagine you would've spent so long at the top of your sport if you were that kind of player. Or person, really."

"My dad's old coach actually sat me down and set me straight. It was a wake-up call of sorts, and he basically said I'd never reach my full potential if I didn't learn to control my temper. He said it was a shame because I had it in me to surpass my dad in titles and wins. That I could be 'one of the greats' if I'd just make the necessary adjustments. I'd always respected the hell out of him, so hearing that from him carried more weight than the others who had tried to tell me similar things. I loved my dad, but when you're a teenager grappling with always being in his shadow and being compared to him on a daily basis, the resentment builds."

"It's so hard for me to picture you as an angry, resentful, hotheaded teenager. It just seems so completely opposite of who you are now."

"Then, I guess I'm proof people change. Or at least that people are *capable* of making and accepting change. They just have to want it enough."

I'm still thinking about our conversation an hour later when we're back at the B&B and in our shoebox room.

"Want some wine?" he asks, pulling me out of my thoughts.

"Hm?"

"Wine? I think that place next door is still open. I can go grab a bottle?"

"Oh. Yeah, wine would be great," I reply. It's been a really long, really weird, really wonderful day, and I should be exhausted. Part of me is. Emotionally, from my meeting with Frank. But that seems like a lifetime ago. A different day at the very least. Because I'm also wound up and not quite ready to let this night with Dominic come to an end.

But then, in the ten minutes it takes him to go next door and back, I made the mistake of answering a phone call that changed everything.

"This is a collect call from Kendra Fitzgerald at Maxwell Federal Penitentiary. Do you accept the charges?"

13

DOMINIC

"*D*ominic, look!" Liam calls, drawing my attention up from my phone. I pop my head up and catch him going down the sidewalk backward on his hoverboard. We're strolling through downtown Arbor Cove, but the streets are unusually calm for a Sunday evening, save for a few families and couples out for walks. Weather-wise, it's been one of those perfect summer days I'm usually too focused on practice or upcoming matches or meetings to appreciate. Even this summer, it's been rare to carve out time to truly relax. But today, I've let myself soak in the sunshine and salty sea breeze that permeates the coastal air.

"Nice," I say, giving him a thumbs-up, though my mind is still on Pierre's text.

"Be careful, and don't go too far ahead!" Tristan yells.

Friday night, the minute I got back from getting the wine, I could tell something was wrong. The bathroom door was closed with the fan on in an attempt to block out the sound of Tristan's cries, but it didn't work. When she came out, face scrubbed free of the paint from the carnival, but red and tear-stained, I didn't even ask before pulling her into my chest and holding her there. I wanted answers but wasn't going to press.

"*My mom...*" she eventually said, but trailed off and shook her head before she could get anything else out. I just pulled her back in and held her tighter, assuring her it was okay, that she didn't have to tell me right now. I spent the night with my arms wrapped around her, wishing like hell I could just absorb whatever pain she was going through.

Yesterday, over the gourmet breakfast she was so excited about upon check-in, she told me her mom had called. It was the first time they had spoken in months, and it obviously didn't go well. She admitted as much but said she didn't want to get into it. So that was that, and we spent the morning exploring a couple of historic homes and landmarks in Rockdale before Isaac called to say a car had arrived to take us back to Arbor Cove.

As soon as the car pulled away from Tristan's, I already found myself searching for a way to see her again before our standing Tuesday twins hand-off. Then Pierre came over, annoyed and cursing me in French for missing our session the day before, and said he'd reached out to a specialist in Baltimore, who was able to squeeze us in for a last-minute appointment at the end of the week. It's a meeting that will help with my recovery, so I was ready to jump on a plane immediately. Except it also means more time away from Arbor Cove. With the North American leg of the ATP tour kicking off, I've been planning to meet Max in Washington, D.C. next weekend, in addition to New York for the U.S. Open at the end of August.

Things with Tristan are in such a precarious state that I'm afraid of what will happen by putting so much distance between us for any length of time. And any time Nash calls and brings up the contract negotiations with Linx, I'm reminded once again what's at stake.

I can feel my remaining time with Tristan slipping through my fingers.

And at the same time, it feels like we haven't even truly gotten started.

"You're awfully quiet," Tristan comments, waving a hand in front of my face as we walk.

"Oh. Sorry, guess I zoned out," I tell her, locking away my thoughts.

"That's okay. I'm sure you've got a lot on your mind. Are you nervous about being bombarded by reporters when you go to watch Max?" she asks, making me wonder if she was also thinking about the fact I'm about to leave town for a week.

"Not really. The statement Gage put out in June gave about as much information as they know to expect from my camp about an injury. I've gotten pretty good at evading questions over the years, anyway."

"Let me guess, by batting your lashes and flashing the million-dollar smile that graces magazine covers and ads?" she teases, making an overly dramatic impression of that scene.

I shrug, laughing along. "Hey, if the tactic works, why not use it?"

An hour later, we're all sitting around an outdoor table that overlooks the boardwalk, complete with seagulls flying overhead, squawking for food, the twins both with giant scoops of chocolate ice cream in their hands. Tristan just broke the news to them that I'm going to be traveling in and out of Arbor Cove for the next month.

"I bet you'll be the best good luck charm for Max," Genevieve offers, sounding way less upset than expected.

Liam sits perfectly quiet, scowling, as he practically attacks his ice cream scoop like it's responsible for this world-ending news.

"Liam? Anything you want to express? Using words?" Tristan asks. Apparently, his therapist mentioned it's been beneficial to have him verbalize his emotions, if possible.

"I'd like to express that this is *bullshit*." He pauses long enough to pin a glare on me. "You *promised* we would have a rematch in basketball, and you *promised* you'd teach me…stuff," he hisses, dropping his voice like he doesn't want his sisters to know what *stuff* he's talking about.

"Liam, that is *not* how you speak to Dominic. Or anyone else for that matter," Tristan admonishes, already looking like she wants to smack the ice cream out of his hand for how he's acting.

"Who cares!" He cries, shoving his chair back from the table and running down the pier next to the ice cream shop. There's a clear view from our vantage point, so Tristan doesn't immediately bolt after him. Instead, she sighs, rubbing her temples.

"I'm sorry. It's not your fault," she says to me, making a move to get up. "I'll talk to him."

"No, let me," I offer, pushing up to stand too. "Really. He's right. I did make some promises that I need to assure him I'll still fulfill."

She sinks back into her chair with a huff and a nod. "Okay. But feel free to haul his butt back over here if he's still behaving that way. Promises or not, he knows better."

I walk slowly, purposefully giving Liam a minute to himself before approaching. He's sitting down, feet dangling off the edge, with his arms still crossed, watching the waves disappear under the pier.

"I know I made you some promises I haven't quite fulfilled yet," I start, easing myself into a sitting position next to him. "But I need you to know I *will* be back. We'll play basketball when I get the approval from my doctor and trainer. As for the other stuff, we'll get to those too. You think I would miss out on the honor of showing you how to shave and how to fix stuff around the house? I can't promise that I'll know how to make all kinds of repairs, but we can definitely look up videos to learn together. How about that?"

A couple of weeks ago, he saw me shaving, and his face fell after a few seconds of watching intently. When I asked, he said he didn't know how to shave and asked how he was supposed to learn with a house full of sisters. It nearly broke my damn heart. So I told him I'd teach him, even though he probably wouldn't need to know how to shave for a few years still. That led to a conversation about all the other things he could think of that he wanted to know about doing. Everything from changing a light bulb to knowing how to mow the lawn.

All the things a dad would typically teach his son.

"Well," Liam mumbles, "I guess that would be okay. You should probably learn some of this stuff too. Life skills are important, even for famous people, you know," he says, looking up to give me a dubious, arched brow expression.

I grin, relieved he seems to be coming back around to his normal self. "You're right. I do need to learn. How about you make a list of the things you want to learn most, and we'll start with the first one or two this week before I leave for Baltimore? Then we can do more when I get back."

"Okay," he says, nodding and reaching out to tap my outstretched fist with his. He looks back toward the table where his sisters are. "How much trouble am I in with Tristan? On a scale from forgetting to do my homework to breaking her favorite lamp, how mad would you say she is?"

As usual, this kid never ceases to make me laugh. I ruffle his hair and shake my head. "Well, she wasn't super happy with how you were speaking to me, but I think it's fixable with an apology."

"I'm sorry," he says with sincerity, looking embarrassed. "I shouldn't have acted that way and said the 'bullshit' word."

I have to bite back a laugh at his word choice. "Apology accepted, buddy. I know you were just upset. But I do promise I'm coming back. And you can text me while I'm gone. Anytime."

After Liam repeats his apology to Tristan, we all stroll down the boardwalk, letting the kids wander ahead, seeing which of them can get closer to seagulls before cracking up and running away.

"I guess I should be glad they're too distracted by the seagulls to want to go into any of the stores for t-shirts or beach toys," Tristan muses, seconds before Gen comes barreling toward us, a huge smile filling her freckled face.

"Look! There's a photo booth over there! Can we *please* get our pictures taken?" she pleads, lacing her fingers together under her chin and sticking out her bottom lip with her big hazel eyes pinned on Tristan.

"Looks like I spoke too soon," Tristan mutters to me, her own smile breaking through. "Okay, but after this, it's going to be about time for us to head home, kiddo."

"Aw, but it's not even close to bedtime! I don't even have camp tomorrow, anyway."

"I know, but I promised Aunt Lorraine I would catch up on some work stuff before tomorrow. And I seem to recall the deal we made for coming to get ice cream requiring a certain set of twins cleaning their rooms…"

"Ugh, I *told* you she wouldn't forget," Liam grumbles as he and Gen take off for the photo booth line, one of them grumbling something about Tristan being a fun-killer.

Tristan and I trail behind, and she catches me trying to hide my smile.

"What?' she asks, coming to a stop around the side of the photo booth.

"Nothing. You're just really good at this."

"At what, being the mean fun-killer?"

"No," I laugh, "I was thinking more along the lines of balancing the roles of parent figure and cool sister. You're kind of a badass."

"Shower a girl with enough compliments the way you do, and she might start getting certain ideas…"

"Oh yeah? Like what?" I ask, coming up with a few ideas of my own. Ideas involving how to get Tristan back into her tiny white bikini again before I leave for Baltimore.

"Like…" she trails off, looking around before grabbing my hand to pull me into the gap between the photo booth and an arcade game. "This." She presses up on her toes and wraps her arms around my neck. I instinctively grip her waist and lower my head, grinning against her waiting lips.

With her body molded to mine, she links her fingers together around the back of my neck and kisses me with the same quiet desperation I've felt all afternoon. Careful of our surroundings, she pulls back much too soon, looking up at me and subtly running her fingers over her lips before swiping my hat and putting it on her head. She flashes me a coy smile and takes two slow steps backward, and the sight makes me groan. Either she has no idea how fucking sexy she looks like this, or she *does* know and is trying to kill me. I take one step and grip her hand in mine, tugging her back against my body.

"Have I mentioned how ridiculously fucking hot you are?" I ask, slipping a hand between the dark waves falling over her neck and shoulders and pulling her in for another kiss. She hums against my lips before parting her own to deepen the kiss; her hands braced on my chest. This time, neither of us pulls away, and I'm vaguely aware this is getting reckless, but the thrumming in my veins makes it impossible to pay attention to the thought.

Until a little voice calls, "Tristan? Dominic?" and we both break apart like we've been caught doing something worse than making out.

Tristan rounds the corner first, smiling at her sister and trying to act casual. "Hey. You guys finished?"

"Uh, actually, we wanted to get one with the four of us. But we'll need another dollar. And also, who was that guy?" she asks, her head swiveling around to look in all directions.

"What guy?"

She shrugs. "I don't know. Just a guy. He was taking pictures on his phone, though."

"Of you two?" Tristan asks, horrified and scanning the area desperately.

"No. *Of you two.*"

Tristan and I share an *oh fuck* look before both turning to search for the mystery photographer in all directions.

But there's no sign of anyone suspicious, and Gen didn't get enough of a look to give any kind of description.

Which means, *oh fuck* was right.

14

TRISTAN

"Oooh, is that a *smile* I'm seeing? " Josie asks, leaning over the table to peek at my phone. I jerk back, trying to hide my screen from her view, but it's too little too late. "Ah-ha, so it *is*, in fact, a Dominic smile. Should've known."

"You are such a snoop," I gripe without any actual annoyance.

"Maybe that's because *somebody* has remained entirely too tight-lipped about a possible romance with a certain blue-eyed tennis star."

On cue, my phone buzzes with an incoming text from Dominic.

DOMINIC: FaceTime?

TRISTAN: I'd love that. Full disclosure, though, Jo is currently reading this text over my shoulder.

Seconds later, my phone rings, and Josie swipes it out of my hand before I can answer, running into the yard with it. All I hear is Dominic's laugh and, "Hey, Josie, how's it going?"

"I warned you!" I yell, not even bothering to go after her. Yet.

She climbs into the kids' treehouse, so I know exactly how to keep her from getting too much time to dig for intel. Or threaten bodily injury if he hurts me. Hard to tell which it'll be with her.

After a minute, I slide the door to the living room open, where the kids are currently glued to the TV, watching Black Panther for the second time this week. "Hey, guess who Josie's talking to on FaceTime from the treehouse?"

"Who?" Liam asks without looking away from the screen.

"Dominic."

They're up and out of their bean bags almost before I even get his full name out, racing across the yard. I watch them go, trailing behind at a leisurely pace, wondering if they'd even be a fraction as happy if *I* were the one out of town and calling.

When did he become their favorite person? *And if they're this excited about a FaceTime call after he's been gone for two days, what the hell will it be like when he goes back to his real life?*

The question makes me freeze outside the treehouse. But even hearing him from a distance, his sexy accent and the cute way he pronounces certain words and phrases sweeps the question under a 'not now' rug inside my head. He says hi to the twins and obliges Liam's request for a tour of his hotel room before asking if I'm around. Liam huffs for a second like he can't believe Dominic would rather talk to me than him before Josie distracts him by asking, "who wants popsicles." I give her a grateful smile and take my phone back, climbing into the treehouse.

"Give me just one second," he says, propping his phone against something next to the bed of his hotel room. Before I can say anything, I see a flash of orange, and then he adjusts the phone to his liking. "There you are," he says, leaning back in the bed of his hotel room with an arm folded behind his head for support. The position gives me a view of his bicep and his shoulders and chest—all bare. And all one sexy-as-hell combination.

"Hey, you," I say, biting back the fifteenth Dominic-induced smile of the day. "Umm, two things. Did you just take off your shirt for fun, or to torture me? And second, are you already in bed at," I check my watch and frown, "seven-thirty on a Saturday night?"

He shrugs. "I'm old, remember?"

"Whatever," I say with an eye-roll. "We've been through this how many times? Thirty-three is not that old."

"Thirty-*four* as of next week," he says casually.

"Oh my god, I can't believe I forgot! August 7, right? We'll have to do something to celebrate when you get back. I'm sure Liam would love to have an occasion to practice some of his new recipes, and Gen says she wants to learn how to bake, so that would be perfect. Are you and Max going to do anything the day of? I guess probably not if he's still in the tournament, huh?"

"Nah, probably not. I don't really care to celebrate it anyway."

I'm about to object when he cuts me off. "But I wouldn't mind a belated celebration with you guys when I get back to Connecticut. I'm so used to being on the road on my birthday; it almost doesn't feel like my birthday if I'm not in tournament or training mode."

"Well, all the more reason to make your belated celebration something to remember."

"Pretty sure it'll be hard to forget if you're there," he says, making my heart do a special kind of dance inside my chest.

"So, how did it go with the specialist guy today?"

He told me via text that they met yesterday and discussed Dominic's progress, his thoughts on the risks of trying to come back to tennis by January, and then ended with wanting Dominic to come back today for a couple of tests for further assessment.

"It went pretty well; he said the tests confirmed what we already talked about—that my recovery is going quicker than most, and I'm on track to be able to compete in January, but any number of things could happen between now and then if I push too hard. But I'm sore as fuck now. I think he and Pierre just wanted to see how badly they could torture me. Sure as hell felt that way, at least. You asked why I'm in bed? Because not even the promise of food would be enough to make me leave this room tonight. I haven't felt this kind of pain and exhaustion since my five-setter at the Australian Open this year."

I shift my position, feeling like I'll be my own kind of sore if I spend any longer in the kid-sized chair I'm sitting in. Moving from the chair to sit in the treehouse's gaping doorway, I offer him a sympathetic frown. "That's great, though, about your tests. I told you you'd be on track to get back to kicking ass and taking names before you knew it."

He winces and scoots up, moving partially out of view of the screen. "Fucking cramps," he groans.

I wince back out of sympathy, hating that he's in pain. "I wish there was something I could do to help."

"Don't suppose you've figured out how to crawl into a phone and come through the other side?"

"No, sorry." I bite my lip as a wildly inappropriate idea hits me. Ensuring I'm alone in the yard, I spin back around until I'm completely concealed in the treehouse again. "But if I had figured it out, I'd be there in a heartbeat, and I'd even offer to massage it and make it all better."

The phone falls over before quickly being moved up, showing Dominic's shocked face.

I smirk. *Exactly what I was going for.*

All last week, our schedules never seemed to align; I was slammed with work, going with Lorraine to meet clients every evening, all wanting to commission very specific pieces from Lorraine. And Dominic had meetings with his sponsors and team, anyway. So, we resorted to increasingly flirty texts and a few stolen moments filled with painfully brief kisses. Without fail, each time we'd start to take things any farther—his hand under my shirt or my hand so much as grazing the outside of his shorts —the universe conspired in one way or another to end things before they could even get started.

Which, truthfully, has led to some *very* intense solo sessions late at night, and I have a pretty strong feeling it's been the same for him. It gets the job done, but at the same time leaves you still aching for the real thing.

"Is—is that so?" he asks, clearing his throat. Need and desire are written in his features, and his chest heaves up and down, drawing my attention to a vein in his neck. "What exactly would you be massaging?"

For a brief second, I bite my lip again and hesitate to take things in this direction. But the sight of him—damp, messy hair, bare chest, electric blue gaze heating me up like he's here instead of hundreds of miles away—already has me hot and bothered.

"Well, I would start at your shoulders, because they look tight too. Then I'd move to your legs and work out the knots and cramps until you don't even remember being sore. I'd start at the calves, slowly easing my way up."

"Fuck, Tristan," he groans, and one hand disappears out of view at the bottom of the screen. "Then what?"

He adjusts the camera, and suddenly his hand reappears, gripping his length, his abs flexing as his hand starts moving.

Holy fucking hotness. If the sight of him like this through a screen can make me feel this desperate, I can't imagine what having the real thing will be like.

I move my own hand down, slipping it inside my shorts. "Then, after taking my time on your thighs, making sure they're not tight anymore, I'd wrap a hand around your cock and show it the same care and attention I did the rest of you." I squeeze my eyes shut, touching myself as the scene plays out so vividly in my head I know it won't take long to finish. "Then I'd start kissing my way down your chest and abs before taking you in my mouth, working both in unison, finding the right rhythm to drive you wild. You'd weave a hand through my hair, holding it back as I increase the tempo until..." I pause, absorbing the sight of him working himself over, eyes closed, a single bead of sweat rolling down the column of his neck, and my own strokes increase to match the pace of his until I'm biting down on the strap of my tank top as my climax closes in.

I realize my eyes squeezed shut at some point because when I peel them open, Dominic's eyes are on me as he pumps himself two more times before finishing with a groan that makes my toes curl.

"Jesus, Tristan," he mumbles, still panting after taking a

minute to clean himself off. "That was…fuck, I don't even have the words to describe what that was. You've rendered my brain useless."

"Bet your legs are feeling better, though."

"Legs?" he asks, laughing. "I'm not even sure I still have those. They stopped receiving blood some time ago."

"Shame," I tsk, shaking my head, "Guess you won't need an in-person version of that if you don't have legs anymore."

"I'm dangerously close to telling Max to fuck off, and I'll catch him in New York for the Open—*that* is how much I need an in-person demonstration of what we just did."

Heat fills my cheeks as a smile spreads across my lips. "What time did you say you're planning to get back next Sunday?"

My name yelled in unison from across the yard interrupts his response, and I sigh.

"At least their timing is improving," he jokes, shaking his head.

"Definitely a step in the right direction. Get some rest, okay? Talk tomorrow?"

He nods through a yawn.

"Sweet dreams," I tell him with an air kiss before hanging up and jogging back to the house, hoping like hell I don't look as flushed as I feel.

"So," Josie says later, pouring us both a glass of sangria. "How was your little *tryst*?"

"Good one," I say, rolling my eyes at her lame attempt at a play on words.

"I thought so. Now, spill, Tris, or you know I will just keep giving you bigger pours until the booze does the talking for you."

For some reason, I haven't given Josie much information about what's been going on between Dominic and me. Probably because a part of me knows better than to read much into it. But now, faced with her inquisitive gaze, I realize I need to tell *someone* about it—whatever *it* even is.

"So…" I start, contemplating how far back to go. "Remember how I told you about what happened at the restaurant?"

She nods.

"Well, I sort of skipped over the part where we almost kissed in that alley…"

From there, I launch into the rest of the day, filling her in completely until finally finishing with a confession about what he and I just did via FaceTime.

She fans herself off dramatically, offering an *ow-ow* at the end of my confession.

"Jo, but seriously, tell me the truth; do you think this is a terrible idea? I mean, what if the twins or Maggie found out? Maggie might already suspect something, but I don't want the kids to get confused. Plus, between the restaurant incident and the mystery guy at the boardwalk, I can't help but wonder if I'm playing with fire as far as the wrong person seeing something. It's just…messy, you know?"

"Messy? Yes. Terrible? No. But I understand your concern about Liam and Gen. And the media thing." She drums her neon pink nails—the same shade as her hair—against the glass table-top. "You said it yourself, though, maybe whoever that guy was really was just taking pictures of the ocean, and the angle made Genevieve think he was looking at you and Dominic. There aren't any photos circulating, so I wouldn't worry about it. I think you should just see what happens. Keep things under wraps, but don't let that stop you from exploring whatever it is you guys have. You deserve fun and happiness, and it's pretty obvious he brings you both. Forget the rest. At least for now—and definitely until you get to experience the real thing."

She winks and holds up her glass.

I let her words sink in and try to play out both scenarios in my head: one where things with Dominic continue down this path, and I don't let fears and negative possibilities dictate the terms of whatever it is we're doing, and another scenario where I tell him we can't do this anymore.

But it's almost not even a choice.

Not when my heart only hurts at the thought of one of those scenarios.

After the workweek that felt like it would never end, I'm finally packing up my bag and already imagining myself sinking into a bubble bath with my Kindle and a glass of wine. I'm trying to recall if I still have the sangria supplies from Josie's visit when the sound of the gallery's door chime makes me internally groan.

"Sorry, we actually close at four-thirty on Fridays now," I call, closing my bag and summoning a fake smile to greet the idiot who can't read door signs apparently.

Except, the second I turn, my smile blooms into a mixture of something real and shocked.

"Oh, I'm sorry," Dominic says, halfway turning back toward the door with a grin. "I can go, if you'd rather."

"Oh my god," I squeal, still in shock as he lets the door close behind him again, coming my way. "What are you doing here?"

When he reaches my desk, I drop my bag and fling my arms around his shoulders, pressing my lips against his without waiting for an answer. He smells like fresh laundry and mint, and I briefly contemplate never letting him out of my embrace.

"Max lost in his quarter-final match this morning, so I told him I had to get back, and he wasn't really in the mood for company anyway. Good surprise?" he asks, nuzzling my neck, his few-day-old stubble scratching roughly against my neck.

"The best," I confirm, pulling back after one last hit of his scent. "Liam spent the day with Kai, and I'm about to go meet him at the basketball courts if you want to join and make his day."

"Let's go," he says, gesturing for me to lead the way.

"I saw a little of Max's match on Wednesday. I was watching when they came and interviewed you from his box," I tell Dominic while we're waiting for Liam at the basketball court.

He dribbles a few steps to his right before pulling up to shoot. "Oh yeah?"

"Yep. When you told the commentator lady what all you thought Max needed to change about how he was playing to come back and win. Gotta say, it was kinda sexy seeing you all in the tennis zone. It seemed to come so naturally to you—knowing and reading the game so well."

"It's kinda what I do," he says with a wink. "But I know what you mean. It's a combination of having been on the tour for almost two decades and being able to assess a match from the outside as if I'm the one playing."

"I can't wait to watch you play," I say without thinking. It's the truth, but so is the fact that him being back on the court will mean he's gone and out of my life, and I won't exactly have the opportunity to jet-set across the globe to watch him play. The closest tournament would probably be the U.S. Open, and that would mean going back to New York.

"Dubai, Acapulco, Indian Wells, Miami, Paris...name the city or tournament, and it's a done deal."

He says it so matter of factly like he's already considered the possibility. Like he *wants* me to come watch him play as much as I want to see him in action.

Which would be crazy...right?

We've never talked about what happens when he gets back to his career. It's just kind of been an unspoken understanding that it would signal the end of whatever personal involvement we have. He promised Liam they'd still talk as much as Liam wants, but I haven't dared consider the possibility of trying to continue anything between us beyond his days here.

He dribbles around a little more, and it takes me back to that first week we met when he hobbled around the court for Liam's sake. It seems like so long ago, and yet...also like the summer has flown by in the blink of an eye.

"So, I've been thinking," he says, taking a second shot from beyond the three-point arc. It sails into the net in a perfect swoosh, and I'm starting to wonder if he *let* Liam keep their game competitive, or if he really was just off because of his injury.

"About...?"

He retrieves the ball and props it between his forearm and waist to meet my eyes. "My trip back home, Max's wedding, and all the festivities that will entail. What would you say...if I asked you to come with me?"

"To the wedding?" I ask, halfway thinking I must've misunderstood him.

He nods.

My mouth falls open. "I'd say you're crazy. Insane. Out of your mind."

"That doesn't sound like a no..."

I unfold my arms and lift my sunglasses to the top of my head before moving my hands to my hips. "You're serious? How can you possibly think that's a good idea?"

"Simple. Because it would mean spending more time with you. And I don't see how that's *not* a good idea."

"You don't? And what about all the raised eyebrows and questions showing up with a date will elicit? Your family? Are you sure they'd be okay with you bringing someone they've never met?"

He uses his free hand to cup the right side of my face. "I don't care about the raised eyebrows. Let me worry about my family. The guest list is small, and anyone who will be there knows to be discreet. Chloe already said there would be a 'no cellphones at the reception' policy. Six days in Provence, at a completely private chateau, without any outside obligations or work or responsibilities."

"What if..." I trail off, chewing on my lip while I contemplate the end of that sentence.

"Don't overthink it," he interrupts, pressing a soft kiss against my lips. "You can't tell me you don't want this too."

"You're right; I can't tell you that because I *do* want this. That sounds incredible. But what about my job? My siblings? I can't just pick up and spend a week six thousand miles away. It would be the trip of a lifetime, but those responsibilities I'd be leaving behind can't just take care of themselves."

He hums in contemplation, but his face is still stoic and determined, totally unfazed by anything I just said. "If I find a way to take care of your job and your siblings, would that convince you?"

"You're not used to being told no, are you?" I ask with an exasperated chuckle, weaving my hands around his back.

"No. But I'll repeat, this doesn't feel like a no."

It's not, but I kinda like making him work for it. Keeping him humble.

"Let's call it a maybe."

"I'll make you a deal." He steps back and tosses the basketball between his hands, coming to a stop several feet behind the three-point line. "If I make this, you come with me to the wedding."

I turn toward him and cross my arms. "And if you miss?"

He scoffs as if he's deeply insulted by such a question. "I'm a professional; I don't miss."

"You're an *injured* professional, and basketball isn't even your sport. It's a valid question, Dominic."

"Exactly. It wouldn't be fair if I was uninjured, holding a racket and a tennis ball. This way, it's more like a coin toss. Fifty-fifty."

"So you're admitting there's a fifty percent chance of you missing?"

"Fine. *If* I miss—but I won't—I will accept the maybe. For now."

"Gee, what an offer," I scoff with a laugh. "Just shoot the ball, big talker."

"And I'll get Liam a signed jersey from any basketball player he wants and Gen a signed racket from Serena."

A smile dances across my lips at his amendment. *Damn it, he's good.* The way he cares about those two and always seems to go above and beyond for them never ceases to make my heart melt. The truth is, I already know my answer. I think I knew it the second his hand met my cheek and his eyes searched mine for answers to questions neither of us could ask. And after the last few weeks, nothing sounds better than a few stolen days with the man in front of me.

When he goes back to his glamorous, jet-setting life as a global tennis star, I'll be able to keep a small part of him in my memories of our time in France.

"Deal."

As soon as Dominic shoots the ball, I leap into his arms, taking him by surprise, so we both miss the outcome of his shot.

"This definitely doesn't feel like a 'no'."

"That's because it's a yes."

15

TRISTAN

ONE MONTH LATER

"*Tristan, it's going to be fine,*" Maggie assures me for probably the fifth time this morning as I frantically run around the house like a crazy person, trying to make sure there's nothing I've forgotten to do.

Twins' and Maggie's school information written down - check. Notes on how to work the house's temperamental stove - check. Money for groceries in an envelope for Aunt Lorraine - check. Notes on schedules/allergies for each sibling left on the counter - check. All emergency contact information and numbers written down and taped to the fridge - check.

Still, it feels like there's something I'm forgetting.

Or maybe that's just my nerves talking. Dominic spent the last two and a half weeks in New York to support Max during his matches and fulfill some contractual obligations for his sponsors, so I'm practically giddy at the thought of seeing him in a matter of hours. But, while I'm dying to see him, it's everything else that comes after that I'm freaking out about. Like meeting his family and friends. I don't care what he says; they're definitely going to have questions, and I can't say I'd blame them. He told his family he's bringing someone to the chateau, but didn't give details, so why wouldn't they be suspicious and curious?

"Tris," Maggie repeats, putting her hands on my shoulders to make me stop walking around the house. "Passport," she says, picking it up off the kitchen island and putting it in my hand. "*That* is what you're forgetting. Everything else is fine. I'll be fine, and I'll make sure the kids do their homework and don't eat seventy-five donuts and nothing else while you're gone. Okay? And Aunt Lorraine will be here too. You're not even going to be gone a full week. We'll be fine. Chill."

Chill.

If only.

But, she's right—I've been over everything multiple times, packed *way* too much for a short trip, and have been over all the pertinent information with Aunt Lorraine already. I've left no stone unturned, and it's not like I'm leaving them to fend for themselves.

"Okay, you're right," I concede with a nod. Before she can get very far, I pull her in for a tight hug. "Thank you for being okay with this. And for all the help you've been with the twins. I owe you."

She squeezes me back and pulls away, shaking her head. "No, you don't. Are you serious? You absolutely deserve a break, Tris. You do so much for us, and it's about time we could return the favor. So please, don't worry about us. Just go. Have fun with Dominic, and enjoy the hell out of every second. I mean, you're staying in a freaking castle for God's sake!"

I grin, still halfway in shock; this is actually happening.

Liam runs into the kitchen with Gen hot on his heels, both squealing, "The car's here!"

"Guess that's my cue. Quick," I tell them, waving my hands for them to come give me hugs.

With promises to bring them back some authentic macaroons and chocolate, I hop in the car that'll take me to meet Dominic at La Guardia Airport, a whole mess of emotions swirl in my stomach.

Touching down in France felt surreal. We flew into Nice, and I briefly lamented the fact we didn't have time to explore more because even a brief drive through the city was enough to pique my curiosity about the coastal town, where Dominic spent part of his youth. A quick drive past the house he lived in and the tennis courts he used to frequent fed my ever-growing curiosity about Dominic's life before becoming a superstar.

But the beauty of the countryside commands my full attention, drowning out any lingering thoughts about Dominic's past.

"Wow," I exclaim, admiring the sprawling hills outside the car's window. "I've never seen anything so...captivating. I can't imagine how incredibly beautiful it is in full bloom." Rolling down the window welcomes in the faint scent of lavender, and I briefly close my eyes and take a deep breath, committing it all to memory.

Before I can ask what he's doing, Dominic slows down and pulls off to the side of the road. I realize his intention and scramble out of the car to take in the full, unobstructed view of lavender fields. Or, at least what remains of them. Even stripped of all the lavender, there's still a certain beauty to be found in the harvested fields. Maybe it's the jet lag talking, but I'm completely mesmerized. Row after row of green lines blend together. In my mind, I can already imagine what it's like to walk through the rows pre-harvest, basking in the sensory overload that would trigger—vivid shades of purple, a soft breeze carrying the distinct scent of lavender, the warmth of the summer sun beating down.

"There's really nothing like it during peak summer months," he says, drawing my attention away from the scene in front of us.

I could probably count on one hand the number of sights that would capture my attention more than the landscape surrounding us, and his blinding smile is definitely one of them. It steals my breath and pulls my lips up until my expression matches his. We spend a few suspended seconds letting our eyes bounce between each other and the view before he breaks the silence. "You should come to Provence in July or August before the fields are harvested. I'm usually traveling all summer, but I promised myself I'd spend the first summer after I retire road-tripping across France. Maybe one day..." The smile slips from his lips, and I immediately know whatever the rest of that sentence was going to be will remain unspoken. I study his features, trying to discern where his head is at, but his eyes hide behind his aviators. His gaze travels somewhere behind me, into the distance before dropping to the ground as he shakes his head.

For a moment, I allow my imagination to run wild, picturing a life where Dominic and I spend countless long summer days together, roaming the lavender fields at sunset without giving the outside world a second thought. A life where we could be together without a thousand complications coming between us.

But I know better than to give in to that fantasy for more than a few seconds.

"We should go," I say, shaking off the visions of extended picnics and lazy smiles we'll never get to share.

Dominic just nods before taking the handful of steps back to the car and opening the passenger door for me.

"So, who all is already at the chateau?" I ask after he pulls back onto the road.

On our flight over, Dominic informed me the wedding, while intimate in the number of guests, will be a weekend-long affair: the civil ceremony will take place on Friday, followed by the religious ceremony, a cocktail party, dinner, the reception on Saturday, and, finally, a farewell brunch on Sunday. As if that wasn't enough, there are also several pre-wedding events throughout the week. I'm already overwhelmed, and I'm not even in the wedding party. But Dominic swears Max and Chloe are down to earth, and it won't be as hectic as it seems.

"I think it's just Max and Chloe, Chloe's sister, Yvette, and us until tomorrow. That's when the real fun will start," he says with an ominous emphasis on the word real.

I raise a brow at him. "Care to elaborate on what that means? Because the way you said it makes me think the exact opposite."

"My parents and grandparents on my dad's side will arrive tomorrow, along with my mom's brother. And Carter."

"Okay…still not following."

"My uncle is a borderline alcoholic who's brash and abrasive on a good day. And Carter as in…Carter Cantrell."

My jaw hits the floor. "*That* Carter? He and your brother are friends? That's…surprising."

From what I've seen, Carter is basically the bad boy of tennis. Or, at least, the sport's most controversial player.

"He and Max crossed paths a lot as teenagers and especially in their early twenties. They used to hate each other, probably because they were so similar in a lot of ways. But eventually, they formed a friendship out of mutual respect, and now they're super close." He pauses, shrugging almost to himself like he still doesn't get it. "I've never personally had a problem with Carter, but some people in the tennis circuit aren't crazy about him. My dad, for one."

"*Oh,*" I say, realization dawning. "So when you said fun, you meant *drama*. I see now. Wasn't he just talked about on Sports Center last week for fighting or something?"

"It's pretty much a monthly, if not bi-monthly, thing for him to get into some kind of hot water with the media. The one you're probably thinking of, though, is that he reportedly punched his coach. Knocked him out. Then left a note saying he was fired. But, as you're well aware, headlines can be misleading, and rarely is the whole or accurate story reported. I wouldn't be surprised if that's not the entire truth, or there's more to it. As much as I think Carter can be a loose cannon on—and occasionally off—the court, he's not stupid."

The explanation makes me frown. Mostly because I already feel bad for Carter; even if he was potentially in the wrong for whatever happened with his coach, being vilified by exaggerated or inaccurate news stories is never fun. "Well, then I'll reserve judgment until after I meet him. Any other drama I should be aware of?"

He's quiet for too many seconds, and it sets off alarm bells in my head. "Dominic?"

"I wouldn't necessarily call it *drama*, per se, but in the interest of full disclosure, I've been out with Chloe's sister. But it was only a few dates. Nothing serious."

I exhale a deep breath, trying not to let the news bother me. "When and how many dates?"

He makes a pffft sound like he has to think. "Last year and three dates. Maybe four."

For a second, I'm tempted to ask if they slept together. But I'm not sure if I want the answer, so I simply nod and say, "okay, then. If you say it's not a big deal, I believe you."

Twenty minutes later, the Mercedes winds down a private drive lined with tall trees on either side that block the view of the estate. But when we get to the driveway's end, it becomes clear the view was worth waiting for. Surrounded by impeccably maintained greenery on all sides, the chateau is a stunning example of 19th-century French architecture with a beige exterior, soft edges, and a blue roof. Stone stairs flanked by matching statues of lions lead up to dual glass doors and to what I assume is the grand entrance.

A butler appears and welcomes us, taking our bags with a bow and smile before ushering us up the stairs. When we step inside, I immediately feel dwarfed by the huge open space of the atrium. With soft yellow walls and intricately detailed arches leading from room to room, and a massive leather couch laid out in a circle, the room is already enough to make me stop and take it all in. Overhead, the space remains open all the way to a circular glass ceiling.

A feminine voice calls something out in French from a nearby room, and Dominic quickly answers back. I look at him in question a second before a smiling brunette comes through one of the arches and squeals in delight.

"You made it! I'm so glad you're here," she says, pulling him in for a hug. She's tall, with straight, dark hair and soft brown eyes — a huge diamond ring dazzles on her left ring finger.

As if she could sense me studying her, she pulls away from Dominic and turns to me with a huge smile. "Hi! I'm Chloe," she says in perfect, unaccented English, holding her right hand out to me.

I smile back and shake her hand, liking her already. "Tristan. Thank you so much for having me. This place..." I look around and shake my head, "it's incredible."

"Isn't it? I still can't believe this is actually happening, that *this* is where I'm getting married," she says dreamily, looking around with me. "Want a tour? It's kind of easy to get turned around if you're not sure where everything is."

Another voice interrupts, this time male, and says something in French from behind us. We whirl around, and I'm momentarily dumbstruck by the sight of Dominic's younger brother. Max saunters into the room, smiling at Chloe as she rattles off something back in French, before pulling Dominic in for a hug. They have a brief exchange in French, and while I find it incredibly hot to watch them, I feel a little out of the loop.

Chloe notices and clears her throat to interrupt them. "Max, don't be rude."

"Oh, that's okay," I quickly say.

"Forgive me," he apologizes, coming toward me and pulling my hand into his. "I'm Max, the better looking Moreau brother," he offers as an introduction, wearing a smirk that looks a lot like his brother's.

I laugh and shake his hand. "Tristan. It's so nice to meet you."

He leans in and does the cheek kisses, making me dangerously close to swooning. "Likewise. So I know Chloe was offering a tour, but like I told her, I just made the same trip you two did a few days ago, so I told her you might prefer to catch a nap now and then get a tour and a rundown of all the amenities after dinner?"

I open my mouth to answer when Dominic cuts me off, quick to say, "I think that's a *great* idea. Let's do that. Where did you say our room is?"

"Yeah, I could use a nap actually." I fake a yawn to cover up how blatantly *unrelated* to jet lag Dominic's comments were. I really do want a tour because *holy house hunters, this place is amazing.* But not amazing enough to pass up the opportunity to *finally* get some alone time with Dominic.

Max barks out a laugh, making it known he's onto us. "Third floor, turn right out of the elevator, fourth door on the left. Right next to Mémé and Pépé's room."

Dominic cuts him a look and rolls his eyes. "Max, tell me you did not actually put us next to our grandparents, in a chateau that has, what, twenty rooms?"

Chloe smacks her fiancé's arm and sighs. "No, your room is not next to Mémé and Pépé. They're on the first floor. Here, I'll show you to the room."

We squeeze into the tiny elevator and ride up to the third floor, and Chloe guides us to the room before telling us dinner will be around six and disappears back into the elevator.

Dominic pushes my suitcase and pulls his into the room, and once again, it's an incredible sight to behold. Rich blue and green tapestry lines the walls of the entryway, with various landscape paintings dispersed throughout the hallway that leads to the bedroom and bathroom.

"Holy shit," I mutter when we get to the bathroom. It's the size of my college apartment, with a large clawfoot tub, separate shower, dual vanities, and a freaking *fireplace*. I drop my bag and hold my arms out to spin around. "This seriously might be bigger than my first apartment. I don't even need the bedroom; if you can't find me, check this tub first."

"Don't need the bedroom, huh?" he asks, arching a brow.

"Uh, *hello*, did you see this tub?" I turn back around to admire the tub of my dreams. "Gen and Liam's bathroom is the only one with a tub at home. Can you blame a girl for daydreaming about alone time in a tub like this?"

"You know...the master at my rental house has a claw foot tub. Pretty similar to this one. You can come over to use it," he says, coming up behind me and pulling me into his chest with his arms wrapped around me. "Anytime."

"Oh yeah? And what's the price of admission?" I ask, wrapping my hands around his forearm. I can feel the ripples of his veins, and I'm suddenly very aware of just how sexy arm veins are.

"Hmm," he muses. "I'd accept sexual favors prior to admission or…an invitation to join you."

Visuals of him wrapped around me just like this, but with a lot less clothing between us, floods my mind and makes my pulse jump.

Yes please.

"You think we'd both fit?" I ask, tilting my head to the side.

"One way to find out."

He unwraps his arms from around me and goes to the tub, turning on the faucet and closing the drain. One of the tiny toiletry bottles gets emptied into the tub, quickly filling the air with lavender and cedarwood.

Never again will I think of lavender the same way.

With purposeful, long steps toward me, Dominic crosses the space, slowly working the buttons loose from his shirt until it falls open, and I'm face to face—face to chest, really—with possibly my favorite view ever. My breath hitches at the sight of his carved abs and broad chest, and before I think about what I'm doing, I'm climbing him like a tree, shoving the button-down all the way off his shoulders as his hands palm my ass to hold me in place around his body.

He moans into my mouth when I trail my fingers over his shoulder blades, toeing the line between grazing gently and scratching with my nails. He tugs at my shirt, and I lift my arms to help until it's joining his on the floor. My bra is next to go. I untangle myself from around him, desperate to shed the last layers keeping me from a gloriously naked man.

Except we don't make it that far.

A knock at the door, followed quickly by the sound of it creaking open, makes me jump back and scramble to locate my bra while Dominic rushes to push the bathroom door closed. A feminine voice calls out in French, and Dominic frowns, spouting something back and rushing to get clothes back on. The only word I recognized is "Mémé," which I think was the word Max used for their grandmother. He shoots me an apologetic look, tinged with frustration, and moves back toward the door.

"Apparently, my parents and grandparents decided to come a day early after all," he explains, rubbing a hand over his face with a sigh. "I'm going to go greet them and help unload the car. You stay, though, enjoy the bath, and I'll be back as soon as I can."

I feel every ounce of the same frustration he does at the perpetual bad timing we seem to be cursed with. But it's not like we can just pick things up where they left off anyway, not unless I want to make a terrible first impression.

"Okay," I reply with a smile that probably looks every bit as fake as it feels.

He takes one last long look at my half-naked body and shakes his head, mouthing *I'm sorry* before leaving the bathroom.

I have no idea how long he's going to be gone, so I take my time in the bath, letting the bubbles and soft lavender scents ease my travel-weary muscles and mind. Beyond the tub, a window overlooks a fountain with a stone lion in the middle and a large rectangular pool behind the fountain. The chateau sits on twenty or so acres, with incredible views of sprawling hills and fields nestled between them, greenery as far as the eye can see. Somewhere on the property, there is a tennis court, a gym, and a private spa. It feels like a fairytale, being in this place, with these views, *with this man*. The idea of going to explore and see the rest of the property and the nearby town makes me jittery with anticipation.

When Dominic doesn't return by the time my fingers and toes turn into raisins and the water is room temperature, I begrudgingly climb out and begin rummaging through my suitcase for something suitable to wear to dinner. And to meet Dominic's family, apparently. I didn't even think to ask what the dinner dress code will be, so I choose a simple red sundress with a high neckline that shows off my legs without being indecent.

I've all but given up on Dominic coming back by a quarter 'til six, and swing the door open, prepared to find my own way to the dining room. I smack right into Dominic, whose hand was outstretched toward the door.

He grabs my shoulders to steady me, his eyes lazily trailing from my curled hair to my red lips to the way my dress flares at the hem.

"Wow. You look..." he trails off, eyes still stuck on my legs. "Like the best kind of temptation, wrapped in the color of sin," he finishes.

His description makes me laugh, but then I notice the glossy appearance of his eyes and the faint smell of alcohol clinging to him.

My brow hitches up my forehead. "Just going to greet them and unpack the car, huh?"

His hands shoot up in surrender. "I should have clarified about greeting them. See, Pépé has this thing where he insists on everyone going around making toasts when the whole family gets together. He's become obsessed with bourbon in his old age, and uses any excuse to show off his newest find."

"Uh-huh," I say slowly, crossing my arms. "And exactly how many of these 'toasts' were made?"

"A few."

"Enough to give you, Dominic Moreau—Mister 'I only drink wine occasionally, no hard stuff'—a nice buzz."

He shrugs, grinning. "Guilty. A nice enough buzz to do this," he says, slipping one hand under my dress to drag his fingertips over the back of my thigh. He groans when he reaches my ass and finds it exposed.

"*Fuck*," he mutters softly against my hair, reaching his free hand up to cup my neck.

The second our lips touch, the elevator doors pop open, but Dominic's efforts to pull away are sluggish at best, until a throat clears, finally drawing our full attention.

"Dominic," the voice's owner greets, flipping her dark red hair over her shoulder and giving him a blatant once-over.

"Yvette, hey," he says back, running a hand over the back of his neck and through his hair. "This is Tristan."

As if just now realizing I'm here, she peels her eyes off Dominic to study me. If looks could kill, I'm pretty sure the one she's giving me would incinerate me on the spot. "Pleasure," she offers curtly like she can't bring herself to speak an entire sentence to me.

We step out of the elevator and into the atrium, awkwardly bypassing each other as she gets in.

"Four dates, huh?" I ask, looking at him from underneath pinched brows. "I'm not so sure she feels the same way you do about things."

He looks back at the elevator and frowns.

But before he can say anything, an older gentleman with white hair and a mustache approaches us and pulls my hands into his. "You must be Tristan. I am Dominique Moreau. But please, call me Dom," he says in thickly accented English. His smile looks exactly like Dominic's, and I immediately see the family resemblance.

"I am." I nod, leaning in as he does for air cheek kisses. "It's so wonderful to meet you. Dominic has told me a lot about you. But he forgot to mention you're the source of the good looks in the Moreau family."

His smile grows as he laughs and wags a finger at me. "I like her," he tells Dominic, holding out an arm so I can loop mine through it as he walks us toward the dining room to introduce me to his wife.

Marie Moreau is petite, with green eyes and honey brown hair cut above her shoulders, and a smile that makes it all the way to her eyes. She doesn't speak much English, but I can tell from the way she talks and laughs with her grandsons that she's full of love for her family.

When Dom finds out I haven't had a proper tour of the chateau yet, he insists on taking me. We walk through the rooms, and he tells me the layout is basically one big circle on each floor before coming to the best part of the entire place—a huge library with floor-to-ceiling shelves all lined with countless books. I make a mental note of where it is, already envisioning myself stealing a few hours in here with my Kindle before Dom leads me back to the dining room.

Loud, booming laughter fills the room and draws my attention to the doorway from the kitchen seeking the sound's source, and it immediately feels like I'm getting a preview of what Dominic will look like in thirty years. Gabriel Moreau stands as tall as Dominic, with thick, caramel-colored hair highlighted by grays, a strong nose, and a slightly less bulky build than his sons, though his body is by no means out of shape. Only a handful of inches shorter than her husband, with shoulder-length blonde hair, soft blue-gray eyes, and a wildly infectious smile, Cordelia Moreau is as lovely as her pictures online make her out to be.

Dominic waves them over to make introductions, and I can already tell they're the reason Dominic is the genuine, caring person he is. Warm and kind, they both make me feel entirely welcome, insisting Dominic and I sit next to them at the table so they can get to know me. Cordelia asks about my life, though I get the feeling Dominic already said something to her about steering clear of certain questions. Wine and appetizers are served while conversations flow around the table, and every once in a while, I'll catch Dominic watching me from the corner of my eye. He gives me a wink or a smile each time, and it never fails to make my heart flutter.

Eventually, Max and Chloe both stand to make a quick 'thank you' toast, Max delivering it in French and Chloe translating it to English for my and Yvette's benefit. All through dinner, it's impossible not to notice how adorable Max and Chloe are, whether it's the laughter they constantly seem to share or the way Max's eyes fill with love every time he looks her way. Dominic was right; despite their differing schedules and equally demanding jobs, they do just seem to have found a way to make their love work.

Hours—and who knows how many bottles of wine and bourbon—later, with my cheeks hurting from laughing at the stories Dom told and the jokes Gabriel made, and from countless drunken smiles aimed at Dominic, I'm on my way back to the patio where everyone is congregated around a fire pit when two voices make me pause.

They're behind a half-open door, and it's Yvette and Chloe, though I can't tell which voice belongs to whom.

"I should tell him, right? He needs to know."

"I disagree. Why does he need to know at all?"

"Because I love him! Not telling him feels wrong."

"Just hold off a few days. You can tell him when this is all over, and everyone's lives go back to normal."

16

DOMINIC

"How you feeling, Ace?" I ask Max, grinning at his haggard state as he enters the on-site gym. His eyes are bloodshot and heavy, and he looks like he slept about as well as I did.

"Fuck you," he replies, rotating his left arm in circles to stretch. He grimaces when he switches to the right arm, muttering under his breath and shooting a death glare my way.

I laugh and continue with my own stretches.

"Who plans a seven a.m. workout for the morning after killing two bottles of bourbon? And, for the record, Pépé is cut off from pouring that shit the rest of the week. If it doesn't kill me, Chloe might."

Truthfully, I regret ever saying anything about a morning workout. I'm not nearly as hungover as he is, but I'm painfully aware of why I don't drink hard liquors anymore.

"Hey, all I said was that I'd be working out at seven, so I could have the rest of the day with Tristan. You're the one who enthusiastically insisted on working out too."

"That's not exactly how I remember it," he responds with a snort.

He's right; I did drunkenly propose some ridiculous challenge, but I didn't expect him to accept. Then again, when it comes to the

two of us and anything competitive, challenges get taken seriously, no matter how big or small.

We stretch in silence and let my Spotify workout playlist fill
the air instead.

Max doesn't break the silence until we're both warming up on
side-by-side Nordic Track machines. "So what's the story with
Tristan? It seems different with her than with your
previous…flings."

"It *is* different with her," I answer honestly.

"So, it's not a fling then?"

I hesitate, adjusting my speed to buy time before responding.
"I don't know, man. It's complicated. Her life is in Arbor Cove—
her *siblings* are in Arbor Cove. What kind of future would there
even be if we tried to make something work beyond my time
there?"

He adjusts his speed too, quickening his pace. Forever trying
to one-up me. "One that takes work. And patience. But it's not
impossible. This might come as a surprise to you, but plenty of
people who travel a lot for their career *do* make relationships
work."

"You and Chloe are the exception, not the rule, though."

"And you don't think that took a fucking ton of work? There
were plenty of times when either of us could've walked away
because it was easier. She could've found some suit with a nine-
to-five who wouldn't have her hopping on a plane to fly thousands of miles only to spend two days together before she has to
get back to work. Look, I'm not saying Tristan is your exception.
But if there's even a chance she could be, why wouldn't you at
least consider giving it a real shot? There has to be a part of you
that wants to; otherwise, you wouldn't have brought her here."

His question sticks in my head, and I can't even pretend to
come up with an answer. He's right. And it's not that I haven't
known for a while now that there could be something real
between us. That it would probably be amazing. But the deck is
stacked against us in so many ways. I'm not even sure it would

matter how much work we both put into a hypothetical relationship.

"There's another problem," I tell Max eventually, bringing the machine to a gradual stop. "That massive fraud case out of New York a while back? The couple who were hedge fund managers and stole a shitload of money from their clients? That ring a bell?"

"Yeah?" he asks, nodding slowly.

"That was Tristan's parents. Two of the clients they fucked over were relatives of Michael Grant."

"Fuck," he mutters, stabbing at the machine's button to slow down. He turns to me before hopping off and moving to a bench for core work. "So, what are you going to do?"

"What *can* I do? I told her I don't give a shit about what her parents did, that it doesn't have anything to do with her as a person. And I meant it. I can separate her from that bullshit because I know she's *not* them. But I'm smart enough to realize what any kind of public relationship between us would mean for my relationship with Michael and Linx."

He nods in understanding. "Does she know?"

"No. And I'm not sure I want to tell her. What purpose would that serve? Make her feel bad about something that wasn't her fault to begin with? Or worse, make her break things off in a misguided attempt to do the right thing?"

I spend the rest of our work out session thinking about our conversation. Eventually, we move to the tennis court and hit around together before taking up positions on opposite sides of the same baseline. I'm hitting lobs and light serves from a stationary position—Pierre's voice echoing in my ears, warning me not to stupidly jeopardize my recovery—while Max seems intent on sweating out all the bourbon, pummeling serve after serve until his basket of balls runs out.

A wolf-whistle from somewhere behind us makes us both turn around.

Chloe and Tristan are perched outside the fenced-in area, coffee in hand. Tristan hitches a thumb at Chloe, selling her out as the whistler. I drop the racket and walk over to the fence, flipping my hat around so I can lean in and summon her for a quick kiss. She leans in, lacing her fingers through the fence over mine, and pecks my lips.

"We're almost done," I tell her.

"Don't stop on our account," she says, trailing her eyes over my body appreciatively. Her gaze lingers on the sweatiest parts of my shirt that make it cling to my body. "I always enjoy seeing you in action."

Max snorts, and I punch him before he can make any kind of crack about her comment. Chloe rolls her eyes and tells him to get his mind out of the gutter.

"What are you two doing today?" Chloe asks.

"I was thinking we'd drive down to Marseilles for the day. Do a little exploring," I answer, watching Tristan's eyes light up at the prospect.

"Fun! That sounds so much better than dealing with last-minute wedding stuff," Chloe says, giving a *humpf* and a frown.

Max opens his mouth to say something, but Chloe cuts him off. "Don't even say it. We are not eloping three days before our wedding, Maximilien Moreau!"

He mimics her in a teasing way, making her scoff and run for the door leading to the court to chase him for payback.

"They're kind of adorable," Tristan says, watching them with a smile on her face.

"Try being around it for a year or two," I counter, "You'll find it less adorable and more nauseating."

"Hm. I don't think you could possibly sound like less of a romantic," she teases.

I gasp and grab my chest like she's cut me deeply.

"Au contraire, ma chérie." In French, I rattle off the plans I've already come up with for our day trip, knowing how much it drives her wild to hear me speaking in French.

She watches me talk and bites her lip. "Wait, did you say something about shopping?"

My brows shoot up in surprise. "You caught that, did you?"

"I might've looked up some basic phrases." She shrugs.

"Marie doesn't speak much English. It seems like everyone here knows French but me."

Her thoughtful gesture makes me smile. I swear this woman will never not surprise me.

"You know," I tell her, walking toward the gate. "I'm an excellent teacher. I could give you *all kinds* of lessons."

"That so?" She folds her arms and laughs when she catches me, wagging my eyebrows suggestively. "What is with you Moreau boys and your dirty minds?"

"Not our fault if the ladies we surround ourselves with give us one-track minds."

"Whatever you say, Romeo," she says with a laugh.

Little does she know, a romantic is exactly what she's turned me into.

Because in a crowd or in my dreams, she's the first thing my eyes search for, even knowing she's not mine to keep.

"Something on your mind?" I ask Tristan, taking my eyes off the road momentarily to study her profile. We're driving back to the chateau after our day trip to Marseilles, and she's been staring out over the hills for minutes on end now. She's beautiful like this, bathed in the late evening light, the breeze from the open convertible blowing through her hair. It's a sight I vow to commit to memory.

She turns to meet my gaze and offers a tight smile. "Just thinking."

"About what?"

"How different things seem to be here versus back in the States. You couldn't even go to a restaurant in New York without people finding out and showing up to stalk you. But here, we walked through the busiest, most touristy areas in the city, and only a few people even stopped you. It's just...completely different from what I would've expected, especially after New York."

After the incident at the boardwalk in Arbor Cove, we've maintained a strict *No PDA* rule, even though keeping my hands to myself and resisting the urge to steal kisses has been a torturous test of my willpower each of the few times we've been in public together. But today, after we left the bistro where we had lunch, she tentatively slipped her hand into mine, flashing me an *'is this okay?'* look. I squeezed her hand in answer, and that was that. We spent the rest of the afternoon with our hands intertwined, or my arm around her shoulders and her arm around my waist, only separating for a handful of brief fan interactions. Each time we were approached, she seemed a little more comfortable with the attention than the last. Especially once she realized there weren't hordes of photographers lurking around after a few photos posted advertising my location.

I nod and remove one hand from the wheel to hold the hand she's using to fidget with the fringe on a hole in her skinny jeans. "I can see why you'd have expected worse. But, honestly, it's usually more like today than it was that day in New York. Of course, it's worse at majors and some of the other large tournaments, but for the most part, my privacy is respected here."

"Even as France's most eligible athlete?" she teases, the corner of her mouth lifting into a half-smile.

"Well, I do have to fight through the throngs of women that throw themselves at my feet everywhere I go, but other than that, I can pretty much fly under the radar."

She snorts and rolls her eyes, and I brace for impact when she pulls her hand out of mine. Her cute fist makes contact with my arm, and I have to swallow my laughter when she winces and shakes her hand.

"Guess I should remember your ego and your biceps are both the size of boulders."

"Those aren't the only parts of my body the size of a boulder."

"To think I used to believe you were a gentleman..." she trails off, making a *tsk-tsk* sound through her laughter.

"Had to lure you in somehow." I wink.

Suddenly, the playfulness is gone from her eyes, replaced by heat and desire. She leans over the center console, giving me a clear view down the front of her tank top before running her fingertips along the hem of it. "And what, exactly, are you going to do now that you've got me?"

Her voice is a husky whisper, and the sound of it accompanied by the way she's biting her lip and slipping a hand up my thigh makes me groan.

"Fuck, you're killing me," I say, both needing her to stop so I don't drive us into a ditch and desperate for her hand to make contact with my cock.

We're only a few kilometers from the chateau, but the second her hand rubs me through my jeans while the other pops the button and works the zipper, it's too much. A volcano erupts under my skin, months of pent up need and longing hitting full-force. I turn off the main road onto what looks like a quiet, more secluded road. Not that I care much right now. We could be parked on one of the busiest streets in Paris, and it wouldn't matter.

As soon as the car is stopped, our seatbelts come off in a mad rush to shed the only thing keeping us apart. Tristan works my jeans open all the way until my cock springs free, not even hesitating to take it into her hand and make languid strokes while I groan into her neck between kisses.

"Do you know how badly I've wanted this?" she asks, her eyes flicking to mine in the semi-darkness. "How many nights I justified using my vibrator to mental images of you, sweaty from working out or just getting out of the pool by telling myself that's the only way things could be? How many times I wondered if you were just as conflicted as I was?"

"Fucking hell, Tristan," I groan, pulling her in for a kiss that hopefully conveys that I *do* know how badly she's wanted this because it's all I've wanted for weeks. Months. The visual of her using a vibrator, touching herself, while she thinks about me is almost enough for me to come here and now.

She pulls back to adjust her body enough to lean over the center console and lowers herself down my body, flashing me one last look before wrapping her lips around me completely. I let out a sharp hiss at the sensation before gathering the curtain of her wind-blown hair and pulling it out of her face. The convertible's space restrictions make logistics tricky, but any discomfort the position puts her in doesn't show. Using one hand to grip the base, she moves both her hand and mouth in tandem, in a torturously perfect rhythm.

"Oh, fuck, I'm about to come," I warn. Instead of pulling back, she increases her pace; the graphic sounds of her sucking me fill the air.

It's the trigger my climax needs to rip through my body and shoot hot into Tristan's mouth.

With one last swipe of her tongue, she releases me with a *pop*, eases herself upright, gives me a shy smile, and uses her fingertips to trace her bottom lip. My head flops back against the headrest, and I'm still panting and trying to unscramble my brain to remember things like how to zippers work and which direction is up.

When the orgasm fog lifts, I look over to find Tristan looking at me, her smirk illuminated by the lights on the dashboard.

"Need me to drive?" she asks playfully.

"I'm considering it," I say with a laugh, shaking my head in awe.

After another minute passes, I pull back onto the road and silently applaud myself for renting a wildly impractical convertible that's capable of getting us back to the chateau in record speed. As amazing as that detour was, it didn't even put a dent in the bone-deep need I feel for Tristan. I lift my right hand off the wheel and twine our fingers together in her lap, using my thumb to trace small circles on the exposed skin of her thigh.

When we finally get back to the chateau, a plan hits me all at once, dictating that I turn down an unlit dirt path leading toward an old building that was used as the servants' quarters. It's protected from the chateau's view by a wall of greenery, keeping our arrival unannounced.

"What are you doing?" Tristan asks, looking back toward the main driveway.

"I have an idea. Come on."

I slip out of the car and carefully close it without making a sound. She doesn't ask questions, just does the same, and meets me around the hood of the car, where I grab her hand and tug her in the direction of the backside of the chateau. "Shit," I mutter when we get close enough to hear voices in the pool patio area.

"Can't we just go in the front if everyone is out back?"

"Worth a shot."

We make it to the front entrance, but one of its heavy glass doors swings open, so I quickly tug her back into the shadows until she's firmly planted against an eight-foot shrub. She giggles, and I bring my mouth down on hers, intending only to quiet her laughter, so our cover isn't blown, but it quickly escalates into a kiss that I never want to end. She slips her hands around my shoulders and pulls my chest flush against hers, making me groan at the contact, before gently tugging my lip between her teeth.

"*Fuck*," I mumble, gripping her hips to meet mine, so she feels every inch of how much she affects me.

A pair of angry voices speaking in hushed tones carry from the front steps, but I'm too lost in Tristan to care what's going on outside of our bubble.

When we separate, chests heaving and breathing heavily, I find her eyes in the moonlight. "For the record, I wanted you even in the beginning. Even when I lied to myself and pretended otherwise. I was conflicted about acting on anything, but never how I felt about you."

She presses up on her toes to seal a kiss against my lips but pulls back after a second. "Prove it."

I lift my head up, looking around, searching for somewhere—anywhere—with a shred of privacy when the perfect answer occurs to me. "Come on," I tell her, grabbing her hand and weaving through the maze-like shrubbery that will get us from this side of the house to the other while remaining hidden from view. We bypass the orangerie, careful to steer clear of the light it emits to the outside, and I pull her toward the side entrance of the gym, slipping through the door.

I haven't had to sneak around with a girl like this since I was a teenager.

And somehow, that makes it even hotter.

As soon as we're safely tucked away in the privacy of the empty gym, I tug her against me using the belt loops of her skinny jeans. Her body crashes into mine a moment before our mouths fuse together, and I grip the back of her thighs to lift her up, so she wraps her legs around my waist.

The lights are off inside the gym, but moonlight seeps in through the window, bathing us in soft light.

"Your leg—" she objects, pulling back and searching my face.

"Is fine," I finish, taking three steps forward until her back meets the padded wall of the gym, my hands gripping her ass through her jeans.

She moans into my mouth and grips the bottom of my shirt, pulling it up and breaking our kiss to rid my body of the cotton like it personally insulted her. With the new access to my body, her hands go wild, raking over my back in a way I know will leave marks.

As good as it feels, it's not enough. I need to see her, to feel her —*all of her*—and I'm done waiting.

Keeping her in my arms, I whip us around and head straight for a nearby workout bench. Lowering her to the bench, so she's perpendicular with it, I get on my knees so we're nearly face to face, before ripping the tank top over her head and off her body. One day—soon—I'll take the time to appreciate the sight of Tristan in the lacy red bra she's wearing right now, but today is not that day. It's quickly shed from her body, my hands on her breasts a split-second after it hits the floor. She braces herself on the bench with one hand, the other weaving through my hair as I suck her beaded nipple into my mouth.

"Oh, god," she moans, hips bucking off the bench when I redirect my attention to the other breast.

Reaching between us, she glides her hand over my erection,

but I grip her wrist and pull it away before she can slip it under my waistband. Instead, I reach down to pop the button and pull the zipper of her jeans. She lifts her hips enough for me to peel them all the way down. I briefly register her thong matches the bra I all but ripped off of her, but like that bra, I see it only as a roadblock. Dragging a finger slowly over the silky material, the wetness I feel there makes my cock swell even further.

"Spread these gorgeous legs a little wider for me, ma chérie."

She obliges, her breath hitching when I pull the material to the side and run my pointer finger over her folds. With my thumb, I find her clit and rub slow circles there long enough to coax a loud moan from her lips. She moves one hand off the bench to grip my shoulder, her nails digging in to brand me with their half-moon shape when I slide a finger inside her, dipping it in and out.

"I love how turned on you are for me right now," I tell her, giving her nipple another tug while my other hand continues to work her slick clit. "Is this what you pictured, all those nights you needed a vibrator to ease the ache?"

She nods.

"Tell me," I instruct, quickening my thumb's pace against her clit. "What were you imagining?"

"*Oh, god,*" she moans, writing under my touch.

I slow my pace, teasing her mercilessly. "What did you picture those nights?"

"You," she huffs, panting heavier. "How hot it would be if, when I came over and caught you mid-workout, you stopped whatever you were doing to make *me* your workout. To use *me* to satisfy that crazed look you'd sometimes get during a workout."

"Jesus," I hiss, wondering how I'll ever make it through a workout without getting hard now, just thinking about her answer.

I hook my pointer finger under the fabric of her thong and tug it free until she's finally, *finally* bare in front of me. I've seen her in a bikini, and I've seen her in just underwear. I've even seen her naked through a screen, thanks to a few R-rated FaceTime calls. But none of it comes close to comparing to the live, in-person version of her here and now, propped on a workout bench, her thighs slick with the wetness dripping down as she spreads her legs for me.

She reaches for my jeans, but I swat her hand away again. "Ah-ah-ah. Not yet. You wanted me to prove how much I want you, remember?"

I silence her protest by kissing my way down her jaw, down the length of her torso, before slowing my pace once I reach her abs. Now, I drag my tongue down leisurely, until she's shaking with need when it stops just above her clit. "God, Dominic," she groans with a silent plea woven into those two words.

At the same time, my two fingers slip into her, I suck her clit into my mouth, fulfilling her unspoken request. Her moan fills the space around us, and it's the hottest sound I've ever heard.

She surprises me—once again—by finding her voice and unabashedly vocalizing exactly what she likes, feeding me encouragement and telling me how good it feels. I'm a quick study and soak up her cues like a sponge, like the information she's giving me is precious. Not to be forgotten.

It's not long before she's writhing beneath me, her head going back as she calls out her release.

Pushing back to stand, I strip off my jeans and boxer briefs, digging to find my wallet for a condom. While I roll it on, Tristan moves so she's in line with the bench, spreading her legs on either side. It's a precarious balance, but she doesn't seem to notice or mind, reaching for my hips to pull me forward as soon as I have the condom in place.

And the second she grips my cock and slides it between her wet folds, thrusting her hips enough to create torturous friction against her clit, I can't be bothered to think clearly either. I brace my hands above her head, supporting my upper body and giving myself the right leverage to make this angle work. She grips my hip with her other hand, using it to help steady herself.

Pulsing my hips forward, she guides me into her entrance until I'm fully nestled inside her, and we both let out loud moans that would've been heard beyond the walls of our room in the chateau if we'd been in there instead. For a moment, neither of us moves. I'm not even sure I breathe.

And when I do move, the bench jerks, sliding back with the movement. She lifts her hands to brace them just below mine before lifting one of her legs and wrapping it around my waist, giving me a deeper angle. I drive into her, my hips finding a rhythm that makes me see stars. Underneath me, her perfect breasts bounce, begging for my attention. I lower my mouth to one, then the other, nipping and sucking with just the right pressure.

"Fuck, Tristan. You feel so fucking incredible," I groan, both never wanting this to end and desperate to push her over the edge once again.

When she starts sliding on the bench, now drenched from her juices, I slip out of her and pull her to stand, maneuvering her body before she can even finish asking what I'm doing. She quickly realizes my intention and hinges at her hips, bracing herself on the bench with her ass perched in the air, legs wide. This time I fill her with one swift thrust before reaching around her body to find her clit. I trace circles over it in time with my movements, and it's exactly what she needs to fall apart, her orgasm tearing through her like a tornado.

Maybe it's the angle, maybe it's watching her fall apart in such spectacular fashion, but I can feel the pressure building, burning at the base of my spine. I chase the fires of my climax for three more pumps before filling the condom with my own release.

We both slide to the ground, our bodies slick with sweat but sated, and I pull her into my arms, still needing some kind of physical contact with her body.

I don't even have words to describe what that was. Nothing seems adequate in any of the languages I speak.

And for several blissful minutes, I hold her in my arms and fantasize that this thing we have, the one we refuse to label or talk about directly, could someday have the chance to grow into something long-lasting.

17

TRISTAN

*T*he next morning, wearing the same smile I fell asleep with last night, I roll over in bed to find a note from Dominic on his pillow.

Early call with my team, then working out with Max and Carter. Come find me out on the court after breakfast.
  -Dominic

After we dragged ourselves out of the gym last night, we managed to sneak into the chateau and up to our room without being seen, which seemed like the best idea at the time. But now I'm wondering how the hell I will be able to look Cordelia and Marie in the eye if they ask about what Dominic and I did yesterday.

By the time I trek downstairs for breakfast, conversations in French and English carry through the atrium, letting me know I'm the last one to make it down. Yvette and Chloe are seated at the far side of the table, but their conversation comes to a halt when Chloe looks up and sees me.

"Morning," she greets with a warm smile. "Coffee, tea, and juice are over there," she points to a small bar area in the corner, "and breakfast should be out any minute. You're just in time."

"Oh, thanks," I say, walking to pour myself a much-needed cup of coffee.

Cordelia and Gabriel are listening to Dom, who's making animated hand gestures as he tells a story I couldn't begin to understand if I tried. Marie turns away from her husband and gestures to the seat across from her, smiling with nothing but warmth.

"Bonjour," I offer in greeting, slipping into the seat. *"Commet allez-vous?"*

Her smile reappears at my effort, and I smile back, hoping I didn't butcher the simple phrase.

"I am well, thank you," she replies.

As if he suddenly registers my presence, Dom turns and abruptly cuts his story off when he sees me. "Tristan, my dear, there you are. We missed you last night, but I trust my grandson showed you a good time in Marseilles?"

Marseilles was fun, but it was nothing compared to the good time he showed me later.

"He did," I say, tucking my hair behind my ear even though a part of me wants to hide my face behind it because there's no way my cheeks aren't flushed. "I love history, so it was incredible to see such an old city."

"Excellent. And what are your plans for today?"

I look to Chloe with a shrug. "I think the guys are doing their own thing, right? So I'm at your disposal to help with anything wedding-related you have left to do."

"Perfect! I'm just getting the gift bags ready to go for the rest of the guests who will be arriving this evening and tomorrow. The rest is under control, and the wedding planner will be here tomorrow to coordinate the rehearsal. So the only other to-do items today involve a massage, mani, and pedi. Then we'll all meet back up for dinner. Sound like a plan?"

"Sounds perfect."

The rest of breakfast passes in a blur of stories as Dom reminisces about what Max and Dominic were like as kids, making us all laugh with his enthusiastic reenactments. It makes me curious about the crazy speech he's sure to give at the reception if he's this lively over a casual breakfast. Something in my chest pinches when I think about how lucky Dominic is to have grandparents—and parents—who so clearly love him with their whole hearts. I'm incredibly grateful to Aunt Lorraine, but my siblings and I don't have any kind of long history with her or even a single nostalgic story from childhood. I didn't even meet her until I was fifteen, and I can count on one hand the number of times we spoke before last year.

After breakfast, Chloe and I follow the *thwack* of a tennis ball smacking against rackets and exchange a raised-brow look when it stops, followed by a loud, "OUT?! THAT'S FUCKING BULL-SHIT, MAX!" and then, "Are you serious?! If you think that was in, you need to get your damn eyes checked!" and finally, "Well, I sure as shit won't be going to *your* optometrist!"

"Yikes," I say with a grimace. "That doesn't sound good."

"I take it you haven't met Carter yet?" she asks, the corner of her mouth lifting. I shake my head, and she laughs. "He's…something else."

I've heard of Carter, sure, but beyond what Dominic said about him, I'm not sure what to make of the guy.

I'm about to ask what she means when we round the corner, and I'm greeted by the kind of sight usually reserved for daydreams and fantasies. Max and Carter are on opposite sides of the court with Dominic off to the side behind Max, watching their hitting session, and between the three of them, there's not a shirt to be found.

Which means there are currently *three* sweaty, impeccably toned torsos—of three impossibly beautiful professional athletes—on display. It's like Christmas for my eyes.

Dominic commands my attention first like I have some kind of internal radar whenever he's around that draws me into him. His backward cap, the way his shorts sit on his hips and highlight the

V of his core, the way the sweat on his shoulders glistens in the sunlight as he motions something to Max about his swing...it's a sight I don't think I'll ever get used to seeing.

Max nods, bouncing the ball while Dominic talks, before setting up his serve. With a sharp smack against his racket, the ball sails over to Carter's side, taking my attention with it. Even with the few features I can discern from here as he darts across the court—caramel-colored skin donning a few tattoos, over-grown brown hair peeking out of the front of his cap, and rippling abs—it's easy to see why he's one of the biggest heartthrobs of tennis.

Carter and Max finish their game within a few minutes, with Carter coming out on top, and based on the enthusiastic fist pump he gives, you'd think it was an actual competition. Max and Carter go back and forth with a little friendly trash-talking before they end up laughing at something Dominic chimes in with.

"Carter catches a lot of shit from the media, but he's really not so bad," Chloe says, shielding her eyes from the sun to watch the guys' interaction. "And if you ask me, he's good for the sport."

"What do you mean?"

"You know how they say tennis is a gentleman's sport?"

I nod.

"Well, typically, there are guys like Max and Dominic in the sport. Not all, and that's not to say Max and Dominic are the pictures of player etiquette perfection, but for the most part, the players don't rock the boat. Max used to make waves with his partying, but that was separate from who he was when he trained and played. Carter...well, there's a reason his nickname is Wild Card."

I give her a dubious look. "And you say that's a *good* thing for the sport?"

She shrugs, flipping her ponytail over her shoulder. "It *can* be. Shakes things up, at least."

"Chloe, you saw that, right?" Carter hollers while making his way over to where we stand outside the fence. "How badly I kicked your fiancé's ass just now?"

She laughs and holds her hands up. "Don't bring us into this, Carter. We only just caught the last couple games."

His eyes skate over to me at her use of the word 'we,' and his lips part into a slow grin as he takes me in. "Hi. I'm Carter. And if there is a god, you are Chloe's single friend," he says, voice teasing and hopeful.

Upon closer inspection, Carter is even hotter than I thought. Strong, expressive eyebrows, a jaw that surely cuts glass, dark gray eyes framed by long lashes. The kind of smirk you feel down to your toes.

A girl could get lost in his charms without even realizing it.

"I'm—" I start, but quickly get cut off.

"She's not," Dominic answers, coming up and shoving Carter. "She's here with me, asshole. So put away the arsenal of pickup lines or whatever the hell it is you have to use to get women in your bed."

I shoot Dominic an *'is that so?'* look at his comment, but feel something flutter inside my chest at the same time. It's not that his words are untrue; I *did* come to France *with* him. But it's different hearing them verbalized in that way. Seeing him show a little possessiveness. It's kinda hot.

Chloe goes to the door through to the court to help Max pick up the rest of the wayward tennis balls, though she quickly squeals at Max's attempt to bear hug her, sweaty chest and all.

"Hey, you," Dominic says with a wink. He weaves his fingers through the fence and leans in, my body reacting on instinct and leaning in too, meeting his awaiting lips through the chain link.

Carter sighs dramatically behind him, making some comment under his breath about needing new friends, and it almost makes me laugh.

"Hi," I say, lacing my fingers through the fence over his after we break apart. "That was quite the show. Though I have to say, I'm sad I missed seeing you in action."

"Haven't gotten tired of watching me, huh?"

I pretend to mull over my answer, which makes him rattle the fence where he grips it. "I guess not…yet."

He laughs, walking toward the fence's door for me to come in and cross the court with him to where their water bottles are.

"Hey, someone's gotta keep you humble, remember?"

"How could I forget?" He winks, making me smile automatically.

Was there ever a time that wink hasn't affected me? It doesn't seem possible.

"What are you guys doing today? I'm helping Chloe with the guest gift packages, then we're having a spa day. I know you're probably *very* jealous."

"I am, actually. But we are doing…whatever Max wants, I guess. We didn't really throw him a proper bachelor party, so we're going to have to make up for that today."

I arch a brow at him. "You three, out for an impromptu bachelor party? Sounds like a recipe for trouble if you ask me."

"Don't worry, Pépé is coming as well."

The news makes me laugh. "And that's supposed to reassure me? You didn't see him at breakfast. He's a riot," I tell him, shaking my head, but smiling at the idea of Dom accompanying them on this bachelor party of sorts.

"That he is."

"Yo," Carter calls from across the court. "I was told there'd be a bachelor party celebration. Or am I the only one who remembers that?"

Chloe unwraps herself from around Max's body, and I'd bet money an eye-roll accompanied her sigh.

"Whose party is it, yours or mine?" Max counters.

Dominic sighs, pressing his forehead to mine. "I actually meant it about being jealous of your spa day. Because the role of refereeing these two gets old—fast."

Somehow, I don't doubt it.

After a few more bickering comments between Max and Carter, Chloe tells me we'd better go finish up the gift bags so that we're not late for our appointment. She instructs Dominic to keep them in line, to which he looks at me and mouths *take me with you.*

"Have fun, guys," I say, shooting Dominic one last smile

before Chloe's arm links through mine, and we head back the way we came.

I don't know if it's the massage, the champagne, or a combination of both, but four hours later, I'm completely relaxed and feel like a new person as Chloe drives us back to the chateau. We all are. Some of the guest gift bags were missing this morning, and Chloe panicked, but now she's laughing and singing off-key to the Spice Girls playlist we made while getting our pedicures. Even Yvette turned into a different person than the one who barely spoke five words to me before today. Once she came out of her shell of bitch-iness, she was actually...*nice* to me. It turns out she has a boyfriend, and he's even flying in for the wedding. I doubt we'll be staying up late braiding each other's hair and swapping stories about our lives, but we're at least cordial now, which I'm counting as a win.

We make it back to the chateau and find the guys in the library, where they've set up a table tennis game.

"Hey," I say, sneaking up on Dominic to wrap my arms around his waist from behind. He's off to the side, watching Max and Carter play an intense, take-no-prisoners game of table tennis almost as competitive as their real tennis practice this morning. "Uh-oh, I'm getting a sense of Déjà vu with these two."

"Yeah," Dominic agrees, but there's something off about his response. Like he's not even registering what I said or what he's saying.

I come around to the front of his body to search his face. When I follow his gaze, I realize he's not watching the game at all, but staring blankly out the window behind Max and Carter.

"Hey," I say, waving a hand in front of his face. "Everything okay?"

He snaps out of it and looks down at me. "Not exactly. There's something I have to tell you."

"There's something we have to tell you." The words my parents

used all those months ago to sit me down and attempt to explain away the charges they were facing echo inside my head, and it makes my heart race.

"What? Tell me," I plead, letting go of his hands to wrap my arms around myself to brace for impact. Nobody ever follows that up with, *"I brought you ice cream!"*

He darts a look around the room, which now holds a few more of the relatives and other guests that must have arrived during our time at the spa. "Let's go for a walk."

"Okay."

The fact he wants to make sure we're out of earshot of other people doesn't escape my notice, and it weighs on me the entire time it takes us to get from the third floor to the outside garden. Dominic walks a few more seconds in silence, even after ensuring we're alone like he's not sure how to broach whatever subject it is.

"Dominic," I call, grabbing his attention from the spot he's studying on the ground. "What is it? You're freaking me out."

That finally fully snaps him out of it, and he takes the two steps separating us to grab my hands in his. "I'm sorry. I probably should've been less cryptic." He squeezes my hand, and it's a simple gesture but surprisingly reassuring. "Do you remember that day on the boardwalk when Liam and Gen wanted to do the photo booth?"

I nod.

"And Gen saying there was some guy taking pictures of us?"

I give another nod when the word 'yes' gets stuck in my throat.

He pulls his phone out and holds it out to me. I'm instantly greeted by the image, albeit grainy and far away, of Dominic kissing me in that gap between the photo booth and an arcade game. My back is to the camera, so you can't make out much beyond my hair color and height. As much as I dread finding out, the need to know what, if any, information is also given propels me into action. The headline reads, *"DID DOMINIC MOREAU FIND LOVE IN SMALL TOWN, USA?"*

"Oh my God," I exclaim, terrified to read the rest.

With my heart in my throat, I grab his phone and start pacing as I scan the brief article, which is really only a paragraph. But there's no mention of my name, just speculation about the possibility that the woman in the photo is a native of Arbor Cove and a note at the end that they'll come back with an update if the woman's identity is discovered.

Rereading it a third time still does nothing to quell the unease coursing through my veins. "Fuck. Okay. This...this is going to be fine," I say, still pacing. "We just...can't be seen in public together in Arbor Cove now. Or anywhere. But that can fix this, I think."

I'm not even sure I believe myself.

"Tristan," Dominic says, bracing both hands on my shoulders to put a stop to my pacing. "It *is* going to be fine. This is just some shitty sports world gossip site. I'm pretty sure Gage is one of probably seven people who see it. They didn't have your name. And Gage is already working to get it taken down."

I hear his words, and on some level, I know they make sense. But flashes of awful, horrible things written on trashy gossip sites about me assault my mind, and all I can think is that it's only a matter of time before somebody puts the pieces together about my identity. On the occasion someone famous dates an everyday person, I've seen the media crucify the average Joe for something as simple as how they're dressed.

I can't imagine what they'd say about me.

I grip the fabric of his shirt and look up at him. The electric blue hue of his eyes has a temporary calming effect on me, but I quickly shake my head and break the spell. "Dominic, I can't...I can't go through that again. Or anything like it. This is *exactly* why I knew I needed to keep my distance from you."

"Breathe," he instructs, cupping my face and forcing my eyes to stop bouncing from spot to spot. "I'm going to take care of this. I promise you'll be okay. *We'll* be okay."

The way he says *we* is adamant and confident and like it's a foregone conclusion there actually is a *we* to be okay.

"How can you say that? You can't know that, Dominic."

My voice breaks on his name, and he pulls me into his chest in a crushing hug, holding me there and absorbing my tears in his shirt. "It'll be okay," he repeats, over and over, kissing the top of my head between promises.

I'm desperate to believe him, desperate for his words and his touch to be the only truths I need.

And for now, I'll pretend we live in a perfect world where they are.

18

TRISTAN

"Gone. Just like that? You're sure?" Dominic asks, pacing the bedroom early the next morning.

He listens for a second, and then pulls his phone away from his face and puts it on speaker.

"...have both been removed from the site. The photo is still circulating around on Instagram, but as far as I can tell, there's not anything more to it than generic speculation. If we're lucky, it'll be old news by the end of the day."

I let out a huge sigh of relief, already feeling the knots of tension ease from my shoulders. The questions and concerns about what potential gossip is floating around Arbor Cove, and what I'll have to do about it come Monday, still loom in the back of my mind, but for now, I'm clinging to any good news I can get.

"But, Dominic," Gage continues, "We do need to talk about... some things."

"*Things* can wait. It's the day before my brother's wedding; I'm kind of busy."

"I realize that, which is why I wouldn't be bringing this up if it wasn't important. Take me off speaker."

Whatever direction their phone conversation takes, though, doesn't seem to be pleasant based on the scowl marring Dominic's features after only a few seconds. He slips out onto the balcony, arguing with Gage about something, so I escape to the oversized shower to give him more privacy.

Eventually, I hear the shower door open and close before Dominic's strong arms wrap around me from behind, pulling me back into his chest.

"Everything okay with Gage?" I ask.

"It will be. He's just being particularly dick-ish today. But it's fine."

He spins me around and sears my lips with a kiss that ends our conversation, and as soon as he does, this moment, right now, is all I can think about. It's the kind of kiss that seeps into my bones, erasing every last thought that extends beyond the walls of this shower. Beyond *him*.

And when he kneels in front of me, slowly leaving a trail of hot kisses down my body, I beg the universe to let me freeze this moment, to let me always remember how he makes me feel.

Our time together might have an expiration date, but that's tomorrow's problem.

Today, I just want to bask in the here and now. To relish the ways he worships my body like it's something sacred to him.

Two hours later, I'm happily nuzzled into Dominic's side in bed, soaking up the last few minutes we have to ourselves before we go downstairs for breakfast and spend the rest of the day knee-deep in all things rehearsal and wedding prep. I'm still riding the post-orgasm high from our shower-turned-bathroom-counter-turned-bed sex-athon, contemplating if we have time for one more roll between the sheets when there's a loud banging on the door of our room.

"Dominic, open the door! Right fucking now!" Carter yells impatiently.

Muttering under his breath, Dominic pulls on a pair of sweats before striding to the door and pulling it open. Carter shoves past him, not even bothering to ask permission.

"What the fuck?" Dominic barks. At the same time, I yelp and pull the sheet tight around myself.

But Carter's not even paying me a sliver of attention. He runs a hand through his messy hair and tugs on the ends, pacing before he turns to Dominic. "Have you checked your phone lately? Max is gone," he says, shoving his phone at Dominic before going back to pulling and twisting the ends of his hair.

"What? What do you mean he's *gone*?" Dominic looks at the phone and immediately shakes his head, tossing it back and going to his own phone on the nightstand. And whatever he sees on it makes his eyes go round. *"The wedding's off,'"* he recites.

"What?" I cry, bolting out of bed, only remembering to keep my grip on the sheet at the last second.

"What the hell happened last night after Tristan and I left?" Dominic asks, looking at Carter like it's somehow his fault this is happening.

"How should I know? I was fucking hammered! I don't remember much after my fifth game of boozy ping pong."

"Who else knows? Have you been downstairs yet?"

"No. I just woke up, saw the text, and came straight down to find you."

Dominic fires off a text before thinking better of it and calls Max instead, putting it on speaker. But it goes straight to voicemail. He barks something in French that sounds really angry and throws his phone against his pillow.

"Did either of them say anything to you last night? I don't understand what could possibly have happened."

Carter's jaw clenches and unclenches as he rolls his lip back and forth between his pointer finger and thumb, thinking back to last night. "I don't think so. The only vague recollection I have is seeing them in the far corner of the library talking. They didn't look happy, but I figured it was just pre-wedding jitters or some shit like that."

The snippet of conversation that I overheard our first night here comes back to me, and I have a horrible, sinking feeling I know whose voice was which now.

"Oh my God," I say, drawing both guys' attention. "The night we got here, I overheard Chloe and Yvette talking. Their voices were muffled, so I couldn't tell who was saying what. And at the time, I thought it might've been Yvette with the problem, but now I'm wondering if it has something to do with this. One of them—I'm guessing Chloe now—said something about needing to tell 'him' something, and that it felt wrong not to do so. But then the other person said just to wait until this is all over and everyone's lives go back to normal before telling 'him' anything. What if Chloe told him whatever the 'something' was, and *that's* what happened to cause this?"

Dominic mutters strings of what I can only assume are French curse words before grabbing his phone and wallet. "Only one way to know. We have to find Max."

"I'll grab the keys to my rental and meet you downstairs," Carter says, already jogging to the door.

After the door closes, I spring into action, throwing on jeans and a t-shirt while Dominic tries calling Max again. It goes to voicemail again. He grips his phone so tightly I'm afraid he's going to break it, so I go to him, wrapping my hands around his neck, so he focuses on me. "You're going to find him, and we will get answers. Sort this out. Do you want me to come with you guys?"

The tension in his shoulders eases just a fraction, and he squeezes my waist in a silent thank you. "Actually...fuck," he hisses, shaking his head, "I don't even know if Chloe is here. If she's not, someone's going to have to explain things to the guests. I'll tell my parents, and they can take care of it. I think it might be better if you stay and...I don't know. If Chloe is gone and happens to come back, maybe you can try to talk some sense into her? I don't fucking know. None of this makes sense."

I can feel the tension building back up inside him, and it's killing me that I can't help him more. "Breathe. It'll be okay," I tell him, echoing his words to me from last night. With my fingers woven through the short strands at the back of his head, I lightly massage the base of his skull for a beat until he exhales a deep breath.

His head dips down until his forehead comes to rest against mine.

"I'm glad you're here," he whispers across my lips.

I press a soft kiss against his lips as my response, letting him know without words that I'm glad too.

One dreadful conversation with Cordelia and Gabriel, an incredibly awkward breakfast, countless cups of coffee, and four hours later, Dominic and Carter still haven't found Max. And nobody has been able to reach Chloe either.

By the time we got downstairs this morning, Chloe and Yvette were both gone too. Everyone had just assumed Chloe and Max were still sleeping. Gabriel and Dom took a separate car to look for Max too. I stayed behind to do whatever I could to help Cordelia. She tried to hold it together when telling the other guests Max and Chloe had stepped out for a bit—not ready or willing to give them the full truth, yet—but I could see the worry in her eyes.

"Here," I tell her, holding out a steaming cup of tea.

She takes the mug with a small, grateful smile. For a woman pushing her mid-sixties, you'd never know it by looking at Cordelia Moreau. The years have been exceptionally kind to her. But the stress from today's developments has seemingly aged her in the span of a few hours. She's standing in front of one of the windows of the massive kitchen with a view out to the driveway, watching like a hawk for any sign of life to approach.

"Can I get you anything else?" I ask, not really sure what else to do or say. Not that there's anything I *can* do or say to make this situation less shitty.

"No. Thank you, Tristan," she replies, only turning to me for a second before going back to watch out the window.

"Of course. Let me know if there's anything else I can do,

Cordelia." I linger behind her for a moment, debating whether I should keep her company or leave her in peace.

But then she turns to me and catches me by complete surprise with her next words.

"I have a confession. I know your history—your family's history, I mean."

I almost choke on my own tea.

She reads the horrified look on my face and shakes her head, reaching out to grip my shoulder reassuringly. "I'm sorry. I shouldn't have said it like that. You see, I asked Ellen to keep an eye on Dominic—and yes, I do realize how ridiculous it is for me to essentially spy on my fully grown son that way. But you have to understand, the pressure Dominic has always put on himself when it comes to tennis hasn't always been an easy thing for me to accept as his mom. Especially when it comes to injuries. Of course, I'm proud of him for the incredible accomplishments he's achieved throughout his career. He's a truly remarkable player." She turns, angling her body toward mine now, and sips from her mug before shaking her head lightly. "But for so long, tennis has been all he cared about. All he lived for. As a former player myself, I understood his drive, his passion. But as his mom, I've always wanted *more* for him."

I offer her a sympathetic smile. "I can understand that."

"So, all of that to say...I asked Ellen if he had been moping around twenty-four seven, as I expected, or if he was finding constructive ways to pass his time that didn't involve obsessing *solely* over his recovery. Imagine my surprise when she told me he had bonded with a pair of nine-year-old twins and was also spending time with their older sister. Ellen, my sweet, dear child-hood friend, told me I was being too much of a helicopter mom, and if I wanted to know more information, I should ask him myself. So I did."

She must see me balk at the last part because she quickly shakes her head, rushing to continue.

"Dominic didn't tell me. I managed to get *just* your first name out of him, and he did mention at one point that you used to live in New York. But he was very adamant about not giving much information other than that, so don't be upset with him. He doesn't even know I know the full truth."

I exhale a breath, still flabbergasted at her revelation. "Okay…"

"I'm sorry; I know I'm rambling. It's a bad habit I have when I'm nervous. But I do have a point to all of this, I promise," she says, wrapping her hands around her mug. "And that point is this: I know life dealt you a truly terrible hand, and I don't blame you for seeking solace in Arbor Cove and wanting nothing more than a simple life of peace and quiet. Now, as far as whatever it is between you and Dominic, it's none of my business what, if any, kind of plan you two have or don't have for a possible future together. But I want you to know, being with him wouldn't have to be an either-or situation. His playing career is one chapter in his life, and there's no guarantee when it comes to that chapter's length. These past few days, I've seen firsthand that he's discovered there is more to live for than just his love of the game. And it's because of you. I'm not saying it would be easy; in fact, I can tell you right now, it would be quite the opposite. But you have to ask yourself what kind of future you envision for yourself. If there's even a chance it would be a future with my son, don't let the uncertainties and fears rob you of that possibility. At the end of the day, your happiness, and Dominic's, is what matters most. The rest can be worked out."

I let her words wash over me and sink in for a minute. "I don't…I don't know what to say."

Hot tears burn my eyes, but I refuse to let them fall. Surprisingly, it's the last conversation I had with my mom—on the phone that night in Rockdale—that's jumping out at me. What a complete and utter contrast it was to the immense kindness and understanding Cordelia is showing me now.

"Don't be a fool, Tristan. Do you have any idea what you're doing by throwing away that money? If you go through with this, your father and I will never forgive you, and we'll make sure your siblings don't either. It

was clearly a mistake to make you their guardian if you can't be trusted to look out for their best interests..."

"Oh, honey," Cordelia says, breaking me out of the memory. "You don't have to say anything. I'm sorry for upsetting you; that was not my intention."

I shake my head immediately. "No, I promise it's nothing you said. It's me. It's just...you're a really good mom. Max and Dominic are lucky to have you."

She sets her mug down and wraps an arm around my shoulder and gives my hand a comforting squeeze.

We stand like that for a few minutes, not talking, just loaning each other silent support in our own ways until my ringtone cuts through the air. As soon as I see Dominic's name, I swipe the screen and immediately put it on speaker, so that Cordelia can hear too.

"Did you find him?" I ask, willing him to have good news.

"We found him," he says a split-second after I ask.

"Oh, thank God," Cordelia says, lifting a hand to her chest. "Where? Is he okay?"

"At some bar in the middle of a town about an hour from the chateau. He's okay," Dominic assures us. "He's completely hammered, but he's in one piece. I'm driving Max's car back, and we'll be back in about an hour."

Cordelia sighs in relief. "Did he mention what happened? Or know where Chloe would have gone?"

"No. So far, he is refusing to talk about Chloe, and most of what he says is barely intelligible anyway. I take it Chloe never came back, and you haven't heard from her either?"

"No," I tell him. "Same story; her phone is off, and there's no indication of where she would have gone. Her bags and belongings are all gone too. Except her wedding dress."

"*Shit,*" Dominic mutters. "What now?"

"Now," Cordelia says, her voice resigned and expression weary, "We cancel a wedding."

19

DOMINIC

"*B*OO-YAH! I told you I'd win this time," Liam cheers, gleefully throwing the basketball into the air and bursting into a crazy dance routine. "Don't feel too bad, Dominic. Sure, you lost to a nine-year-old, but I'm a future NBA Finals MVP, so that should help you sleep at night."

His antics make me laugh and shake my head. *This kid.* "Already calling it now? What happened to being a chef?"

"I'll do both." He shrugs and looks to Kai and Gen across the court. "Kai and I will open a restaurant, and I'll spend my off-seasons there, and he can handle it the rest of the time."

Kai nods in agreement. "And Gen can be our sous chef!"

Admittedly, they've become quite the powerhouse cooking trio this summer, watching countless YouTube videos and Food Network shows, then begging Tristan, Ellen, or me to let them try recipes. And most of the time, their food turns out arguably better than anything I could make.

Gen arches a brow at Kai, jutting out a hip with her hand on it. "Uh, no. I will be the owner; you two will work *for me.*"

"We'll see about that," he replies.

I look at Tristan, who watched the exchange with the same amusement as I did, and she just shakes her head.

"I guess strong opinions run in the Fitzgerald family, huh?"

"Maybe a little," she says, brow arched at me the same way her sister's was.

I walk over to where she's sitting on the bench off to the side of the court. Sitting next to her, I sweep the hair behind her shoulder and lean over to whisper, "I'd say you were more than *a little* vocal with your strong opinions last night."

Her cheeks flush, and her breath catches, and I know she's fighting the urge to make me pay for making her squirm in public. Last night, Ellen picked the twins up, and Maggie slept over with a friend, so we took full advantage of the first full night of alone time we've had since getting back from France two weeks ago. She showed up at my door wearing only the white bikini and black stilettos, which made for a hot as fuck combination on her body, but an even better one on the floor.

She hums but refuses to acknowledge the effect my words have. Instead, she reaches over and steals my hat—my *favorite* hat—and puts it on her own head instead. I make a fake growl sound in my throat, but the truth is, seeing my logo on her will never get old. "I wish you didn't have to go to New York. But I'm keeping this for safekeeping until you get back."

She flips her hair back over her shoulders and winks up at me from under the brim of my cap.

So. Damn. Sexy.

"It looks better on you anyway. But I wish you were coming with me," I counter, though I understand why she isn't.

The fundraiser—the one with my face splashed across various posters from the photoshoot in July—is tonight, and I've already contemplated every possible way to get out of going. But, short of threatening my life, Nash pretty much made it clear that's not an option. I've never been one to skirt my responsibilities when it comes to my sponsors, but after spending at least part of every day together for the last three weeks, spending the next twenty-four hours apart seems unfathomable.

She slips her pinky finger around mine and squeezes. "We talked about this, Dominic. You know why I can't."

Since the boardwalk photo incident, Tristan has been adamant about not letting things drift beyond *friendly* between us in public, which I both understand and hate. Reporters called Gage, trying to get information about the mystery woman and how long I planned to stay in Arbor Cove, but he was able to spin things to give the impression I'd already left for good. Some even managed to track down the address of my rental house, but the neighborhood security guard at the gate called Ellen, who worked her magic to convince them I'd already left town permanently.

Logically, I know why being seen together at a very public event is not the best idea unless we're willing to accept the consequences that would inevitably entail.

But with less than a month left in Arbor Cove, my desperation is drowning out logic. I can already feel her slipping away with each passing day, and I'm not even remotely ready to let her go.

As if in tune with my mood, the sky darkens, and somewhere in the distance, thunder cracks, warning of an impending storm heading our way. Parting ways with Ellen and Kai, the four of us scramble to get back to their house before the rain catches us. The rest of the morning passes in a blur of dance parties, which Maggie even emerges from her room to join in on—and baking, which Gen insists is the perfect way to spend a rainy day.

It's been the kind of morning I never knew I wanted in my life.

In-between dancing and taste testing brownies and cookies, I find myself distracted, searching for a way to keep this—*them*—as a permanent part of my life without asking Tristan to give up the peace she's fought so hard to find in Arbor Cove. And without losing my biggest sponsor.

I refuse to believe there isn't a way to make it work.

Maggie and Gen are in the middle of their rendition of, *"I Knew You Were Trouble"* by Taylor Swift when my phone's alarm cuts through the air, letting me know it's time to leave for New York.

"Come on; I'll walk you out," Tristan says, leaving Liam to measure out the ingredients for his next batch of cookies.

As soon as the door closes behind her, she slings her arms around my body, burrowing into my chest. I wrap my arms around her shoulders, holding her in place. By now, I can't remember a time when it didn't feel right to have her in my arms like this.

With the rain still coming down, we linger on the porch until my snoozed alarm goes off a second time.

She reluctantly pulls away, taking the soft lavender scent of her new body wash with her. I sigh and lean in to press one last kiss onto the top of her head.

Her head falls forward onto my chest, and she grips the fabric of my t-shirt. "You're not making this any easier, Dominic."

"I'll be back tomorrow," I remind her.

But we both know *this* doesn't just mean my overnight trip.

She nods. "I know. I just...I wish I could go with you. As your date. *Publicly*."

My chest fills with something new and unfamiliar at her words, and it's on the tip of my tongue to tell her, *"You can. I want that too."*

Instead, I give her a reassuring smile. "It's okay. I understand, and you were right last night, this is the best way. For now. I can be patient, Tristan. For this. *For you*."

Her eyes gloss over, but before I can get a word out to address the impending tears, she presses onto her toes and seals her lips over mine, letting a kiss do the talking for her.

"Okay," she mumbles into our kiss before pressing against my chest to put space between us. "You have to go. I don't want to be the reason you're late."

Tearing myself away from her feels like torture, but she's right. I'm already cutting it close to avoid being late to the cocktail hour before the gala.

Rain seeps through my t-shirt as soon as I leave the shelter of the porch, soaking all the way through before I make it halfway to my SUV. When I glance back, Tristan is still perched against the pillar of the porch, hugging her arms to her waist and watching me go. She lifts a hand to blow me a kiss.

It's then I realize she's still close to tears.

And that's all it takes to make me turn around and go back to her.

"What are you doing?" she calls, but I'm already climbing the four stairs up to the porch.

"That was a lie—I can't be patient. Well, I *can* be. But I need you to know that I don't want this—whatever this is between us —to end next month. In private, under wraps or splashed on the front page of a newspaper...I'm in, Tristan. *I'm all in.* Whatever you're comfortable with." She opens her mouth, but I shake my head, sending water flying in all directions, and cut her off. "You don't have to say anything. I didn't tell you that to pressure you for a response. Just think about it, and we'll talk tomorrow when I get back."

I lean in and kiss her cheek before turning to go back down the stairs.

But she calls my name, leaving the cover of the porch to grab my hand the second I leave the bottom step.

Standing on a stair to put us eye-level, she flings her arms around my neck and pulls me in, not even hesitating to meld herself to me completely.

"I'm in too."

I pull back from her embrace and find her blinking away the water as it clings to her lashes. I can't tell if the liquid is rain or tears.

"I don't want this to end, either," she adds.

Now it's her turn to shake her head and cut me off, this time with a searing kiss that's anything but chaste. She twists her fingers through my hair, drawing a moan from deep in my throat, and I grip her hips to pull her closer—close enough to feel my cock, hard and desperate for her. She grinds against me for friction, and it's enough to make me forget any and all sense of responsibility. Wrapping my hands around the backs of her bare thighs, I lift her up and urge her legs to wrap around my waist.

I don't even think, don't even try to talk myself out of this, I just carry her to my SUV and pop the back open. She kisses her way down my neck, already pulling at my shirt while I fumble with the back row, trying to flatten it with only about half of my brain working properly.

With the seats down, we climb in and close the door, tugging and pulling at the rest of each other's clothes like it's a race to get the other person naked first—not an easy task when those clothes are soaking wet and sticking to every inch of skin.

Finally, I hover over Tristan's perfect—and perfectly naked— body just long enough to admire the sight before taking one nipple into my mouth, earning a loud moan from her lips. She arches into me at the contact, pressing her hips up and rubbing herself against my erection, so her wetness soaks the tip of my cock.

"Fuck, it's so sexy how turned on you are right now," I tell her.

"You tend to have that effect on me. All the time." She wraps a hand around my length and slides it through her folds, slowly. It's agony and ecstasy—enough to make me fight the urge to drive into her in a single motion right here and now. "What kind of effect do I have on you?" she asks, flashing her eyes up to mine as she pulses up just enough to glide the tip of my cock into her. "Show me, Dominic."

Her plea undoes me.

I push in completely, filling her all at once, and she replies with a loud moan that I feel down to my bones.

The rake of her nails down my back is all the encouragement needed to spur me into action. I grab one of her legs behind the knee, lifting it to give myself the angle I know will drive her wild, before driving into her again and again. Her teeth trap her bottom lip in an attempt to contain a scream, but when I tug her lip free, it's not a scream she gives me; it's pleas. *Harder. Faster. Right there. Don't stop.*

It's not the first time she's been direct about what she wants during sex, but this time, I can anticipate the things she wants before she even expresses them. I press down on her clit with my thumb, circling and rubbing it relentlessly until she shakes beneath me, announcing her orgasm in moans and unintelligible nonsense I'm not even sure contains real words.

She's still riding the waves of her orgasm when I find mine, pulling out to spill my own hot release on her stomach. Leaning back to sit on my heels, I reach over to tug a towel out of my workout bag and clean her off.

She pushes up on her elbows and shakes her head, biting back a smile, and reaches for her bra. "Guess I'm going to be the reason you're late, after all."

I laugh and tug a dry shirt from my bag over my head. "Maybe so, but you'll never hear me complain about being late if it's related to sex."

"Good to know," she says with a wink.

Not only did I miss the entire cocktail hour, but I stroll into the hotel's ballroom two minutes before the first speaker extends a thank you to all who helped make tonight possible, calling my name out among the others. A few guests nearby crane their necks around, offering me a head nod or a silent raise of their glass in acknowledgement.

I nod back and offer tight smiles, even though I probably don't deserve more acknowledgment than any of the others who donated to the silent auction. Weaving my way through the crowd to find the table where Nash is, I take my seat and keep my attention locked on the stage to avoid the daggers Nash is staring at me for being late. The speaker—some executive for one of Rolex's partner event sponsors—drones on for long enough to make me wish I had stopped at the bar before finding my seat.

Finally, the speaker reminds everyone the silent auction bidding will remain open until one hour before the night ends, throwing in a comment about loosened wallets increasing your chances of winning.

"So," a blonde to Nash's left begins, eyeing me in a way that tells me she likes what she sees. "You're *the* Dominic Moreau."

"That's right," I say, trying to remember if Nash had told me anything about his date for tonight. Though, last time I was in a similar predicament, I guessed the wrong name, which went over about as well as you'd expect. "And you are...?"

"Nina," she purrs, offering me her hand.

I make some small talk with Nina and meet the other two people at the table—a nice couple from Ohio who owns a chain of car washes. Dinner arrives, and I indulge in their questions about my life, what motivates me, what it's like having a whole family of tennis stars, and so on. The kinds of questions I've gotten so often that I could probably answer them in my sleep.

Nash's attention whips up from his phone for the first time practically all dinner, and he glares at me. "I'm sorry, baby, I need a minute with Dominic," he tells her, leaning over to kiss her cheek. He pushes back in his chair to indicate I'm supposed to follow him.

She shrugs and takes another sip of her champagne, already turning to talk to one of the car wash owners.

Nash leads the way out of the ballroom and into the foyer before turning to me with an incredulous look on his face.

"Tell me this is not fucking true," he explodes, shoving his phone at me. I don't even have time to get a good look at the screen before he explodes again. "Tell me you are not screwing Tristan fucking Fitzgerald!"

My jaw clenches, and I immediately shush him, shoving him deeper into a deserted corner of the open space. "What the fuck is wrong with you that you'd announce something like that where people can hear?"

"This is not sounding like a 'no', Dominic."

His tone makes me clench my hands into fists.

"As my agent, my personal life has nothing to do with anything pertaining to your job. And as my friend, you're really pissing me off right now."

"*Nothing to do with my job?*" He snorts, and I can practically see steam pouring from his ears. "It sure as hell has *everything* to do with my job when you are fucking the one person in the world who will singlehandedly ruin this Linx contract. Did you even think of that?"

I fold my arms across my chest, ignoring his question. "How did you even find out? What did you do?"

"Gage called me after the leaked photo incident you conveniently forgot to mention to me. Wanted to know if I had any information about who you could possibly be seeing because you wouldn't say."

"Oh, so you *both* want to get yourselves fired, I guess." I uncurl and curl my fists, fighting every fiber of my being that's begging me to take a shot at Nash right now.

And then, as if tempting fate, the asshole laughs.

"For almost locking down another record-breaking contract for you with Linx? Do you hear yourself? Dominic, I am *this close*," he holds up his thumb and pointer finger an inch apart, "to having that contract finalized. You *know* that. So why, *why* are you willing to throw it all away for this girl? I told you about the Michael Grant connection to her parents in July, for fuck's sake!"

"She is not her goddamn parents, Nash!" I bellow, realizing a second too late I need to lower my voice. "And I'm well aware of the Michael Grant connection. That's all I fucking think about some days. Michael has been great to me, and I'll always be grateful to him and to Linx for the partnership we've had the last decade. But I won't let this contract dictate my private life. If Michael has a problem with my personal relationship that he lets affect our professional relationship, maybe our partnership was never as strong as I thought. I'll talk to him myself if necessary."

"And if you lose Linx? Rolex? Others? We've already lost Gatorade. You know the facts. We knew your injury, combined with your age, was going to put us at a disadvantage with contract negotiations. You're playing with fire, Dominic."

"Maybe she's worth the burn, Nash. Did you even consider *that* is why I'm willing to let Linx go? Or were you too busy prematurely mourning the contract for selfish reasons?"

"Are you sure about that? That she's worth it?" he asks, studying me carefully. "Did you know she met with her parents' attorney a while back? And shortly after that meeting, she lost a massive amount of money that was conveniently being kept in an off-shore account. As in, what I assume to be all of the money her family had left. She's broke, Dominic. How well do you really know her?"

"I don't think I like what you're implying. How the fuck do you know all of this anyway?"

He shrugs, picking lint off his tux like this conversation isn't one that's about to land him in the emergency room. "I have a P.I. who does great work. Discreetly. Now…it's a simple question: can you say with absolute certainty that she isn't with you for your money?"

I let my glare serve as my only answer for a second, so he continues, "What about the photo that was taken of you two by the ocean? Can you honestly say you know she wasn't behind it? Maybe she was hoping someone recognized her, shared her name, linking her to you, as a way to get her name back in the press?"

"No way," I answer, but his questions swim in my head, jumbling together in a flurry of confusion. "You don't get it. She doesn't *want* any kind of spotlight or attention from the media. I'm not even sure when she'll agree to be seen with me in public."

But then I think about today, about the dramatic shift between us.

He reads my hesitation as doubt and pounces, surging on with his unrelenting questions. "So she's given you no indication that she wants to go public as a couple? No reason to think she'd have any particular motivation to want that? Let me ask you this: if you two are so close, did she tell you about the meeting with her parents' attorney? About the money? If not, you need to ask your-self why."

His questions are valid, on some level, at least, especially because I know he is genuinely trying to look out for my best interest. I'm stumbling over my thoughts, trying to sort them and offer explanations, trying to shut off the tiny voice in my head that says maybe I *should* ask why—why she didn't tell me about losing all of her money, why, after weeks of keeping distance between us in public, she kissed me out in the open…*why she let me fuck her in my car where anyone could see.*

"Dom, I'm begging you," he continues, "don't throw away this Linx contract if you're having any doubts about her at all." He shakes my shoulders like he's willing me to snap out of Tristan's spell, and turns, nodding toward the ballroom to indicate we should go back. "Look, I get that you care about her, but lust, infatuation, even incredible sex, isn't worth jeopardizing this kind of money over."

Seconds tick by before I finally snap out of my silence, realizing I'm an idiot for even entertaining those questions, for letting Nash—who knows nothing about Tristan or our relationship—get inside my head. It's on the tip of my tongue to tell him that what I have with Tristan is so much more than any of those things.

But I never get the chance because we round the corner and my heart smashes into pieces at the sight in front of me.

20

TRISTAN

$\mathcal{M}$y face must portray exactly how I feel, which is that I don't even know him. After we both laid our cards on the table this afternoon, I came here thinking we were on the same page. That we wanted the same thing. Felt the same way about each other. *That I could trust him.*

The decision to come to New York and surprise Dominic was impulsive, but for once, the prospect of being seen or photographed with Dominic in public didn't make my heart rate skyrocket. I spent the entire drive here mulling over different scenarios about how tonight would play out, how we'd eventually handle going public, what that would mean for my life back home. No matter what scenario played out, I was certain I could handle whatever happened. Even if it meant being thrust into the spotlight.

But the last three minutes are making me question everything from my judgment to his sincerity.

"God," I groan, "I'm such an idiot! This was a huge mistake."

"Tristan, I—" Dominic says, taking a step closer to me, but I take a step back and cut him off.

"Do you actually think I would be responsible for that photo of us getting out? Or that I would want to be with you because you're rich? Because being with you is a way to somehow clear my name and have another fifteen minutes of fame I don't even want?"

"*Of course not!* I've never questioned your intentions."

"That's funny because your silence just now seemed to imply the opposite. If not that one, then what part was it that clearly has you questioning things? Questioning me?"

He steps into my space, lightly gripping my arm and holding my eyes captive with his. "Tristan, no. Let's just...go talk about this somewhere else," he pleads, looking around for somewhere more private.

I know he's right, that this isn't the time or place for this conversation, but the rage pumping through my veins makes me want to defy anything he says right now.

And I need answers.

"What did he mean by the Michael Grant connection?" I ask, my eyes flitting from Dominic to his agent, the asshole who clearly believes the worst of me. "And the Linx contract?"

I'm answered with silence from both men, who are locked in some kind of wordless exchange, eyes narrowed and jaws clenched.

Nash finally turns his attention to me, a look of utter disapproval fixed firmly in place. "Michael Grant was a friend of your father's in college. He wasn't an FFG client, but he referred his brother and nephew to your parents, and they lost everything. Michael Grant is also the CEO of Linx, which has been Dominic's biggest sponsor for the last decade." Each sentence feels like a lead weight pressing down on my chest, but I force my eyes to stay on him, waiting for the rest of an explanation I can already tell will crush me. "His highly lucrative, *eight-figure* Linx contract is up for renewal in December. Want to take a guess how those negotiations will go if and when Grant finds out about the two of you?"

His question hits me like a physical blow, the weight of its answer an albatross around my heart.

"Nash, that's enough. You've made your point," Dominic snaps, cutting him a razor-sharp glare.

"Someone had to give it to her straight because apparently, you haven't been," he offers with an unapologetic shrug.

Dominic's eyes flare in warning, and he takes a menacing step in Nash's direction. I haven't seen this kind of anger from him since the day of the French Open finals, and my instinct is to rein him in so he doesn't do something stupid, but I'm not the picture of composure right now either, so I stay put.

"If you like being my agent, I suggest getting the fuck out of my sight. Now."

Nash's eyebrows lift, and his mouth opens to respond before snapping shut. "I hope you know what you're doing, Dom," he says, shaking his head as he takes slow steps in the direction of the ballroom.

"For the record," I start once Nash is gone, "That meeting with my parents' attorney when we came to the city *was* about an offshore bank account they had opened in my name. It had an exorbitant amount of money in it—*money I gave up,* to be distributed to the families of clients my parents stole from. I didn't tell anyone because I don't want an ounce of recognition for doing what any person with a conscious would've done. I *hate* that my parents even put me in that position. I'll never not be horrified and ashamed of their actions. As fucked up as it is that *I* would need absolution for *their* actions in the eyes of some, I've dealt with enough bad press to know it's a battle not worth fighting. I'm happy with the life I've built in Arbor Cove; why would I risk messing that up for the sake of rebuilding a reputation I don't even care about? So, despite whatever anyone might think, seeing my name or face in print is the last thing I want."

"I know. You don't have to explain." Before I can protest, he closes the distance between us. I'm immediately tense, wary of potential prying eyes seeing our exchange, but he's completely unbothered by the possibility we're flirting with disaster. He's so close, his cologne—a heady mixture of sandalwood and leather—surrounds me and temporarily steals my sanity. But then I remember where we are and force myself to snap out of it and take a step back.

"*I'm sorry,*" he continues. "I swear to you, none of what Nash said reflects how I feel. I *know* you're not with me for money or fame. I know that, Tristan. Please, please believe me."

His eyes search mine, begging me to accept his words as truth. They're filled with absolute sincerity, and I can already feel my anger dissipate. But that doesn't change the facts.

"You didn't seem so sure a few minutes ago," I point out.

He winces, his Adam's apple bobbing on a swallow. "You're right; I should have shut Nash down immediately. I guess I was just surprised you didn't tell me about the money. I understand not wanting to make it public knowledge, but that's not the same as telling *me.* I could've been there for you. You shouldn't have had to deal with it all on your own."

He's genuinely crestfallen, and I'm starting to think maybe my decision to keep him in the dark was a mistake.

"I just...I've gotten used to handling things on my own over the last year. Keeping everything close to the vest. Especially where my parents are concerned."

"You don't have to carry it all, Tristan. You can talk to me. About anything. Everything," he implores, squeezing my hands for emphasis.

"I could say the same to you. Why didn't you tell me about your contract?"

"Because it's irrelevant. I meant what I said." He drops my hands in favor of moving them to cup either side of my face, the pad of his thumb lightly tracing my jawline. I melt into his touch, unable to summon the will to pull back even though a voice in my head warns me we're begging for trouble. "I won't let my career dictate my personal life. I'll find a way to make it work. I'll talk to Michael, make him understand. And if he doesn't," he shrugs, as if losing a huge contract worth millions isn't a big deal, "There are other companies who would jump at the chance to sponsor me."

I frown, knowing it's not as simple as he makes it seem. "But you're...you can't lose Linx because of me. That's insane. You'd lose millions."

"So? I *have* millions. I don't care about money. For the better part of two decades, I've dedicated my life to my career, with little room for anything else. I was happy because it meant I was accomplishing everything I set out to do professionally. But one day, when it's all said and done, and my career comes to an end, accolades and a house full of trophies aren't going to bring my life joy. If there's one thing the last few months have shown me, it's that *I want more.* More than another title, more than another endorsement deal, more than an Athlete of the Year award. You, Tristan—*you* are more. And I can't lose you because of Linx."

"Dominic...I don't...I don't know what to say." I shake my head, my mind spinning from everything he just said. I want to tell him he's crazy, that he can't throw his Linx deal away for someone he's only known a matter of months. But I can't. Because his words have wrapped around me like a blanket, filling me with warmth and hope and making my heart beat a little faster. His confession has given life and roots to the underlying feelings I've refused to label lately, only because I know once I give them a name, it's game over for my heart.

"Say you'll forgive me for being a complete and utter idiot, and you'll let me make it up to you." He pulls out a room key, making his intentions clear, and my mouth goes dry at the thought.

Wild ideas start racing through my head.

Ideas for *exactly* what he can do to make it up to me. Starting with a striptease, in his tuxedo. I give his entire frame a slow, drawn-out perusal and try to envision what kind of moves Dominic's strip routine would consist of. *Chippendales would have nothing on him.*

A smile slowly pulls at the corners of my mouth before I bite my lip to hold it in check. "I forgive you. But you've got your work cut out for you if you really want to make it up to me. And I'm not talking about the mini-fridge I'm about to raid," I tell him before plucking the room key from his hand and walking toward the elevators.

He gives me a questioning look, and I shake my head. "I think it might be best if I skip the gala. It's just that there's no putting the cat back in the bag once it's out, you know? You might be willing to lose Linx, but I'm not willing to let you. Not tonight, at least."

"I get it. I hate it, but I understand. I have to go back, but I'll make the rounds and duck out in an hour and meet you up there."

"Okay." I slide my hands along the smooth fabric of his tux to grip the lapel and grant myself a few seconds to appreciate the curl of his dark lashes, to study each individual shade of blue filling his irises, to admire the harsh cut of his jaw. It's like Dominic is proof that God plays favorites when distributing features; there's not a single flaw to be found, and I both love and hate that about him. Without thinking, I press up on my toes and seal my lips against his. His hands slide to my lower back and pull me into his body before deepening the kiss. It's wild and reckless and *everything*. He kisses me like we're living on borrowed time, and he's afraid what the end of this moment will mean.

I'm lost inside this kiss until a throat clears somewhere behind me in an obvious *excuse me* fashion. My face heats as I glance over my shoulder to find a blonde woman glaring at us. She tilts her head to gesture the elevator buttons, which Dominic and I are standing in front of, blocking. I quickly step back, and Dominic does the same. All it takes is a flash of his smile and, *"Oh, I'm so sorry. Going up? I've got it,"* for her scowl to melt into a smile. I resist the urge to roll my eyes because, *of course*, he wields that kind of power with nothing more than a few words.

She continues staring at him with thinly-veiled interest, completely ignoring my existence despite the fact she *just* saw us making out until the elevator doors slide closed between us.

Dominic's quiet laughter draws my attention, and I whip my gaze over to him.

"You should see your face," he says, head shaking in amusement.

I school my features to go back to neutral. "I have no idea what you're talking about."

"If you say so. One hour," he repeats, squeezing my hand before letting me step into the elevator. His eyes drift over me, making my skin break out into goosebumps before he gives me a wink.

I opted not to join him in the ballroom mostly because I need a few minutes alone to decompress and regroup after the last few minutes. Plus, considering how delectable Dominic looks in his tux, I don't trust myself not to blatantly eye-fuck him all night without even caring who sees.

With an hour to kill, I take my time perusing Dominic's suite, admiring everything from the marble fireplace to the oversized bathtub in the middle of the room. When that only takes ten minutes, I steal a shirt from Dominic's overnight bag and ditch the evening dress I borrowed from Jo. Next, I make good on my comment to raid his mini-fridge, grab an exorbitantly expensive tiny bottle of wine and a bar of chocolate, and scroll through the TV guide before settling on a random sitcom for the sake of background noise. Once finished with the chocolate and wine, I call Josie for a distraction. Earlier, I went to her apartment to get ready, and she practically couldn't get rid of me fast enough. But when I asked about her plans for tonight, she shrugged and said it felt like a good night to get Chinese food delivered and have a *New Girl* binge-athon. Then she changed the subject completely. Her phone goes to voicemail—*twice*—which is another red flag because she practically lives with it attached to her hand.

A few minutes later, I pull up Instagram (I caved and reactivated my account when Dominic was traveling, and I missed seeing him. Pathetic, I know) and quickly realize the reason for Josie's evasiveness. "No fucking way," I exclaim, shooting up from the bed to study the details of a photo her douchebag ex-boyfriend just posted.

...*from a restaurant on Josie's block.*

I try calling her again.

Voicemail.

"Seriously, Jo? JORDAN?! I don't care how many times he apologizes, what he buys you, or if his dick has magical powers, you cannot be considering giving him another shot. I swear to God, if you don't send me a timestamped picture of your TV paused on a scene from *New Girl* to prove you're not doing what I think you're doing, I'm going to come smack some sense into you."

"What is it with you and phone conversations about dicks?"

The suite's door clicks closed, and I spin around to find a smirking Dominic. The sight of him—looking just as dapper as he did an hour ago, though his hair's a little disheveled now like he ran his fingers through it one too many times—is enough to instantly overrun my frustration with Josie.

It really is a shame he doesn't wear tuxedoes more often.

"You mean my *private* voicemail message you eavesdropped on?" I counter, smiling at the memory of the first time we had this conversation.

"Well, you *are* in *my* hotel room." He tosses his jacket over the back of a couch and stops at the foot of the bed to take off his shoes.

"Guilty." I run my fingertips along the hem of his shirt, where it sits on my thigh. "I'm also in *your* t-shirt."

"As much as I enjoy seeing you in it, I think I'd prefer you *out* of it." His eyes fill with fire, and he starts to loosen the bowtie from around his neck before slowly crawling up the bed toward me.

I lift up a foot and stop his movements, shaking my head. "Ah-ah-ah. You're supposed to make up for being a, quote, complete and utter idiot, remember? And I know exactly how I want you to start."

"How?"

"I want your best stripping routine. I'm talking, pretend you're auditioning to star in the next *Magic Mike* movie. *That* is what I want."

He shakes his head with a laugh, probably already regretting his decision. "Couldn't take it easy on me, huh?"

"Easy? Nah. Besides, you're the one who taught me easy is boring."

In a single movement, he grips my ankles, yanks me down the bed until I'm flat on my back, and hovers above me. "That's right; it is. And I don't do boring."

He drops down to plant a searing kiss on my lips before pushing off the bed and flinging the bowtie my way.

For the rest of the night, he repeatedly proves he *definitely* doesn't do boring.

21

TRISTAN

*E*ven though we hardly slept last night, sleep is the last thing I want after spending the entire car ride with Dominic's hands on me in some way—massaging my shoulders, holding my hand, resting on my thigh, fingertips lightly grazing the back of my neck. With a few hours until I'm supposed to pick up Liam and Gen from their playdate with Kai, all I want is to hold on to the fleeting time we have to ourselves.

But when I pull into view of Dominic's house, we're greeted by a huge party-bus parked in his driveway.

"What the fuck?" he asks, not wasting any time before jumping out of the car and charging toward the house.

I scramble out and follow behind him. The closer we get, the louder the rap music gets, coming from somewhere behind the house. He follows the path around the side of the house and throws open the gate to the backyard. Loud music pulses through the outdoor speakers, there's a full makeshift bar set up on the patio, the pool is full of people on floats, and a group is gathered around a table, locked in a beer pong battle.

Dominic scans the scene in complete shock.

I don't know what I was expecting to see, but Reggie Smith, the star quarterback for the New York Giants, is definitely not it. Upon closer inspection, I realize two of his teammates are also here, along with three Victoria's Secret models and several other people I don't recognize.

"Max!" Dominic shouts, storming toward the beer pong table. "What the hell is this?"

Max whirls around and holds his arms out, a beer in each hand, and replies in French.

"No shit," Dominic fires back. "I meant, *why* are you having a party at *my* house? You haven't bothered to answer my calls, now you show up and throw a fucking party?"

"Yesterday was Reggie's birthday," he explains, nodding toward Reggie across the table. "We were partying at a club last night, and someone said we should go to the Hamptons. But then I mentioned this place, and everyone agreed it sounded better, so we paid the party bus driver a grand to bring us here. I thought you'd still be in New York."

"Jesus," Dominic mutters. He takes another look around and shakes his head, pulling Max a few feet away from the table. "Do you even know anyone here other than Reggie?"

Max shrugs like he hadn't really thought much about it. "I met most of these guys last night. It's just a party, Dominic. Lighten up."

"You've brought two dozen strangers to my house, and you want me to *lighten up*? When you know damn well I came here for the sole purpose of having privacy. Unbelievable. I know you're going through some shit, but this crosses the line."

Max rolls his eyes and waves off Dominic's question. "You act like one little party is going to make a difference. This might come as a shock, but the world doesn't revolve around you, brother."

"Max, enough. You're drunk," he snaps, and I can tell he's struggling to rein in his temper.

Max still won't talk about what happened in France, and I know Dominic is worried about him. He withdrew from all tournaments for the next month and sent a single text out saying he was fine but needed space and disappeared.

Clearly, Dominic was right to worry.

"I'm fine," he asserts, downing the rest of one of his beers.

"You're not." There's a vein sticking out in his neck, and his jaw clenches tight. He steps into Max's space and swats the second beer out of his other hand. "This is not going to ease your pain, Max," he says, his voice dropped low.

"*Don't*," Max snaps. He cuts Dominic a warning glare, and I'm tempted to step between them because this is going downhill fast. "You don't know the first fucking thing about it, so just *don't*."

"You're right. I don't know. Because you won't even talk about it, you'd rather drink the pain away, apparently. But that's a Band-Aid on a bullet wound, and you know it. Don't be this version of yourself, Max. You've come too far."

By now, their scuffle has garnered the attention of a few guests. Reggie's beer pong partner, Seth Timmons—a rookie wide receiver for the Giants—has his phone out, trained on the scene.

Before I can yell at him to put it away or warn Dominic, Max fires off an angry-sounding response in French. Dominic's eyes go wide, and he fires something back, gesturing toward me. Max looks at me and shakes his head, and I'm cursing myself for not knowing French because whatever is said is only making things worse, with nobody to deescalate the situation. Neither brother pays any attention to the growing crowd; they're too consumed in whatever they're yelling back and forth.

And then everything happens in the blink of an eye. Max takes a swing at Dominic. He ducks in the nick of time and then lunges forward to tackle Max. They spiral into a chaotic mess of swinging limbs and muttered curses.

Now everyone is watching. Several drunken idiots cheer them on. The scene has become a total disaster, and I seem to be the only one actively trying to stop them instead of fanning the flames.

I surge forward the second there's a gap between them. I press a hand to each of their chests, keeping them apart, and volley a stern glare from Max to Dominic. "Stop! This isn't going to solve anything. And you have an audience," I add at a whisper-yell, redirecting my gaze to Seth with his phone still trained on us.

That part gets their attention and instantly sobers Max up.

With wild eyes and heaving chests, they finally snap out of their fog of anger and look around. Registering the situation, they take a few steps away from each other and brush off the grass and dirt clinging to their clothes.

The crowd disperses, and only a handful of people linger to see if there's more drama to come. A girl looks from Max to Dominic to me, and I overhear her say something about a love triangle. A snappy retort sits on the tip of my tongue, but if there's one thing I've learned, it's not to give in to the temptation to react to speculative bullshit. All it does is fuel the rumors.

Max's eyes narrow at Seth as he spins, giving his audience a 360-degree view of the yard and everyone in it. "Reggie, what the fuck? Thought you said everyone knew the phone rules."

Reggie mutters something under his breath before storming over to Seth and grabbing his phone. He studies the screen for a second before his eyes go wide. "You were doing a *fucking live?!* Phones are banned at my parties for a reason, you idiot."

A beat passes before the reality of the situation sinks in.

And when it does, I feel sick.

"You put that shit on Facebook?" Max exclaims.

Seth shrugs, not even remotely apologetic. "What's the big deal? Fans love getting a glimpse behind the scenes. It's not—"

"*What's the big deal?*" Dominic echoes in bewilderment, cutting him off and leveling him with a razor-sharp glare. "Do you have any idea what you just did? Of course, you don't because you're fucking hammered."

Dominic takes a menacing step toward Seth, but Max immediately puts a hand on his shoulder to pull him back. "Dom, no. I'll take care of it."

He turns to Max and shakes off his hand. "Yeah, you will. I want everyone out. Now."

"Aw, come on, man; don't be like that," Seth starts, turning toward the beer pong table and grabbing a cup.

Dominic's hands clench into fists at his side, the muscles of his arms bulging—everything about his posture is filled with tension. I take a step in front of him and press a hand to his chest. "You said it yourself; he's hammered. Max can handle things out here. Come on," I tell him, wrapping my hand around his fist and tugging him toward the house.

After a second, he nods and lets me lead him away from the party. When we're safely inside, I finally expel a shaky breath and start pacing the kitchen while Dominic pulls out his phone and watches the video. It's not long—less than two minutes—but by the end, Dominic is silent for a moment before muttering a string of curses.

I grab the phone from him, thinking I must've missed something, and my eyes immediately zero in on the screen.

For some reason, a small part of me thought maybe it wasn't that bad, that maybe we'd get lucky somehow.

A scan of the comments shatters that illusion. Some express disappointment in Dominic for having poor judgment; others speculate the fight is because Max had an emotional breakdown after his broken engagement. A few make light of the situation, saying it's not a big deal.

But those aren't the ones that make my heart jump into my throat.

Isn't that Tristan Fitzgerald? Are they seriously fighting over HER? EWWW.

    Wonder which one of them she conned into thinking she cares about them.

    Wouldn't put it past her to go after both. $$$$
    What he said ^

Can't blame them, she's hot AF.

Hope they're keeping an eye on their money. Sticky fingers are probably a Fitzgerald family trait!

One word: RUN!

Guys, she's probably a really nice person. SIKE. The only nice thing about her is her tits.

I don't care what anyone says, she's guilty too. That whole family is bad news.

"Oh, my God!" I cry as panic engulfs me. Now I'm the one pacing, trying to fight off the flashbacks and memories those comments summon.

"Don't read that shit. People are idiots," Dominic says. He puts his hands on my shoulders to stop me, and I freeze, meeting his eyes.

Under normal circumstances, like when Liam refuses to do homework or Maggie forgets to pick the twins up, those cool blues and the strength he emanates with a single touch are enough to ease my mind and calm my racing heart. But right now, they have the opposite effect. His lips are moving, and I know he's trying to reassure me, making promises to fix things, but the sound of my heart thrumming away in my chest is drowning out everything else.

"I can't..." I step out of his grip, put some space between us, and move toward the front door. "I have to go."

"Tristan, don't. We can figure this out. Just stay, and I'll call Gage and come up with a way to fix this. Don't go."

I shake my head, wishing like hell it was that easy. "I just...I can't do this right now."

"This isn't like before," he calls, stopping me in my tracks. "You're not alone this time."

That's the problem; I want to tell him. Instead, I swallow the words and run.

22

DOMINIC

*T*wenty-four hours.

That's how long it takes after Tristan walked out of my door for me to crack under the need to do *something*. Right after she left, I called Gage and filled him in on the situation. He barely got three words in before I made it clear Tristan was my priority; whatever he wanted me to do or say to mitigate the fallout would have to wait.

"Dominic, I'm telling you, let me handle this. Do not leave Arbor Cove," Gage pleads. *Too late.* In the background, I can already hear him angry-typing. I check the rearview mirror before switching lanes, shaking my head even though he can't see me.

"I've got things under control too," Nash chimes in from his end of the conference call. "Give us a little more time. I've spoken with Monica. I've got a call scheduled with Gatorade, and I'm waiting to hear back from Linx. Just lay low for now."

Since Tristan left yesterday, she hasn't answered my calls or texts. Maggie told me Tristan had called her right after leaving my house, explained the situation, and asked her to keep the twins. She said something about needing a day to herself to sort things out.

Without a plan, without even knowing where to find her, I

jumped in my car and started driving. I have no clue where Tristan is, but I know who will.

Josie.

Calls and texts are too easy to ignore. I'll camp outside her door if that's what it takes.

I just need to know that Tristan is okay.

"Look, I'm not just going to sit around. I don't expect or need you two to understand. You don't even have to like it. But you do have to listen and accept what I'm saying. I'm not laying low or keeping my distance from Tristan. I thought I made it perfectly clear where my priorities stand, but in case I haven't, let me spell it out for you both. *Her*. She is the only part of this I care about right now. Period. End of story. I trust you two to handle the rest."

One of them sighs through the phone, and then Gage says, "Okay. I hear you loud and clear. I hope you at least kicked Max's ass in private for causing this shitstorm."

"It crossed my mind. But he's going through enough already. Trust me."

As tempting as it was, I knew going for round two with him wouldn't actually accomplish anything. He's dealing with his own issues.

"Dom, listen, I'm sorry about the other night," Nash says. "I didn't know you felt this way about her. I just thought—"

"I know. It's fine."

"Just let me know if I can help."

"I will. For now, just keep doing what you're doing. I know this might have fucked things up with Linx, but I don't care."

"Let me worry about that. I'll handle them. You do what you gotta do, and I'll update you later."

An hour later, I tug open the door to The Lantern, the restaurant where Josie works, and search the space from the bar to the door leading back to the kitchen. It's halfway between lunch and dinner, so it's not overly crowded, and it only takes a few seconds to spot a waitress with light blue hair.

Before I can take more than a few steps into the seating area, the hostess stops me. "Can I help you?"

"Yeah, uh, I need to speak to Josie. It's rather urgent," I tell her, tacking on a smile to help my case.

"Oh, um, sure, I'll let her know. You can wait right over there," she offers, pointing toward a bench behind me.

"Thanks," I say, taking a seat. For the thousandth time, I pull out my phone to check for a text or call while I wait. I've gotten a dozen texts and missed six calls, but none of them is from Tristan, so I shove my phone back into my pocket.

"Dominic?" Josie calls from across the entryway, drawing my attention. Her eyes go wide when she sees my face. "Don't take this the wrong way, but you look like shit. Which is saying something because you're, well...you."

I jump up and go to her, ignoring her remark. "I need to see her, Josie. I know you know where she is. Did she come to you? Is she at your place? I need to fix this."

She frowns, placing a hand on my arm and shaking her head. "No, she's not at my apartment, and I honestly don't know where she is. I was actually going to call Maggie to get your number on my break. She texted me last night, but she didn't elaborate much. I'm worried about her. She's never just up and disappeared like this."

"*Shit*," I say, sighing heavily. I wasn't expecting that answer. "So she didn't tell you where she went? Not even a clue?"

Josie shakes her head and pulls her phone out of her pocket. She looks down and reads off, "I don't know what to do, Jo. I think I just need some space to figure it out. Clear my head. I'll call you later." She looks up and cuts me off before I can ask. "No, she hasn't called, and that was the last text she sent."

"So she told you what happened?"

She nods. "I saw the video before she texted. For what it's worth, she's not upset with *you*...just the situation. It's a lot, you know?"

"Trust me; I get it. I just...there has to be something I can do to make this right."

A guest waves a hand in the air to flag her down, and she nods in acknowledgement. "I have to get back, but my shift ends in two hours. Meet me out front then, and we'll come up with a plan."

"Make yourself at home," Josie offers with a sweeping gesture toward the couch. "Ignore the mess. I lost track of time last night and didn't have time to pick everything up before work this morning."

"It's fine," I assure her, looking around.

The mess she's referring to consists of textbooks and note-books splayed open and scattered on a dining-table-turned-desk, and an overflowing basket of laundry next to the couch. To call her apartment small would be an understatement. It might even be a stretch to call it an apartment. The kitchen, living, dining, and bedrooms are all melted together in one open space with all of the furniture pieces practically touching because they're so close.

"Can I get you anything? Water? Coffee? Something stronger?"

"I'll stick with water. Thanks."

"So, I was thinking," she says, getting my water and pouring herself wine. "What do you know about how everything went down before? When she was dealing with the fallout from her parents' arrests?"

I let out a breath and shrug. "Not much. Just that she dealt with a lot before finally drawing the line when things spilled over and affected her siblings. Work too."

"Yeah. You'd be surprised at the kind of shit she dealt with. At first, she brushed off the outrageous accusations—the insults slung at her by perfect strangers, even the outright lies written online by insane keyboard warriors. She carried on with her life as usual—or as usual as she could, given the circumstances—and didn't let any of it get to her. What *did* get to her was having people she cares about affected. Having them look at her differently, like they almost weren't sure what to believe. And it didn't help that strangers and reporters would wait for her outside their apartment building, even when Liam and Gen were with her. Some even found her at work. Can you believe those assholes actually accosted her at a children's hospital? Some fucking nerve, right?"

"Jesus, that's awful."

"Yeah." She takes a sip of her wine and nods. "As if that wasn't enough to deal with, they fired her the next day because of all the, quote, bad press her name carried. She didn't even get to tell the kids goodbye."

"Wait, that's it," I say, practically leaping off the couch.

Josie looks at me expectantly, waiting for me to elaborate. "What's it?"

"The kids. She once told me that was the worst part of the fallout she had to deal with—leaving and losing the kids she worked with at The Happy Hearts Foundation. She hated that they might think the worst of her."

"Yeah…"

"We're going to show her they don't."

23

TRISTAN

*C*oming to Rockdale wasn't intentional. At least not at first. I didn't have a destination in mind when I drove out of Arbor Cove two days ago until I saw a sign that told me Rockdale was 67 miles away, and before I knew it, I was parked in front of the 24-hour diner. Peanut butter pie didn't solve my problems, but it did bring me a few minutes of peace.

Now I'm sitting at one of the tables in the breakfast room of the same B&B where Dominic and I stayed, trying to figure out where the hell things go from here.

"A watched phone never rings," Lois, one of the owners, says before taking the seat across from me. "They say those things work both ways, you know."

Oh, I'm painfully aware of that. I've picked it up to call Dominic countless times. But I stop cold when I realize I'm no closer to fixing this mess than I was two days ago.

"So I've heard." I tear my eyes away from the device and flip it over, so it's face down on the table. Instead, I survey the room, studying the framed family photos on the wall behind Lois.

She watches me studying the photos and smiles. "Those are some of my favorites."

"You and Kevin are adorable together. You both look so

genuinely happy," I say, nodding toward a candid shot of them laughing as Kevin pushes her in a swing.

"We were. Still are. We've been married for forty-seven years and together for fifty."

"Fifty years," I echo, shaking my head. "Wow. I'm sure you get this question a lot, but what's your secret?"

She lowers her hands to the table, turning to look at the wall behind her, and hums. "I don't know that it's a secret so much as a recipe, of sorts, that makes a relationship successful. Maybe a little bit of both." She turns back around, offering me a smile full of warmth. I gave her the gist of my situation last night at dinner, but she was sweet enough not to press for more when I didn't elaborate. "You've gotta have boatloads of patience, for starters. Trust. Communication. And at the end of the day, you just have to commit to choosing each other, every day. There will always be trials and obstacles to overcome or reasons to walk away and call it quits. The couples that endure the test of time are the ones that simply say, '*I choose you*' over everything else."

I let Lois's words sink in for a second, committing them to memory. "A recipe...I like that."

"Now, that's not to say it's an easy feat. Quite the opposite, actually. Lord knows we almost didn't even make it down the aisle."

My brows fly up, and my eyes flit to the photo of them on what appears to be their wedding day—Kevin in a suit and Lois in a simple white dress and holding a small bouquet. "What happened?"

"Kevin's parents didn't like me. Didn't think I was good enough. I suppose you could say I was from the wrong side of the tracks. They were wealthy and had always wanted him to become a doctor like his father. Had hopes he would marry the daughter of someone in their social circle. They tried everything to convince him not to marry me, even writing him out of their will. But you know what my sweet Kevin told them?"

I shake my head.

"He said none of that mattered. That money wouldn't make

him happy. And that was that. He'd made up his mind, and they could accept it or lose him."

"What happened? Did his parents eventually come around?"

"Eventually. They realized there's more to me than where I came from, that what mattered was their son's happiness."

"Would it have made a difference if they hadn't? Would you have done anything differently?"

She thinks about it for just a moment before answering, "No. Of course, it hurt that they didn't like me. But I realized—after a year of trying to win them over—you'll never please everyone. If there's one thing I could tell my younger self, it's that my own happiness is *mine* to control. No one else's."

With that, Lois excuses herself to go check on things in the kitchen, leaving me alone with my thoughts. It's eerie how closely Lois's story parallels mine in some ways—something I'm sure didn't escape her notice. I study the photos on the wall through a new lens, thinking about what they had to overcome to get to their happily ever after.

It makes me think about my own future.

My own happiness.

Dominic's future.

His happiness.

I've been so focused on all the wrong things. So worried about what could go wrong instead of how *right* things could be. Lois was right; there will always be obstacles. But at the end of the day, what matters is choosing happiness. Choosing each other.

Choosing love.

Took L&G to Dominic's.

I peel Maggie's note off the front door and turn right back around, heading for my car with a smile firmly in place. My plan was to stop by the house, check on my siblings, and ensure they hadn't burned the house down before hauling ass to Dominic's as soon as possible. This works out perfectly. I don't have all the answers or know what exactly our future looks like as a couple, but I do know I'm willing to find out.

When I get to Dominic's house, I don't even bother going in, opting instead for the side gate leading to the backyard. Fall might officially be upon us, but Dominic's pool is heated, so there's no keeping Liam and Gen out of it just because the temperatures have dropped.

But it's empty.

"*Hellllloooo,*" I call, sliding open the glass door from the patio.

Silence.

I frown, totally mystified. In all the times I've come to pick up the twins from Dominic's house, I've never been greeted by silence upon arrival. But then I look over and find a note on the couch that says to meet them in the theater room.

It's also empty.

The remote has a note that says to push play. I do as it says and take a seat on the couch to find out whatever it is these three are up to.

But when the video starts, I'm immediately brought to tears.

It's a home video of Dylan, a seven-year-old I met last year when he was in the hospital for a kidney transplant. *"My favorite thing about Miss Tristan was that she always made me laugh,"* he says with a huge smile.

Then it cuts to Aisha, an eight-year-old with cystic fibrosis that I got to know over the course of her many hospital visits. *"Miss Tristan always brought me gummy bears and let me braid her hair."*

Next is Nicole, a ten-year-old with leukemia. *"Miss Tristan introduced me to Nancy Drew books and made scavenger hunts for me."*

Half a dozen more clips play, all of children I worked with during my time at Happy Hearts.

And at the end, there's a picture of Dominic holding a sign that says COME BACK TO THE LIVING ROOM in his block letter handwriting.

When I get there, the tears start all over again. Dylan, Aisha, Nicole, and a few other kids are in the living room, along with their parents, my siblings, Dominic, Josie, and my old coworker from Happy Hearts.

"What...? This is..." I shake my head in disbelief, looking from Dominic to the rest of the group and back. Before I have a chance to get a full question out, I'm quickly engulfed in a group hug from all the children. I rein in the waterworks and exchange hellos with their parents before everyone eventually breaks off into their own conversations.

Dominic meets me off to the side, and I don't even hesitate before throwing myself into his arms. For a second, he holds me tight, and I let him, temporarily at a loss for words. I want to tell him this is the sweetest, most incredible thing anyone's ever done for me, but none of those words feels sufficient. Instead, I link my hands together at the back of his neck and press up on my toes to convey it all with a kiss.

"How in the world did you pull this off?" I ask when we finally break apart.

"I reached out to a few friends who helped with the details and logistics. I knew Happy Hearts couldn't disclose personal information of patients, but I knew they *could* pass along my information and request for a phone call to those patients' parents. These kids adore you, Tristan. That won't change. Not when they know the real you. And their parents were eager to help when I explained what I was trying to do. Everyone I spoke to had nothing but admiration and appreciation for you." He stops and looks around, squeezing my hand. "I know this doesn't fix everything, but I just wanted to—"

"It's perfect," I interject, shaking my head. "You, Dominic Moreau, are too good to be true. I can't believe you did this."

He tugs me close enough, so his lips brush the shell of my ear. "I told you...I'm all in."

My response gets cut off by Liam, who proudly announces that lunch is served.

"Talk later?"

He nods, and we both follow the group to the kitchen to dig into Liam's homemade pizzas.

After lunch, the crowd eventually dwindled until it was just the five of us. The twins swim while Maggie and I watch from the patio, and Dominic takes a call from Nash. Dominic and I haven't had the chance to talk, but each time I happened to catch him watching me this afternoon, I had to fight the urge to drag him away from the party and keep him all to myself. As amazing as today has been, I'm ready to run inside and bolt the door if that's what it takes for us to finally get some time alone.

"Hello? Tris, are you listening?" Maggie asks.

I'm not. I have no clue what she's even talking about because Dominic catches my eye from the doorway, where he's perched against the frame, arms crossed as he studies me with a look that makes my stomach dip. It's mischievous and sexy and sweet all at the same time.

It's a look I hope he never gives anyone but me.

I arch a brow and mouth *what?* to him, fully convinced he has something else up his sleeve.

He pushes off the door frame and slowly mouths three words that make everything that's not him disappear. Three words that have been dancing on my own tongue, waiting to be set free.

Three words that make everything else irrelevant.

I push up from the table to go to him, but he's already made it to the table. "Mags, mind if I steal Tristan for a walk down to the beach?" he asks, eyes still trained on me.

"Sure. I'll keep an eye on double trouble."

"*Heard that!*" Gen and Liam yell in unison.

For a minute, we walk in silence, my heart beating wildly inside my chest. I open my mouth half a dozen times to say something, but nothing makes it past my throat. When we get to the sand, I take off my booties and socks, letting my toes sink into the cool sand. I pull my cardigan a little tighter and cross my arms. It was a beautiful early fall day today, but with the sun setting, the temperature drops.

I grab Dominic's arm to stop his movement, turning to face

him. "Wait, what happened with Linx? Was that what you were talking to Nash about?"

He nods, dropping down to sit. "The deal's done. I sign tomorrow."

"What? Just like that? How?"

"Well, I called Michael last night to come clean and tell him about us—and to let him know I'd be happy to go to Nike or Adidas if he had a problem doing business because of my personal life. As it turns out, little Nicole," he nods his head back toward the house, "is Michael's niece. Nicole's mom sent him the video we made, and he said he was going to call me himself this morning to work things out. Everything came together quickly after that."

"Wow. That's amazing. I'm so glad it worked out. Congratulations, high roller." I wink and bump his shoulder with mine.

"Thanks. I'm glad it worked out too, but I meant it, Tristan," he says, turning to me. "You're worth more to me than any contract. I hope you know that."

"I do know that." I bring my hands to his face, the light stubble along his jaw tickling my palms, before leaning in to press my lips against his. He slips his hands around my waist, holding me close to deepen the kiss into something a lot less innocent.

This kiss, this moment—*this man*—is too much.

Too perfect.

We eventually break apart before things veer into R-rated territory and one of the neighbors gets a free show.

We sit in comfortable silence for a moment, and I watch the waves crash in front of us. Until now, I hadn't realized how much I've come to love all the trappings of summer in Arbor Cove—the warm salty air, long days and late nights, the scent of coconut sunscreen and chlorine, walks along the beach. But I also realize the reason I feel that way about those things is sitting next to me.

I walk my hand closer to Dominic's in the sand and link my pinky finger with his. "I love you, too, y'know."

His gaze whips to mine, and he smiles. "Oh yeah?"

I nod. "I know your life is crazy and takes you around the

world, and I know we have a thousand things to figure out. But I learned recently that making love last means choosing each other, over and over. And it doesn't matter if the obstacle is dealing with the price tag of your fame or you being halfway across the globe most of the year. I just know I want to choose you."

"My life *is* crazy. But I swear to you, we can make this work. And hey, I'm old and injured, who knows how much time I've got left until the big R. Could be next year," he jokes.

"You're *not* old!" I counter, smacking his arm. "I bet you've still got five more years in the tank. And I'll be your number one fan until the end, whenever that might be."

He gives me a wink and studies my face with a hum. "You know…a true fan would get that painted on their face."

"Is that so? Make it to the finals of the French Open next year, and we'll talk."

"Finals, huh? What if I lose in the semis?"

"Ah, good point. Guess you'll just have to try again the next year. And the one after that. Then again, by that point you *will* be old, so maybe I should amend—"

"All right, okay," he cuts me off, reaching out to make me pay for that. I squeal and try to dodge him, but he's too fast. I'm pinned under him, laughing and squirming when he stops, the playfulness gone as he lifts a hand to brush my hair back. "Whether it's one year or five years from now when I walk off the court for the last time, I won't be thinking about how much I'll miss tennis. I'll be thinking, *how lucky am I to have found someone who actually made me look forward to the day I hang it up.*"

EPILOGUE
DOMINIC

"*C*an you grab the rest of the gifts?" Tristan asks, gesturing the pile to my left on her way out the door.

I nod and pick up the presents before following her to the balcony where there's an obnoxious number of safari-themed decorations strewn about. We're at my parents' house in Nice, spending one last summer all together before Maggie moves to California.

Tristan takes the gifts from me and arranges them on the table with the others. I wrap my arms around her shoulders and pull her into me so her back is against my chest, and we both watch the scene below.

"I can't believe we officially have a one-year-old," I say, shaking my head. My mom is on a float with a giggling Tyson in her arms while my dad pulls them around the pool and Liam chases them. Next to the pool, Genevieve and Maggie are on lounge chairs, flipping through bridal magazines in search of ideas for Maggie's wedding next year.

"I know," she says, gripping my forearm and settling into my embrace. "And what a year it's been."

I hum in response, thinking about all the changes the last

twelve months have brought our family. Maggie graduated from the University of Connecticut and got engaged. Liam and Gen started their own cooking channel on YouTube that went viral. As for me…

Tyson was born two weeks after I won Wimbledon last summer, and a week after his birth, I formally announced my retirement from tennis.

"Any regrets?" she asks, spinning in my arms and looking up to search my eyes.

I move my hands and cup her face, studying her in return. *God, she's beautiful. Even more beautiful than the day we met.*

"About retiring?" My brows pinch together, and I shake my head. "No. Never. It was time. I get to put my son to bed every night and wake up next to you every morning; how could I ever regret that?"

"Good." She smiles, wrapping her hands around my wrists and leaning in to kiss me. I groan against her lips, already contemplating the possibility of pulling her back inside to have my wicked way with her, and she slips her arms around my neck, pressing herself against me.

"Hey! You love birds ever going to join us?" My mom calls from the pool, breaking the spell.

I reluctantly pull back and mutter a few curses under my breath, making Tristan laugh.

"Hey, at least they're not tagging along on the road trip," she offers as a consolation.

"Good point."

Now I'm thinking about our upcoming road trip through Provence, and how blissfully alone we'll be for ten glorious days. Though, I have my doubts we'll make it the whole ten days away from Tyson.

"Yeah, yeah," I call back to my mom. "On our way."

"We're about to pick teams for volleyball," Liam shouts. "Gabriel and I are team captains. We all agreed you two aren't allowed to be on the same team, so you're with me, Dominic."

I nod down at him, more than happy with the arrangement. *I'll take any chance I can get to watch my wife splash and bounce around from across the pool.*

Tristan grabs two more towels from the basket my parents keep by the stairs and makes her way down the stairs. She stops at the bottom when she realizes I'm not behind her, looking back up to where I'm still leaning against the rail.

Her brows furrow with a frown. "Coming?"

I snap out of my daze and nod, giving her a smile that instantly puts an identical one on her face. "Be right there."

I meant what I told Tristan—I miss tennis, sure, but I'm also incredibly proud of the career I had. Five years ago, I had no idea how much time I had left to give to the sport, much less if I'd ever make it to another major final. But then, the following year, I made the finals of the French Open—and won (and Tristan made good on her face paint promise). After that, I vowed to just savor the journey. Titles are great—nobody plays without the hope of winning them—but I felt like I was playing on borrowed time anyway; might as well enjoy the time I had left. And I did. Especially when Tristan and her siblings joined me for whatever tournament they could. But Tyson's arrival felt like the perfect time to transition from that chapter of my life to this one.

I spent more than two decades striving to stay at the top of my sport, to be the best, to win every match. But now?

Now, my definition of the perfect match has nothing to do with tennis and everything to do with the woman who made me want more out of life than titles and trophies.

ACKNOWLEDGMENTS

If you're reading this, my first thank you goes to YOU! I can't tell you what it means to me that, out of all the books to choose from, you've picked this one up. It has been such a crazy, exhausting, stressful rollercoaster of a year, and writing this book was both a labor of love and a much-needed escape from the real world at times, and I hope it gave you a fun escape for a few hours too. Whether this is the first or fifth book of mine you've read, I'm so glad you're here!

Huge thank you to my sweet husband for putting up with both my crazy pregnancy hormones along with my writing-induced stress. You're the best, and Quinn, Harper, and Apollo and I are so lucky to have you.

To my beta readers—thank you for being SO patient with me; I know I took approximately 342 weeks to finish this book. Let's hope the next one doesn't take as long ;)

Autumn—thank you for keeping my author world spinning, especially lately! I'm pretty sure this book would still just be a WIP if not for you.

To all my author friends—I mean it when I say you guys are rock stars, and I'm so glad the whole book world has brought us together. Whether it's texts/messages about blurbs, covers, writing struggles, or GIFs that make me laugh, I don't know what I'd do without you!

Bloggers, bookstagrammers, readers…I'm forever grateful you take the time to read/review/post beautiful photos of something *I* wrote. Seriously. Y'all amaze me every day with your love and support of my books, and I'm so happy to be a part of this book world and to have found you.

ABOUT THE AUTHOR

C.R. Ellis (Caitlin) is a contemporary romance author with a serious addiction to lattes and HEAs. She lives in Texas with her husband, new baby, and two lovable dogs. If she's not writing or reading, she's probably daydreaming about her next travel destination or going to a concert with her husband.

For more information visit www.crellisauthor.com.

Follow Caitlin on Instagram (@authorcrellis) and Facebook (Author C.R. Ellis), for information about her upcoming releases!

Be the first to know about my upcoming releases, giveaways, and sales by signing up for my newsletter!

Come hang out in my Facebook reader group, Caitlin's Brew Crew, to chat all things books (and coffee)!

You can find all of my books on my Amazon author page.

ALSO BY C.R. ELLIS

The Forget Me Knot Series:

Why Stars Chase the Sun

When Light Leads to You

What it Takes to Fall

Where I'd Rather Be